WARPED WORLD

PACK OF OUTCASTS - BOOK 3

EVA CHASE

Warped World

Book 3 in the Pack of Outcasts series

First Digital Edition, 2025

Copyright © 2025 Eva Chase

Cover design: Sanja Balan (Sanja's Covers)

Ebook ISBN: 978-1-998582-48-8

Paperback ISBN: 978-1-998582-58-7

I

Periwinkle

I pride myself on being able to look on the bright side of almost every situation. But there really is no way to put a positive spin on a gigantic tidal wave of shadow energy crashing over an entire city.

I stand there gaping next to my colleagues, watching the filmy darkness churn amid the buildings half a mile away. The murk courses from the ground all the way up to the sky beyond the tops of the tallest skyscrapers, including the once-gleaming, now-dimmed Diamond Victory Tower.

My jaw hangs slack. My mind seems to be stuck in a loop that can only declare, *Bad, bad, bad.*

Good job stating the obvious. What the heck are we supposed to *do* about this massive badness?

After what feels like hours—but is probably only a few seconds, since I don't think I've even blinked—a flood of emotion rebounds from the crash. Even from all that distance away, a slurry of acid-sharp panic and rancid-banana-peel distress smacks into me from the hundreds of thousands of humans living in the city.

I jerk out of my shock with a yelp. Words start tumbling off my tongue without consulting my brain—which is probably fair considering my gray matter wasn't being much use anyway.

"We have to help them! Whatever that stuff from the rift is, it's scaring people—hurting them. They have no idea what they're dealing with."

"And we do?" Hail mutters in his typical cool tone, but the winter fae draws his slim frame straighter at the same moment. "How the fuck does a rift grow like that? How the fuck does it collapse?"

Rollick, the demon who's been running our now-a-gazillion-times-more-complicated mission here, lowers his phone from his ear and shakes himself into action. "It isn't just here. At least two of the other strange rifts have just collapsed in the same way—but neither of those are affecting more than a few humans. Luckily they were a lot farther from any area of civilization."

He jabs his hands this way and that to direct his assistants, his light brown hair rippling with a thrum of his supernatural power. "Let's get in there! Stay discreet, but move the humans and other mortal creatures out of any affected areas you can. If you start to feel any significant effects, back off and take care of yourself first. And watch for any signs that might tell us what we're dealing with."

Despite his take-charge attitude, tension winds through his tone and wafts off him in bitter trickles. Rollick is the most powerful shadowkind I've ever met, thousands of years old, but I think this problem might be too big and bad even for him.

His phone starts ringing again. He glowers at it as if he dreads answering.

As he lifts the device to his ear, Jonah sweeps his well-muscled arm toward the rest of us. "Come on, team."

Our sorcerer sprints toward the nearest van. It's a good thing the human among us moved fastest, because he's the only one out of our group of five who can drive that thing.

As he dives behind the steering wheel, my other three men, a few of Rollick's assistants, and I leap into the shadows to dart after him. I'm vaguely aware of Sorsha and her men racing to their strange RV and of the shadowbloods who've been working alongside us dashing to another of the vans.

I tumble into the back space of Jonah's van and pop back into physical form to gasp out, "We're all in!"

Jonah guns the engine before I've gotten more than the first word out. With a slam of the gas and a sway of his wavy black hair, he jerks the vehicle around and peels down the highway toward the city.

The rest of my teammates solidify around me. Raze wraps a brawny arm around my petite but pudgy body as if shielding me from the hazards of speedy driving. His eyes have narrowed, ominous even with the green contacts covering his naturally pure-black basilisk irises.

"Is part of the shadow realm coming right through into the mortal realm?" he asks. "How could that even happen?"

On the bench across from us, Mirage flicks his fox ears from his bright red hair. "Mix and match. Let's hope it doesn't hatch!"

He grins at his rhyme with a flash of his canine fangs, but his golden-brown face looks tight. I don't think the playful fox shifter can see any more of an upside to the current development than I can.

The strange rift that was sending warped creatures out into the mortal realm was already bigger than any I'd ever seen, but even then it was only about the size of a house. Its sudden growth spurt blew it out thousands of times bigger—and made it lose its balance along the way.

Remembering its dark face toppling over onto the city sends a shudder down my spine.

"What matters the most is making sure everyone gets out of the mess!" I declare. "Then we can worry about what the mess is made of."

Hail gives me a teasing poke of his elbow where he's materialized at my other side. "Spoken like a true cream puff."

The nickname is only affectionate now, holding none of its previous disdain. But when the winter fae glances toward the front of the van, his skin turns even paler than usual alongside a wobble of lemon-jelly uncertainty.

I can taste my teammates' emotions even more easily than any other beings' thanks to the glowing marks I accidentally blazoned onto all of their chests, which thankfully we've all ended up agreeing are a welcome addition. None of us are feeling all that confident right now.

Hail's gaze slides back to me, butterscotch-sweet fondness drizzling over his anxiety. "Don't rush in too fast, Peri. We'll all help, but we should stick together. And we need to pay attention to our bodies—if the mess starts weakening us, we have to get out before it does any real damage."

The tenderness the normally icy man now offers me leaves me a little giddy even in the midst of a catastrophe. I lean my head against the side of his shoulder. "We'll all watch out for each other."

With a squeal of the tires, Jonah brings the van to a stop. He peers through the windows, his stance rigid. "I think we need to go forward from here on foot."

Hopping out of the van, I can't argue with his decision. A wall of the hazy darkness drifts up from the road just a few feet from where he parked. It stretches as high as I can see, turning the structures on the other side wavery as if we're looking at them through murky water.

Murky water that's not actually water, that we need to dive into if we're going to rescue the people within it from drowning. Or whatever it's actually doing to them.

A thrum of dissonant energy radiates down from above. I squint at what I can see of the sky through the haze. "Is the rift still up there? I thought it… broke."

Could it have bounced off the ground and up to the clouds, vomiting shadows as it went, like some horrifying trampoline act?

Does that mean it's going to spew out even more of this murky mess?

Raze's muscles ripple uneasily. "I can sense it too. I guess it didn't totally collapse, then?"

Hail scowls. "Is that better or worse than if it did?"

None of us can answer that question.

I swallow hard and gather all my gumption. "The mortals have even less idea what's going on than we do. Let's get to them fast."

I stride forward, ignoring the initial pinches of pain that prickle through my feet and ankles. My companions hustle after me.

Stepping into the murk feels like walking into a shower of cold porridge—and feels about as comfortable as that sounds. Even lukewarm porridge would be an improvement. Add a little maple syrup—

My thoughts scatter with another swell of frightened emotion from the city's inhabitants. I keep walking on as fast as the porridgey sensation allows, peering through the haze at the buildings we're passing and checking my leather-jacket-and-sundress clothed body to make sure the unpalatable breakfast isn't eating *me*.

My nerves keep jittering with the same sort of unnerving push-pull vibe that emanated from the rift before it graduated from slightly-larger-than-usual portal to city-swallowing void. One positive: the rift's massive growth spurt seems to have diluted the effect a little, so the sensation is more like it tickling my skin than nibbling into it.

I'd still rather be eating warm maple porridge.

The structures we pass don't look all that pleased to be encased in the shadowy sludge either. Lampposts and telephone poles lean at odd angles; a couple are doing their best Superman impressions floating sideways off the ground. Some windows look as if they're dripping into the walls that are supposed to be holding them. Rooftops undulate like they're ready to send ships off to sea.

"Row, row, row your boat," Mirage murmurs in his singsong voice, and shivers. "Everything's gotten muddled."

That includes some of the living beings. We pass a few humans lying sprawled in the street beyond rescuing, one whose leg has migrated to his chest and is stretched upright like he's in the middle of a synchronized swimming routine, another who appears to have misplaced her hair on the soles of her sneakers. A stray dog lope-hobbles past, its limbs drifting in a slow merry-go-round along its torso, one ear dribbled to its chin.

That animal is still less weird than the shadowkind creatures roaming between the buildings. A scaly-winged pelican with sharklike teeth swoops down at us, forcing Raze to punt it away. Something I'd think was a kangaroo if its skin wasn't translucent and glisteningly wet—and if it didn't have three bat wings unfurling down its back—thumps by.

There *are* other people nearby, though—people who are alive. Their terror washes over me in waves from all around.

Maybe the fallen bodies are humans who were outside and faced the worst of the initial impact. It doesn't look as if the shadows are damaging their bodies more, at least not quickly enough to see at a glance. Jonah is still striding along beside us, his mouth twisted but his pace steady.

I lift my voice so it'll carry into the buildings. "Everyone, I know it looks freaky out here, but you've got to leave the city! Come out and head north. It's safe once you get past the outskirts, I promise. No more… no more terrorist gangsters from outer space or anything like that."

I falter with that last statement, my conviction wavering.

Rollick told us we couldn't let humans know that shadowkind exist. The few who already do know about "monsters" like us mostly want to murder us, so I can see his point.

But when do we decide there's no excuse people will buy for a weirdness this immense and throw in the towel on the subterfuge?

I don't have to make that call, because a few humans are already poking their heads out of nearby windows.

"What the hell is going on?" one man hollers down. "What is all this crap?"

I suspect claiming it's terrorist sludge from another galaxy isn't going to comfort him.

Jonah speaks up before I have to. "We don't know yet, but it's definitely not good for you. Grab whatever you can take that's important to you and let's get out of here!"

A woman stares down at us with an expression as frazzled as her frizzy hair. "Are you from the government? You don't look like anyone official."

I guess we wouldn't, not me with my vibrant turquoise hair, Raze with all his hulking brawn, or Hail with his nonchalant posture. Even though Mirage is keeping his ears and tails hidden, he's bouncing on his feet with a mix of restless and nervous energy it'd be hard to call professional.

Hail pitches his voice upward in a dry tone. "We're as close as you're going to get to an authority right now. But if you'd rather we go save someone else, we can leave you alone to melt."

"Melt?"

There's a gasp and a whimper from somewhere beyond the windows, and the faces vanish. It only takes a minute before the first several figures hurry into the street. More pour out on both sides of the road in their wake, like a heap of raisins dumped into the porridge.

With his immense stature making him particularly visible, Raze takes the lead in pointing the humans down the road toward theoretical safety. "Just go that way, as fast as you can. Keep walking until you're out of the darkness."

A man in a ratty jacket points at a car parked by the curb. "We could drive out faster than walking."

My gaze sweeps over the line of vehicles, noting the way one windshield has swirled into the roof and another's tires have condensed into a massive lump of rubber in the middle of its undercarriage. "I, uh, don't think that's the best idea."

Who knows whether they'd drive or implode?

The man follows my gaze and must come to a similar conclusion. "Right."

"We'll salvage everything we can!" Jonah adds. "For now, just worry about keeping yourselves safe."

Doubt and confusion dull the currents of raspberry-cordial relief, but the hope of safety wins out. The humans set off in nervous clumps, clutching handbags and backpacks tight as if the sludge might try to mug them.

Which isn't a totally invalid fear, because the procession has barely made it five paces before a snarling, feathered bear-piranha shadowkind charges out of an alley.

Shrieks break out through the crowd. The humans scramble out of the way, some of them stumbling over the curb.

I dash forward automatically, reaching to the swell of determination inside me. Then I remember that I can't use my power.

Just this morning, my marked men and I discovered that I can cast out the glow of my most passionate emotions to prevent harm. But I can hardly throw around radiant beams of supernatural light without all these humans realizing something unearthly is going on.

Hail makes a subtle flick of his hand, and the shadowkind creature skids on a patch of ice that formed discreetly beneath its paws. Unfortunately, the winter fae didn't dare outright freeze its limbs, so the beast simply spins around and careens toward one cluster of humans.

With a growl of consternation, Raze hurtles toward the creature. His fingers twitch as he must restrain the urge to extend his basilisk claws.

He rams the fish-headed feather-bear with his shoulder but only a portion of his monstrous strength. The creature merely lurches to the side when I know Raze could have flung it all the way into one of the nearby buildings if he'd let himself.

"I'll help!" Mirage pipes up. His posture tenses with concentration.

The shadowkind creature sways and then sits down with a dazed air. It looks at its paws as if wondering what it's doing with its life.

Apparently Mirage has used his illusionary powers to give the beast an existential crisis.

At least none of the humans can pick up on what he's done. Those closest ease around the bizarre creature, muttering nervously to each other.

"It's all okay now!" Mirage crows with a clap of his hands —and a flash of his teeth.

One of the women freezes and jabs her finger toward him. "That—that man has *fangs*. He's a monster too!"

A jolt of my own panic shoots through my veins. I hold out my hands. "It's just—a fashion statement! They're pretend, for fun. Like Halloween! You don't have to worry."

Several gazes in the crowd jerk toward me. Eyes widen. And all at once I notice the nervous yellowish tint that's wavering across the haze around me.

A man swings his duffel bag around as if to shield him from me. "That one—her hair is fucking *glowing*. Maybe there really are terrorist aliens—right here!"

He sprints off down the street, and the rest of the humans stampede after him with a chorus of sobs and squeals.

2

Periwinkle

I stare after the fleeing humans as the anxious glow fades from my hair. "At least… they assumed we're aliens and not monsters? And they're running in the direction we wanted them to go."

Mirage nods vigorously. "Might as well look on the bright side!"

One of Rollick's assistants who helped usher some of the humans out of the buildings stops near us with an expression like he swallowed a lemon whole. "Rollick isn't going to be happy about this."

"There isn't really anything about this situation to make anyone happy," I point out. "What's the point in hiding our shadowkind powers when the whole city's flooded with weirdness? They can't be mad at us after we help them get out of the disaster safely, can they?"

On second thought, maybe I don't want that question

answered. But if the choice is keep our powers hidden while the humans turn into mutated synchronized swimmers or risk them realizing they've been saved by monsters while actually saving them, I'll take the latter.

Jonah turns to Mirage, his expression tensing as if he's coming to a similar conclusion. "Mirage, you can use your supernatural skills to downplay *our* weirdness, right?"

The fox shifter twirls his hand, and the piranha-bear spins like a ballerina before lumbering off in the direction he pointed it. "I can make them focus on what they really *really* want that's down the street. Even if it's not quite what they think it is."

"That'll do."

Hail's jaw clenches. "You want us to fling around our powers in front of the mortals? Maybe fox boy can deflect some of the panic, but we're talking about a whole city full of humans."

I set my hands on my hips. "Let the glass be half full for once! We're not going to meet even a tenth of all those humans. And if they start freaking out, then we'll figure out a new plan. Right now, I'd just like us to get on with the plan of Getting The Humans Out Of This Place Before It Turns Them Into Surrealist Art."

Raze gives a sharp huff. "I agree. There isn't much point in us even trying to help them if we aren't going to use the advantages we have. Now let's get going." He gives his massive, sinewy frame a shake. "This stuff feels like dried mud that won't flake off."

That doesn't sound any more pleasant than cold porridge.

I point down the street in the direction we were headed. "Let's get some more humans out of here!"

We set off with renewed vigor, aiming our calls to flee at the windows all along that street and the next. Raze tackles another huge shadowkind creature that charges into our midst, and Hail walls off a few smaller ones in temporary door-free igloos.

There still isn't a whole lot I can add to the evacuation efforts with my powers, so I stick to cheerleading, which is more my forte anyway. I smile and wave to the humans poking their heads out and emerging onto the sidewalks. "It'll be okay! Just a brand-new kind of flood. Very exciting, but better to watch it from outside the city than inside, all right?"

I'm not sure how much they believe me, and several gape at Raze's abrupt shows of strength and the flashes of ice Hail casts out. But with a few whirls of Mirage's bushy tails, they seem to forget all about our monstrous strangeness—including those tails—and drift off toward the edges of the city.

It isn't just the humans who go. Many of them squeeze out of the doorways clutching pet cats or with dogs trotting at their heels. The cats just peer at us with their ears laid flat, but barking bounces between the buildings.

"Don't let them go chasing after any squirrels!" I holler after them. "They might not be the kind of squirrels you're used to."

Hail halts in his tracks. "What the fuck is *that* rodent up to?"

A vole-like creature with a ridge of spikes down its back is hurling itself at the wall of a nearby building. Its body smacks against the bricks to no effect. After the first few batterings we witness, it lets out a disgruntled huff and starts scrabbling at the bricks with its claws.

I frown. "It seems like it really wants to go inside. What's so exciting in there?" I cock my head, contemplating the building, but it looks like a perfectly regular apartment complex to me. I wouldn't have thought any shadowkind creatures were in the rental market.

As he watches, Raze's forehead furrows. "It's kind of like Viscera, isn't it? Smacking and shredding everything around. Except… she was a lot better at it."

I guess we should be grateful that the spiky vole is nowhere near as talented in the destruction department as that higher shadowkind was.

The comments the rogue woman made echo through my head—all her talk about the city drawing her in and then shutting her out…

A shriek carries from around the corner. We dash over to find a woman poised on the threshold of her building's lobby —gaping at the front step which is swiveling as if on a hinge. One corner sprouts upward in a concrete bramble.

Raze leaps over and smashes the cement fixture with a slam of his fist. The woman flinches backward as if she finds his assistance as distressing as the shifting concrete, but the flow of her neighbors behind her brings her stumbling out into the street.

"Get out of the flood!" I shout. "There's safety outside the city! Just keep walking as quickly as you can, and your limbs should stay where they're supposed to be."

The humans don't look especially comforted by my reassurance, but they get moving anyway.

Another small shadowkind creature slithers across the road toward us, its round pink tongue slurping at the shadows and its furry torso rustling against the asphalt. Two puffy feet protrude partway down its body, adding a lurch to its progress with every few winds of its body.

Dodging it, I continue our foray down this new street. "Come out, come out, wherever you are! It's no good staying —you can't shut out shadows. We'll do what we can to send the weird ones back where they came from!"

Hail lets out a flat laugh. "Don't make promises we can't keep."

"I said we'd do what we can. I didn't say it'd work."

But I really hope it does. With every block we traverse and every new cluster of humans we send hurrying out of the city, the gloom of the shadowy atmosphere wears at me. The porridge is congealing.

What if *we* end up stuck in this stuff? Who's going to dig us out?

I grit my teeth against the ache creeping up my ankles and keep walking.

At the next cross-street, Jonah jerks to a stop with a strangled sound. Mirage leaps to his side first and shivers before tutting his tongue. "That's not playing nice. Hail might need to put that one on ice."

"What?" Hail demands, striding over. He and I come into view of the full scene at the same time.

My gut lurches. A shadowkind creature like a scaly, eight-legged rat is squirming *inside* the carcass of what used to be a sheepdog. The dog's head lolls against the road. Its shaggy fur is drenched red around the gouge that runs down the middle of its belly.

The shadowkind creature is drenched too even as it tries to cuddle up to its victim's innards. Its razor claws rake through more flesh as it snuggles deeper.

It doesn't look as if it wants to eat the animal. The faint emotional vibes it's giving off taste oddly warm and sweet, like melted toffee. Like it wanted to show its devotion by getting up close and personal—and that was a little too close for its target's comfort.

More humans are venturing out into the street farther down. Raze scoops up the corpse-creature combo and tosses them under a parked van that's starting to slump on its tires.

"What was that?" a man calls over.

I paste my smile back on. "Nothing to worry about! Just

a few hitches with the new atmosphere. We'll get them cleared up as quickly as we can!"

As Mirage ushers the current crowd of humans onward, a damp flick against my ankle brings my gaze snapping down.

The furry, bipedal snake has followed me. Before I can react, it twines around my calf. With those two clumsy paws, it manages to catch hold of the bottom of my dress and scramble up to wrap its tail around my arm next.

I wince and move to shake it off, but it blinks eyes that are way too wide and pleading to belong on a snake's face at me. With an emphatic wriggle, it flings itself up to my shoulder and slurps its puppy-ish tongue across my jaw.

Jonah is staring at me now. A choked sound bursts from his throat. "Um, Peri, are you adopting a new pet?"

"I think it might have adopted me." I grasp the furry but sinuous body and try to peel the creature off, but it lets out a whine that's as puppy-ish as its tongue. The waft of eagerness to please, tangy with desperation like well-sugared grapefruit, washes over me.

I'm probably a sucker, but I find myself saying, "Maybe I should hold on to it. There might be something different about the creatures coming from this new version of the rift. Rollick will want to study them."

Hail clicks his own tongue chidingly. "You just don't like to make anything sad."

"At least it's not burrowing into anyone's intestines."

For now, I add silently. *Let's hope never.*

A beast that seems much more inclined toward intestine removal hurtles out of a building a couple of blocks ahead of us with a reverberating roar. Its arrival provokes a chorus of human screams.

Raze mutters a curse vehement enough that I wonder if I should cover my new snake-puppy's ears—does it even *have* ears?—and charges off to deal with the actual monster.

As the rest of us rush after him, my heart thumps. Could I generate another ring of light like the one that surrounded Viscera to stop her from committing any more city-smashing? Maybe I could stretch it around each group of humans to fend off any danger?

But that first ring required all of my men concentrating alongside me. I'm not sure that's the most practical use of our current manpower.

Especially since having Raze simply heave the aggressive creature away while Hail freezes its legs solid seems to solve the problem pretty efficiently.

The humans keep stampeding down the street anyway. A few more shrieks ring out when my new self-declared pet lifts his fuzzy serpentine face from my shoulder to peer at the people passing by.

"He's just curious!" I tell them. "He's a nice one."

On the wake of their sprint down the street, another figure materializes on the sidewalk across from us. Rollick peers after the fleeing humans with one eyebrow arched and then contemplates the rest of our surroundings, including the blended rhino-bat creature that's currently snorting at its legs in their new icicle-esque state.

"It looks like you've been dealing with quite a few not-nice ones," the demon remarks in his usual droll tone. Despite his emotional control, tension streams off him like black coffee poured to overflowing. "Good to see the humans are moving in the right direction, though. Those few, anyway." He lifts his chin toward the half-frozen beast. "You've been showing your powers in front of them?"

"We had to," I insist. "It'd be too hard to protect the mortals otherwise. Even with that… It's taking too long."

My gaze veers toward the vast sprawl of the city ahead of us. We've barely penetrated the suburbs.

One of Rollick's assistants who's continued trailing

behind us pipes up. "I tried to tell them you wouldn't approve—"

I spin toward him, setting my hands on my hips. "Well, I don't approve of all the humans drowning in some weird rift's shadow-vomit."

Rollick sounds as if he's stifled a guffaw. "And it's a good thing I don't either. Desperate times… We can feed them some kind of story afterward. They'll probably be too bewildered to trust their memories anyway."

Jonah clears his throat. "Should we keep going, then? It seems like the rift is up overhead now—is there any sign of it sucking the flood back in like it did the smaller ones before?"

"No. Not yet." His former boss hesitates for a moment—a very un-Rollick-like thing to do. Even the demon's confidence has been shaken.

He drags in a breath. "Keep sending off as many mortals as you can. And I think I'd better summon some assistance."

He gestures to his assistant. "Get me the numbers for every shadowkind contact I have in a hundred-mile radius. We're calling them all in."

3

Mirage

I've never seen so many bewildered beings.

The shadowkind creatures that pop out of the murk here and there don't seem to know whether they're coming or going, heading up or down, forwards or backwards.

Over here, one pounces on a mailbox and squirms inside it only to thrash at the metal box until the beast tears straight through the middle, as if it was offended at finding itself inside.

Over there, another creature careens through a second story window, thumps to the ground in the middle of the road, and immediately spins around and scrambles to the doorway to yowl at it like it's demanding to be let back in.

We pass a gaunt, goat-like creature rubbing itself against a telephone pole to the point that it's bleeding essence in smoky puffs from its raw flesh. Then a squishy thing that might be made out of living marshmallows chewing chunks off a tire between wheezy gagging sounds.

Around a corner lies another poor human who's been cut up by a beast. The beast in question is sprawled out across the bleeding body like a dog on a mat. As we approach it warily, it nuzzles the woman's lifeless face as if trying to prod her awake.

It'd have more luck with that goal if it hadn't killed her first.

"They're even more topsy-turvy than usual," I remark as Raze shoos the bloody hound away from the corpse. "Inside and out. Act like a lout."

The rhyme doesn't give me even the brief flicker of comfort they usually do. I find myself nibbling at my lower lip, which is generally a bad idea when you have non-removable fangs.

Peri touches my arm with a waft of mingled concern and reassurance. "The rift is a gazillion times more warped as it was before, so it makes sense that the creatures are too. We just need to figure out how to help them."

Hail grimaces. "Or put them out of their misery as quickly as possible, if that's what absolutely has to be done."

His pained expression shows how much he dislikes that idea. But we have a lot more pain to worry about.

"Time to come out, everyone!" Peri calls to the buildings around us. Her own weird creature squirms around her feet with its puppy-ish tongue flopping around, but thankfully it doesn't seem to be in an eviscerating mood. "Hide-and-seek isn't a safe game right now. We're going to play follow the leader and get out of this place."

To punctuate her words, a nearby store awning partly collapses. One end smacks into the sidewalk while the other flips upward. It wobbles there on its side like a fabric sapling swaying in a breeze.

The shadowy substance around us ripples against my skin. My nerves wobble just like the toppled awning.

Everything about this strange flood of darkness itches at my being. I can't shake it off, but I can't settle into it either.

These aren't the same sort of shadows we're made out of, not exactly. There's something a little too sticky-solid about them.

Trickles of humans emerge from the doorways on either side of the street. Jonah waves them down the road, toward the spot where one of Rollick's assistants is now acting as Pied Piper.

"We'll get you out of here safely," our sorcerer promises. "Please follow my colleague out of the dark area as quickly as you can."

The humans start to shuffle toward the assistant, looking as bewildered as the shadow creatures have been acting—but at least they're not rolling around in anyone's entrails.

As the trickles of humanity widen into thicker streams, more and more people hustling out to potential safety, the shadows shift again. A swell of denser darkness rolls off one of the rooftops and plummets toward us.

All five of us flinch. Hail whips his hand up with a gust of icy wind; a flare of yellowish light bursts off Peri toward the sky.

I can't help simply lashing out with my hand, my claws pricking from my fingertips, multiple fox tails swirling uneasily behind me.

A shudder runs through the mass of shadow—and through the connection I can feel between me and Peri. Peri's light contracts in a snap while she winces.

The blotch of darkness heaves across the faces of the

buildings rather than hitting us, but several of the humans are yelling or shrieking.

Jonah rushes over to reassure them. "Just keep moving! You can get away from it before it gets worse."

Can they?

He glances back at me, his eyes wide, and I remember the main part I'm supposed to be playing. Tensing my body, I summon the images I've been projecting into the minds of the mortals we've encountered throughout the city.

Let them see a soft, welcoming glow just up ahead—always moving farther as it urges them through the streets. Let them hear a cheerful pop beat to keep their spirits up. Let smells of rich chocolate and savory steak waft from that ever-retreating glow.

I'm not sure which part of the illusion calms most humans enough to get them moving. It might be something slightly different for everyone. I just hope no one's too disappointed when they don't find actual steak and chocolate at the end of their travels.

As our latest procession of humans shuffles off toward the promise of the light, our team draws back together.

Hail peers at Peri, his mouth slanted downward. "Did you feel something strange when that big blob of shadow almost hit us? It looked like you reacted."

Raze's face turns grim. "*I* felt something. Like a quake through our connection. My sense of Peri's emotions scattered for a second."

Jonah nods slowly, and a chill prickles through my chest that I can't blame on Hail. They all noticed the same thing I did?

Peri hugs herself and rubs her arms. "There was a little… jolt, or jitter, or something. I've never felt anything quite like that before. But everything's gotten pretty weird, hasn't it? I can still pick up on your emotions just as well as I used to."

She pauses. "Don't worry so much. We're still a team—we're still okay."

She manages to beam her shiny rainbow smile. The unshakeable center of our strange bond.

I don't want any weird shadows messing with the energy that glues us together.

With a tsk of my tongue, I throw my arms around her and whirl her in a circle. "We can make our own jolts and jitters. Show the shadows how it's done properly."

Peri laughs, but Jonah puts on his stern teacher face, which he shouldn't be allowed to do when he isn't a teacher anymore. "We've got a lot more people to evacuate. Come on. And Mirage, be ready with those illusions. It's getting harder to keep people calm the deeper we get into the city."

It's getting harder for me to impress the illusions on people's minds the farther they have to linger before those people are safe, but I salute him and don't mention that part. Peri shouldn't have to worry either—definitely not about me.

As we march a couple more blocks down the street, the pressure of all the power I've already expended drags at my mind. Images of bright sunlight beaming down over us shift into imagined fields of smiling sunflowers waving their leaves—

No, I think that'd send most of the humans running screaming in the wrong direction.

As we call the next swarm of refugees out of their apartments, I sweep my arms through the air like a conductor. Another guiding light gleams in the distance. Why not a sprightly folk tune this time? Hot buttered popcorn and roasted pork belly…

The illusions pass through my own mind sharply enough to leave my mouth watering. But as the humans hurry past me in a daze, the glittering brilliance of the moment fades.

I'm tricking them to send them someplace safer. To make

sure they don't panic and get hurt. So it's not at all like the shadowkind I unwillingly manipulated into the clutches of the scientists who once caged me for their awful tests.

But in some ways it's exactly the same. We want to help these people—to be friendly with them. To prove we're not actually the monsters they might take us for. Only… technically, we are those monsters.

Pulling the wool over their eyes and bamboozling them seems like a questionable strategy for forming any kind of alliance.

I don't know what else to do, though, so I keep pouring as much supernatural power as I can into enticing sights, sounds, and smells. A little of the pressure loosens as earlier groups reach the edge of the city and my illusions can dissipate. But then I heap more on with the next batch of humans trudging off, the bunch of them looking perplexed though hopeful.

A prickling sensation runs down my back, as if someone's jabbing thorns into my spine one segment at a time. Which is very inconsiderate of them.

I shake myself, but the growing discomfort only digs deeper. How much longer can I keep this up before I have to admit I'm done?

Peri is already glancing over at me, her brow knitting. "Mirage? If you need a break—"

I push my smile wide, ready to dredge up whatever energy I can to get her smiling in return again.

At the same moment, a dozen new shadowkind figures materialize out of the filmy darkness around us.

They're higher beings and, to their credit, not looking particularly murderous. One steps forward with an authoritative air, two gazelle-like horns protruding from his straw-pale hair.

"Rollick called us in. He said you need reinforcements. Let's get these humans out even faster!"

Is our demonic leader losing faith in us? I lift my chin, digging even deeper into my reserves of power to fulfill our mission.

There's still a lot more city to go.

4

Periwinkle

My new snake-puppy sounds the alarm first. We're just waving another crowd of humans off on their journey out of the city when it lets out a snort and squirms against my shoulders where it's currently perched.

When I glance over, it winds down my arm to slurp its tongue across my hand. A wisp of essence trickles up from my skin.

In an instant, Raze is barging over. "If that thing is hurting you—"

The shadowkind creature—which I've found myself calling Falkor in my head after this human movie I caught a snippet of once, though that Falkor was a lot bigger and also better at conversation—is staring at me with its plaintive eyes. My gaze flicks over my body, and I cut off Raze in the middle of his threat.

"I don't think it hurt me. It's showing me that I'm getting hurt. Look."

I lift my other hand, and a small puff of essence drifts off it too. When I give the collar of my jacket a shake, a larger waft drifts off me as if I've been sitting too long and gotten dusty.

The creepy-crawling feeling that's been nibbling at my skin since we first entered the shadow-drenched city shivers down to my bones. "I think the rift's flood is starting to eat away at us." I look around at my fellow shadowkind, and my heart skips a beat. "Mirage, you're bleeding a little too."

Mirage whirls his tails, and a thread of essence spirals into the air. He hops to one side as if he can dodge the effect. "Bad shadows."

Hail peers down at his hands with a grimace. "We can't help people if we're falling apart."

Jonah takes charge in his usual steady way, but his expression has tensed. "Let's get to the fringes ourselves so you can all recover. We can carry out the evacuations in shifts now that we've got reinforcements."

He signals the group of newbies Rollick sent who are now a couple blocks away, raising his voice so they'll hear him. "We're heading back to base camp. Keep an eye on your essence and get out of the city if the atmosphere gets too toxic."

The horned being who's been leading the new group gives us a thumbs up in acknowledgment. One of his companions brays at the surrounding buildings. "All right, everyone out! Time's a-wasting."

I hustle along beside my teammates through the streets we've done our best to clear. My skin is crawling even more now that I know it's literally starting to creep off my body. "Do you think the new team will be able to convince the humans? I don't know if any of them have talents as good at comforting people as Mirage's."

"I'm sure they'll do their best," Jonah says.

Mirage nods. "There are lots of different roads to the same place."

A tendril of relief reaches me through our connection, tinged with exhaustion. He's been trying to hide it, but I think projecting all those illusions has been wearing him out as much as the strange darkness has.

My feet are aching from their old wounds. We all need a rest. If this shadowy murk can break down shadowkind bodies, who knows what it's doing to Jonah?

Mini Falkor has slithered back up to my shoulders. His head bobs in time with my steps, as if the thumps of my feet are a dance beat. At least one of us is enjoying himself.

Or herself. I'm not sure if the creature even has a gender. But his namesake is male, so I'll stick with that.

Raze eyes my hanger-on with open suspicion. "What if that thing shifts and gets mean? They all seem to do that eventually."

"He's been stable so far," I say, and focus on the creature's inner state. The emotions wavering off Falkor taste like frothy cream, mild curiosity and excitement. Apparently he thinks we're going on an adventure.

But also— "I'm not sure he is one of the warped creatures. There must be some regular shadowkind around too, right? He doesn't have that twitchy vibe the warped ones usually give off."

Hail raises his eyebrows. "Lesser shadowkind don't normally go all groupie on the rest of us."

"Maybe he was scared." I give the snake-puppy's neck a scratch, and his two paws wiggle where he's clinging to my jacket. "He needed someone to look after him."

Jonah clears his throat. "I think being scared is a pretty

appropriate response right now. Looks like we've got a whole pack to deal with."

Several misshapen creatures have emerged farther down the road. One of them is rubbing its belly against the asphalt. Another rams its head repeatedly into a shop's doorframe—if it moved just a little to the right, it could actually go inside!

The others aim menacing glances our way. A few slink forward to meet us. A feathery, beaked horse sort of thing lets out a squawk that doesn't sound like a friendly greeting.

Jonah holds out his hands. "We can all get along here."

He switches into the sorcerous syllables that make my skin shudder almost as much as the weird shadows do.

The force he's putting into the sounds rings through his voice, but only one of the approaching creatures falters. As it veers toward the sidewalk, the other three keep prowling forward.

"So much for sorcery," Hail mutters. He raises his hand with a puff of frost whirling around it.

Raze tenses to spring—but the warped beasts launch themselves at us first.

Hail heaves a stream of ice at one's legs, and Raze hurtles into another. The third careens straight toward me.

With a yelp and a jolt of terror, I throw out my own hands.

A surge of dark energy smacks into the parakeet-horse and shoots past it to shake the darkened atmosphere beyond. The creature topples backward with an indignant screech.

And the connections between me and my men give a hitch as if they're elastic bands someone's just flicked.

I reach toward my teammates instinctively as if I can restore balance to our bond by touching them. Before I've even finished raising my arms, the flow of emotions between us has settled back into its usual stable current.

Still, the fact that it wavered at all has left my nerves

wobbling even more than earlier. The sensation felt like when we shoved away that cloud of shadow an hour or two ago.

Who gave this murky flood permission to fiddle with my powers, and how can I revoke it?

Raze tosses the parakeet-horse through a high window like a basketball player making a three-point shot and then whirls toward me with a furrow in his brow. His concern echoes the uneasiness passing into me from my other marked men—and presumably pouring in the opposite direction too.

Before we can comment on the odd effect, another form ripples out of the shadows. A spindly man only a few inches taller than my diminutive height eases closer to us, raking his twig-like fingers through the air. His voice is scratchy. "You —you're proper shadowkind."

He gives off a vibe of cranberry-sharp wariness and fishy discomfort, not flavors I'd mix on purpose but totally understandable given the circumstances.

I cock my head. "So are you. You didn't come out of this rift." I swirl my hand toward the gaping maw that stretches all across the sky above the city.

The higher shadowkind peers up at the hazy darkness and trembles like, well, a twig in a breeze. "I think I did. Not very far from here. I was moving through the shadow realm, and all of a sudden, it was as if the ground dropped under my feet. Except the shadow realm doesn't really have a ground? So I don't understand…"

As he trails off, his gaze slides to the lesser creatures still on their feet: the one banging its skull against the door frame and the other that's now squirming around on its back as if trying to wriggle straight into the road. His lips purse. "I *really* don't understand all the other shadowkind around here. Did someone give them mushrooms?"

I can only guess what kind of mushrooms he's talking

about. Maybe Hail has experience with that mortal-realm feature, given his wry chuckle.

Jonah beckons the stick-like man. "Come with us. We're heading out of the rift area. I don't think it's safe for any beings to hang around here very long." He pauses. "You couldn't go back to the shadow realm where you came through?"

The man shakes his head and frowns at the sky. "I tried to leap back through the shadows, but as soon as I got close to the rift it flipped me over again, and I ended up back here."

I peer at the obsessive creatures as we pass them, mulling over our new companion's words—and the things Viscera said to me before her essence burst apart. The warped shadowkind all seem to think there's something waiting for them here that they can't get at. And now the rift is spitting out beings who didn't even want to come.

It's got to add up to a bigger picture, but right now that picture is looking more like a Dali than a Da Vinci.

We hurry on to the edge of the city through the streets we've already cleared. After a few more blocks, Falkor half-scrambles, half-winds around my torso and leaps to the ground to slither-bound along beside me. I guess he wanted to stretch his paws… and stomach? It's hard to tell which is doing most of the work propelling him along.

As the haze up ahead brightens where the flood of shadows must end, a few more regular higher shadowkind slip out to join us. They all sound as puzzled as our twiggy friend, as if they fell asleep on the bus and ended up way past their expected stop. Except none of them were actually asleep.

"The shadows crashed all around me, and I fell right through them," one woman says with a smack of her hands together. "What in the realms is going on?"

Mirage hums. "Dropped from the sky; let's not cry."

When she shoots him an even more bewildered look, Jonah steps in. "We're trying to figure that out. None of us expected something like this to happen."

Over the past week, the rift had been getting bigger and spewing out small floods. But this escalation was jumping from a pond to an ocean in one go.

What if the portal does suck all its shadows back in like it did the last couple of times it vomited? Will it siphon up everything in them too—including us?

Then again, we've been marinating in its sludgy porridge for hours without it backtracking. Looks like it's all spew, no suck this time.

We pass a few familiar factories, picking up our pace at the increased brightening ahead. A few thicker puffs of essence drift off my exposed skin, and I shove my hands in my pockets.

Maybe if I collect the smoky stuff close, it'll stick back onto me when we're out of this mess.

We step out of the murky haze into early morning sunlight. For a moment, I gape at the rising sun. I didn't even realize we'd been working through the whole night.

The fresh air fills my lungs like the sweetest honey. I drink it in, reveling in the faint tingling that spreads over my skin as my physical body knits back together in the places where the strange shadows gnawed at it.

Tents ranging from campsite to circus size poke up from the ground for miles in front of us, with a sprinkling of trailers and camper vans in between. Hundreds of figures walk or, mostly, sit slumped in my view, most of them humans who've been ushered out of the rift zone.

"Peri! Good to see you back." Sorsha jogs over to join us, her bright red ponytail swinging behind her. The phoenix shifter stops a few paces away. "Rollick's been wondering how you were getting on. We've heard a lot of stories from the incoming humans about the 'shiny short woman' who sent them here."

Falkor takes one look at our friend, darts around my feet three times, and scurry-winds back up to my shoulder. Sorsha does a double-take and then laughs. "It looks like you've been adopted. It's not so bad being a steed—you get used to it."

That's right—she has a shadowkind creature like a little dragon who stays with her. Maybe Pickle can show my puppy-snake the ropes.

Jonah has already moved on to more serious matters. "We wanted to evacuate as many people as possible, but we started noticing some ill effects after staying in the rift area for so long. I'm not sure if it affected me, but my shadowkind teammates were losing essence."

Mirage nods and flutters his fingers up from his arm. "It was just breezing away."

Sorsha's good humor dims. "We definitely don't want any of you disintegrating. You'd better get a little rest before you head back in, and we'll alert the other teams on duty to keep an eye on themselves."

Her gaze slides past us to the dark, hazy barrier less than ten feet away down the road. "Wonderful. Here come some more of the warped ones."

A couple of particularly disjointed creatures have just emerged from the thicker shadows. It's hard to call what they're doing "walking." One hobbles along on four legs, two of which are short and stubby as an aardvark's and the other two slim and long as a greyhound's. The other has possibly hundreds of legs and possibly none—I can't tell whether the blobs rippling along its jelly-ish sides are individual limbs or just bulges of its torso.

The blobby creature has a face that's all mouth, which it

holds open wide as if vacuuming up all the air around it and then suctioning at the ground. The aard-hound notices someone's evacuated Goldendoodle trotting past and surges forward with an *urf!* that might be a threat or a welcome.

It could use a little work on its delivery.

Raze steps into the latter creature's path to block it. It halts and then bumps its round, scaly head against his leg. Either it wants scritches or it's really bad at playing battering ram.

The basilisk shifter backs up a step. "What are we doing with the ones that aren't aggressive so far? It doesn't seem right to kill them."

Sorsha sighs. "The ones that come out of the rift area, we've been sending back in. They seem to prefer being at one with the strangeness. Rollick has beings patrolling the outskirts. I don't know what to make of these lesser shadowkind. We found one that suffocated a human by squeezing him too tight and seemed pretty distressed about it, and another that kept digging through every wall it encountered. I have no idea what it was looking for."

Like the ones we've seen—trying to get as close as they can to different parts of the mortal world. As if they feel like there's supposed to be a place for them here—the way Viscera did.

She got so angry when she couldn't figure out how to fit in…

As if stirred by my thoughts, the aard-hound growls and twists its body. The blobby thing shudders and sprouts sudden fangs from its vacuum mouth.

My pulse hiccups, but I tense against the urge to panic. They're upset because nothing makes sense and everyone's pushing them away.

What if we gave them a real welcome?

I care about these creatures, don't I? I want to see them thriving just like every other being from both realms.

Hail steps forward, his jaw tightening as if he's bracing to use his magic.

"Wait." I put all my attention on the pang of affection I can summon for these poor beasts.

The turquoise glow that beamed out of me yesterday spills forward again. I aim it at the two creatures, summoning even more tenderness and compassion for their plight.

We're glad you're here. We want you to stay. We'll help you find your place.

Sorsha sucks in a breath. Hail lets out a sputter. "Well, fuck."

Both of the creatures sprawl out on the road like cats before a hearth, but I don't think that's what my companions were reacting to. When I flick my gaze upward, my lips part in surprise.

My loving glow has seeped far enough to touch the edges of the rift's shadowy flood. Where it brushes the darkness, the haze has taken on a faint glow too. The murky stuff hasn't shrunk, but it feels thinner somehow, not so ominous.

Less like it's about to swallow us whole.

As I stare, my light contracts back into me. The closest patch of darkness remains a bit lighter and more vibrant. I seem to have given it a cheerful makeover.

Sorsha moves closer. "That's something, all right. I don't suppose you have enough of that shiny power to spread it around the whole city?"

I choke on a nervous giggle. The patch of murk I've altered is maybe one-millionth of the whole flood. "I don't know."

"Well, it can't hurt—"

The phoenix shifter is cut off by a rolling rumble that

reverberates from above. We spin around to see a huge military helicopter descending by the edge of the makeshift refugee camp—flanked by two smaller copters and with a horde of trucks and tanks approaching from farther beyond.

"Shit," Sorsha says. "It looks like the cavalry's arrived."

5

Periwinkle

By the time we've reached the stretch of flat, grassy terrain where the helicopters are landing, a dozen army trucks and half as many tanks have already roared up around it.

A bunch of the evacuated humans drift over, looking dazed or nervous. The wave of anxiety wafting off them collides with a current of aggression emanating from the new arrivals, leaving me adrift in a sour-and-spicy soup.

Soldiers pour out of the ground vehicles, guns at the ready. One of them spots a shadowkind being with a prominent cat-like tail who's moving between the tents and shouts, "It's one of the mutants!"

Mutants? That's a new one. I think I prefer "monsters," or even "terrorist gangsters from outer space," but there's no time to debate with the armed figures about proper terminology. The uniformed man next to the one who shouted opens fire.

The cat-tailed woman yelps and dives into the shadows, leaving only a puff of essence behind. The rest of us flinch, even the humans.

"Where the fuck did it go?" the first soldier yells.

I'd feel more like telling him if he wasn't looking to fill us with bullets. My stance stiffens.

Rollick pushes to the front of our increasingly frothed-up crowd with his usual air of authority—and a crackle of power I have to think the mortals can sense at least a tad.

The demon fixes the soldiers with a cool stare. "What do you think you're doing? Everyone here is already safe—or they were until you started shooting."

Another soldier twitches, aiming his gun at Rollick. "Are you one of *them*?"

The demon doesn't appear fazed by the threat of being pelted with ammunition. "One of the people who's been helping evacuate this city so as few civilians as possible get hurt? Yes. What kind of 'them' were you expecting?"

A soldier farther along their swarm points to a being who's just poked his spike-dappled head from a tent to see what's going on. "There's another one! Everyone, get away from it."

As she levels her gun, Rollick holds out his hands. "There's no reason to be afraid of Spur. I can't say he smells the best, but he's a very amiable conversationalist. No offense, Spur."

"None taken, boss!" the shadowkind calls out as he ducks out of view again, preferring to remain bullet-free.

Mutters pass between the soldiers, and several more rifles swerve toward Rollick. "Stay right there," one orders. "No sudden movements."

Rollick rolls his eyes. "I don't suppose anyone here is really in charge?"

The back ramp of the huge helicopter has just swung open with the stilling of its blades. "That would be me. Everyone, hold your fire—for now."

Not one but two men clamber down from the body of the helicopter. If they were illustrations in a book of opposites, they couldn't look more perfect.

The man who strides forward first—the one who spoke —is built like one of the tanks he apparently commands: tall and wide and with lots of blocky edges. He's even got a long, pointed nose that could stand in for one of their jutting guns. His skin is almost the same color, a dull brown. Bits of sandy brown hair poke from beneath his official cap. The crest on the hat shines very prettily—I'll give him that.

Hustling behind him comes a figure at least a foot both shorter and slimmer, whose close-cropped black hair gleams in place of a cap and whose pale features look sanded smooth. He comes to a stop at the bigger man's flank, snapping to strict attention while his companion flexes his broad shoulders.

I wonder what you'd get if you could mush them together. The most perfectly average specimen of all humanity?

Unfortunately, at that moment a shadowkind creature like some kind of slimy elephant comes charging toward the helicopter with a blare of its two trunks. The big brown man spins and swings his arm toward it.

Booms of gunfire reverberate through the air. The creature gives a bugling sound that manages to sound consternated and simply barrels onward, looking even more unsettling with several streaks of smoky essence trailing behind it like party streamers.

"That's not how you deal with them!" Hail snaps, but his

voice is lost in another deluge of gunfire. His stance tensing, he whips his hand forward.

The slime-ephant jerks to a stop with frost lacing its four legs. Letting out a trumpet that's more startled than anything else, it tips over on its side, crushing the hood of one of the trucks.

But none of the soldiers. We should get points for no loss of life.

The military folks look like they don't want to declare anyone except themselves winners. The guns flick toward Hail next.

With a disgusted curl of his lip, the fae man steps into the shadows before anyone can attempt to shoot him. I wince inwardly.

He already resented humans enough for killing his mentor. They're hardly setting the stage for a brand-new friendship.

The soldiers press closer to the refugee camp, their guns twitching left and right as if they think the weapons can detect who's shadowkind and who's human. The humans who are among us might look even more bewildered than they did before, which is an impressive feat.

"Where's the freak who threw around his weird powers?" the tank-like man demands. "Harboring criminals is a crime too, you know."

Rollick claps his hands. The firm sound radiates through the camp like a thunderclap. It holds enough supernatural power to set the hairs on the back of my neck on end.

If it comes down to demon vs. tanks and machine guns, I'd like the chance to step aside before I'm caught in the crossfire.

"Enough!" our leader says. "*We* aren't your problem. My icy colleague just saved at least a few of your lives when none of you managed to do it. The actual problem is over there."

He jabs his hand toward the city in its cloak of darkness that not even the brightening sunlight can penetrate. "Do you want to help us deal with that, or are you here to add to our problems instead of fixing them?"

Mr. Tank does his best to loom, although he looks like he might tilt right over. "Listen up. I'm Colonel Hueber of the U.S. Army, and I'm in charge of this situation from here on. Who—and what—the hell are you?"

I get the impression he's trying to shoot Rollick with his eyes. Thankfully the colonel doesn't appear to possess any supernatural powers of his own.

Rollick smiles mildly. "We'll be glad to have your assistance, Colonel Hueber. I think it'd be best if we worked together. It's clear your associates don't have any experience dealing with the sort of threat this catastrophe poses."

"You haven't answered my question."

"You can call me Rollick. I'm a resident of this country as much as you are. Some of us here may be something other than what you think of as human—I won't deny that. But we're looking to help, not to harm, and as soon as this mess is cleaned up, we'll disappear and you can pretend you never knew we existed."

Colonel Hueber's jaw works as if he's chewing over Rollick's suggestion—and doesn't think it tastes all that good.

"From what I hear, things like you have something to do with this threat." He waves toward the city. "All this shadowy smoky stuff. It comes out of you too, doesn't it?"

I can't keep quiet. "The same blood comes out of you as would come out of a terrorist gangster!" Although possibly not one from outer space, I suppose.

Several pairs of eyes, including the colonel's, jerk toward me.

Oops—I wasn't looking to become their new target.

I lift my hands in surrender, and Falkor squirms around one of my arms all the way to the other.

Hueber's lips part in momentary astonishment before he regains his grip on himself. "What the fuck is that thing on you, lady?"

The slender, softer man next to him clears his throat. "I don't think she's actually a lady, sir, at least not in the traditional sense."

"I can figure *that* much out for myself, Major Yin. I was being polite. Don't know why I'm bothering with these damned mutant freaks or whatever they are."

I peel my self-declared pet off my arm and tuck him against my chest, where he deigns to coil up in my embrace. "We aren't mutants or freaks, and we do appreciate politeness. We can be polite too. I don't know what this little guy is, but he hasn't hurt anyone either."

Raze sounds as if he's swallowed a growl. "Don't you think we should focus on the actual dangers here, like Rollick said?"

Hueber squints at us as if recalibrating, trying to work out just how many of the figures he's faced with are inhuman. "You've rounded up all these people from the city. What do you think you're going to do with them? Are you casting them out so you can take over the place for yourselves?"

Jonah steps up next to Rollick. "*I'm* human. I'll bleed for you if you need me to prove it. And I can tell you that our allies in this catastrophe can't survive in whatever's happened to the city either. The creatures that've been coming out of it are different from anything any of us are used to. We're just trying to protect as many people as we can. Isn't that what you want to do too?"

Again, the colonel appears to deliberate. I'm not sure that is what he wants. But it would probably sound bad if he claimed to be more interested in spraying us with bullets indiscriminately, which works in our favor.

Before he can say anything else, one of the shell-shocked evacuees meanders forward. She swipes her mussed hair back from her forehead and darts a nervous glance toward Rollick and my team before speaking. "They're telling the truth. I didn't know what to do—I was feeling sick, but everything outside looked just as awful—they came and helped us leave."

Her voice quavers but doesn't falter in her declaration of support.

Another of the humans pushes toward the soldiers with an energy that's almost manic. "Yeah. Even if they're freaks— *we* were totally freaking out without them. They've been looking after us. Got us food, gave us a place to lay low now that we're out. That one even stopped one of those real monsters that was going to pounce on me." He points a shaky hand at Raze.

Murmurs of agreement ripple through the refugees who've gathered to watch the confrontation. Threads of wariness still lace their moods, but relief and gratitude sweep over me faster, comforting as a hot cinnamon bun.

As more voices are raised with their own accounts of how various shadowkind helpers came to their aid, a tingle spreads over my scalp. I realize my hair must be glowing my happiness at the same moment as Major Yin's eyes widen in my direction.

Colonel Hueber notices before his underling can say anything. "What in the blazes—"

He jerks up a pistol he was holding at his side. Even as I flinch, the major jumps in with a brisk but warm tone. "Look, they're even providing a light in the darkness. That's fascinating. Who would have imagined talents like that actually exist outside of movies? They could make pretty handy allies in more than just this situation."

I don't love the way Hueber's expression turns thoughtful, but he does lower his weapon.

The colonel motions to the gathered soldiers without acknowledging Major Yin's words. "Let's speak to some of the city's residents and get their full accounts. As long as none of the… strange ones interfere, we can—"

One of Rollick's assistants pops into view and bursts out a desperate warning. "Over by the rift—a whole swarm of the warped creatures just barged out, and they look like they're on a rampage."

6

Jonah

You know you've got a problem when the humans around you are scarier than the monsters.

Had I enjoyed observing the violently fucked-up shadowkind creatures we'd come across while evacuating the city? Hell, no.

But even when those beasts were behaving in ways I couldn't make sense of, I knew they were driven by instinct and self-preservation, however warped those instincts might have become as well.

When it comes to the soldiers stomping down the street around me? The glint in their eyes and the sheen of their guns makes my stomach flip over.

They're on board with self-preservation too, sure. But they're also consciously choosing violence before they know it's necessary. That's their go-to strategy. They've *already* tried to shoot at a few totally innocent higher shadowkind who they'd have found out were on their side if they'd bothered to listen first.

I'm not totally convinced that they won't decide to try to shoot *me* if they object to my tone or my expression or who knows what else. Unfortunately for me, I can't dive into the shadows like most of my colleagues can.

"Bullets won't do much good against these creatures anyway," I call out to the squadron around me. "You might slow them down a bit, but you have to let us bring our powers into the mix too."

"We'll follow our orders," the man closest to me retorts.

The thunderous warble of a helicopter passing overhead makes any further conversation impossible. Not that my new sort-of allies seem interested in chatting.

Peri pops out of the shadows next to me, her arms jerking up in a gesture of surrender when several soldiers flinch. "I come in peace! I'm one of the good guys!"

She sidles closer to me, an uneasy yellowish glow wavering over her teal hair, and drops her voice to a murmur. "Are we sure that more is definitely merrier?"

Despite the situation, my mouth twitches with the start of a smile at her wry tone. Her anxiety quivers into me through our connection, but also all the warmth of her trust and affection.

The mess we're investigating has gotten bigger than any of us could have been prepared for, but I couldn't be happier with the closest companions I have on my side.

I lower my voice to match hers. "I think I need more data before I draw definite conclusions."

Peri lets out a soft giggle and grasps my hand in a brief squeeze. Her odd new pet offers a chirpy sort of woof where it's bounding along by her feet.

If it's jealous, it'll just have to deal.

For that one moment, I have the strange feeling

everything's going to be okay. Why shouldn't we be able to conquer whatever weirdness the world throws at us next?

Then the horde of rioting shadowkind creatures hurtles into view from beyond the row of factories up ahead.

Beasts both big and small, their clashing features making them even more alien than regular shadowkind, barrel toward the mass of soldiers. So much good my advice did—most of the uniformed figures open fire without a second's hesitation.

As the creatures jerk and swerve, flitting into the shadows and back out again, our shadowkind allies emerge on the flanks of the squadron. I catch a glimpse of Raze charging into the creatures' midst, smashing one into the ground and hurling another aside. Ice glints from bolts Hail flings from his hands, aimed to disable the beasts rather than outright kill them.

I suck air into my lungs and holler out a string of sorcerous syllables with all the power I can put into them. *Go back to where you came from! Stay away from other living beings. Do no harm.*

The energy of my magic reverberates through my chest and into my voice. I can feel the impact it should have, can practically see the way the shadowkind I've pitched the commands towards should whirl and dash away.

A few of the smaller ones do, skittering back and forth and then fleeing toward the city. I think I see a couple of the mid-sized creatures stumble in momentary hesitation.

But mostly they keep charging toward us, shrieking and bellowing, snapping their teeth and slashing their claws.

My stomach sinks. The one talent I have that should help against these creatures is a total flop.

Not only that, I think I see a couple of regular shadowkind who joined our efforts darting away, accidentally hit by my words. Slight miscalculation.

I don't have time to stew over my failure. The soldiers are failing too. Despite all their bullets, several of the rampaging shadowkind are pouncing right into their midst.

I dodge sideways as a spiny leopard springs past me. A soldier yelps as it digs its fangs into her shoulder and gasps when a cracking surge of electricity knocks the creature backward. She glances behind her at the higher shadowkind who came to her aid, and for the first time, I catch a glimmer of actual respect.

"Thank you," she rasps out… and pelts the leopard-thing with a bunch more bullets that just turn it into a smoking leopard-thing.

It's close enough to the source of the bullets that a few more rounds send it slumping into a heap of smoldering essence on the road. The same can't be said for its swifter companions.

Shouts ring out all around me. A bull-like creature races toward me with its horns lowered, and some kind of slippery ferret sinks its fangs into my ankle. I stagger sideways, managing to dodge the hurtling horns, and snatch at a lamppost before I fall to my doom by ferret.

A shadowkind on our side hurtles by and smashes the ferret creature beneath one forceful foot. More beings run this way and that, heaving out powers and yelling suggestions to each other.

My arm tightens around the lamppost in a tighter embrace than I'd usually offer anyone other than Peri. Sweat breaks out on my forehead. I'm abruptly aware of the booming of my heartbeat.

No. I'm going to be okay.

I can't melt down in the middle of a battle. My friends, my colleagues—everyone needs me.

What they need me to do, my scrambling mind can't quite identify. I hurl a more focused command directly at the bull, and it actually trots backward a few steps before its glowing eyes flare with renewed rage. Which does at least give Hail time to freeze its legs out from under it.

I kick aside a rattish creature, sending it skidding across the asphalt. A giant newt roars at me, and I fling myself around the other side of the pole.

My breath is coming in short bursts now. Even with my eyes open, images that have nothing to do with the scene in front of me flash through my vision.

Shadowy forms lunging from the corners of a room. My mother's body falling—blood spilling everywhere. Snarls and cackles—my body flung through the air and raked by claws—

I clutch the post even harder and try to focus on the ground beneath my feet the way my therapist back when I was a preteen used to teach me. Staying physically grounded can help keep my mind grounded too.

I'm not in the past. I'm right here.

Right here in the middle of a torrent of violent shadowkind.

Mirage pops up next to me, and my hand flings out automatically. I catch the shove just before my hand smacks his chest.

The fox shifter blinks at me and cocks his head. "Do you need help? You look sick, maybe. This doesn't seem like a good place to take a rest."

No. No, it's not. And somehow just looking at him, taking in the ruddy conical ears poking from his hair and the glint of fangs in his mouth makes my pulse pound harder.

Somewhere deep inside my body is the knowledge that he's one of *them*. One of the monsters.

Somewhere deep down, I don't quite trust even him.

The shame of that recognition twists around my throat. I force out an answer. "I think I should go back to the camp.

I'm not helping much here. Don't worry about me. The rest of you… You should keep pushing the warped creatures back."

Mirage's forehead furrows. He reaches for my arm as if to help support me and freezes when I flinch away.

"They need you," I say hastily to cover my reaction, and jab my hand toward the fray up ahead.

The combined efforts of the army and the gathered higher beings has started to push the warped creatures' assault backward. And I'm really not any use if I'm distracting my allies from the job they need to be doing.

I turn and fix my gaze on the next lamp post down the street. When I reach it, I aim for the next one after that. My pulse keeps thundering through my veins. The ground feels as if it's teetering beneath my feet.

The wail of sirens brings a weird mix of relief and apprehension. As I sway onward, three ambulances careen into view up ahead.

A couple park farther down near the tents. One zooms until it screeches to a halt just a few paces away from me.

A team of paramedics emerges from the back doors. A couple of them grab my arms and haul me toward the ambulance. "Hey, we've got you now. Where are you injured?"

My words hitch on the way out. "No injuries. Just—just something like a—panic attack."

They don't appear to believe me. One tuts to himself while the other bustles around pulling equipment out of boxes. She nudges me down to sit at the back of the ambulance.

"The reports coming in from here are crazy," the man says as he checks my pulse. "Panicking seems like a normal reaction. Your breathing's erratic. You haven't inhaled anything toxic?"

I shake my head, and the world sways. "Nothing—nothing like that. I'm really okay." Or I will be, once I get a hold of myself. "There are other people you should be helping."

"Everyone matters." The woman shudders. "They're saying there are *monsters* out there? What the hell is going on? Here, lie down for a minute."

I don't know how to argue with her. They are monsters, in one way or another.

I sink down on the ambulance floor and stare up at the white ceiling. Fainter visions of the past flit past my eyes.

The ones who killed my family, who ripped me from our little village and terrorized me while they decided how to use me—they were monsters in every sense of the word.

They're gone now. They can't hurt anyone anymore. Rollick and Quinn and the rest of them made sure of it, nearly twenty-five years ago.

But now there are so many more, with ripping teeth and rasping claws…

I close my eyes. "They weren't trying to be here. They're confused. It isn't their fault."

The man snorts. "Right. Not their fault they're tearing apart a whole city."

Part of me wants to argue with him. Part of me knows he understands what's happening far less than even I do.

But from that place deep inside me, a quiver of uncertainty rises up.

How could something *this* bad happen just by accident?

There've always been shadowkind who preyed on the mortal world, even if it wasn't most of them. Are we making excuses and giving the benefit of the doubt when we really should be treating this disaster as a declaration of war?

Periwinkle

Rollick paces back and forth at the head of the table as if he isn't sure where he wants to stand. I'd suggest to him that he shouldn't worry about it because it doesn't really make a difference, but he finally makes up his mind and spins toward all of us gathered in the trailer meeting room.

The gathering is a swarm now. He hasn't included the random higher shadowkind who tumbled out along the fringes of the warped rift, even though several of them helped us finish evacuating the city, but the trailer is still packed.

Alongside me and my team, Sorsha and her men, and the shadowbloods are a couple of the academy's administrators and many of the level 4 and 5 students, plus some lower level students whose problems I guess were more about hiding their true nature than risk of them doing harm. Fen and Brine have squished in next to me, Fen periodically squeezing my arm. I'm not sure if it's more for her reassurance or mine, given the sprinkling of nervous water that often dampens her palm.

There's no point in trying to hide our presence here at the rift now. The cat's out of the bag about us being inhuman with the military folks and many of the refugees. Making sure the weirdo rift's flood doesn't spread any farther than it already has is the most important thing.

I can sense various other beings watching from the shadows to avoid cramming us even more tightly in the enclosed space. I think they're Rollick's assistants and various other associates who are used to doing his bidding without much of a say.

"Well," Rollick says. "The good news is that this is the only place in the mortal realm where the shadows have collided with an area of high human occupation. The bad news is they *have* collided with the mortal realm in several other locations."

My heart skips a beat. "The other strange rifts?"

He nods. "All of them expanded and collapsed over the surrounding terrain much the same way ours here has. I'm getting reports from the beings I had monitoring the other rifts. Thankfully the humans nearby have been smart enough not to go diving in where they obviously have no business going, but my people are having trouble holding back the deluge of new creatures emerging. I've sent the other administrators from the academy to pitch in along with various helpers, but it's a difficult business."

Riva frowns, twisting the end of her silvery braid around her finger. "Do they need more people pitching in? We shadowbloods could split up again—"

Before she can finish her offer, Rollick cuts her off with a raised hand. "The situation here is by far the most urgent. We've got mortals with large guns prowling all around the camps. Tens of thousands of humans getting at least a glimpse of shadowkind."

He sighs and rubs his forehead. My stomach twists like it's trying out for a gymnastics team.

The demon is thousands of years old. To see even him this taken aback by the catastrophe here… Are there words for something even more dire than a catastrophe?

And what do you do to de-catastrophize it?

Sorsha's partner who sometimes turns into a magma-laced hellhound clears his throat, his expression even grimmer than Rollick's. "Have the Highest had anything to say about the… incident?"

The Highest—the immense, ancient beings who hold a vague authority in the shadow realm and over shadowkind who venture mortal-side. At the thought of them, a fresh chill sweeps over my skin.

I hadn't even considered their perspective. I've never encountered any of them myself. But from the murmurs I've heard over the years, they get a bee up their butts about shadowkind catching human attention.

It's not as if it was our idea for a messed-up rift to bellyflop all over a city. Will that matter to them?

Rollick shakes his head, provoking a flutter of relief in both me and the various beings around me. "Not much. They've been notified, of course, but I think the news is so bizarre they're more concerned about their own safety than anything else. The last I heard, they're hiding even deeper in the depths of the shadow realm to avoid any strangeness from these rifts, demanding the rest of us keep control over the situation however we can."

"We have made some progress there," Sorsha points out with her usual optimism, but I can't help noticing the furrows in her forehead too. "At least the soldiers aren't opening fire willy-nilly anymore."

"Yes. We're being riddled with fewer bullets than we were yesterday. And we've gotten all the humans we could locate out of the city. Let's celebrate the wins we have."

Rollick's chuckle doesn't sound particularly celebratory. He holds his emotions close, but I'm still picking up a vibe of uneasy frustration as unpalatable as days-old black coffee.

A hand shoots up in the midst of the crowd, as if we're still at school. Rollick motions for the owner of the hand to speak.

A female shadowkind I recognize as one of my old bullies —one of Gloss's friends, before Gloss got banished for nearly murdering me—pushes a little closer with a flick of her gleaming hair over her shoulders. "Why do we need to worry about the humans at all now that they've got their own authority-type-people to help them? Let the soldiers stay around the humans who left the city, defending them with those guns, and we'll focus on the rift."

Rollick's tone turns dry. "That would be fine, except I don't think Colonel What's His Face and Major Second In Command would agree. They barely trust us to wipe our asses, let alone contain what they see as some kind of level one-million biohazard."

Sorsha's hellhound shifter raises his eyebrows. "We could incinerate them all, and then we wouldn't have to worry about them to begin with."

As Sorsha elbows him chidingly, Rollick shakes his head. "Our new 'friends' may be frustrating, but I don't think they've earned a massacre. And they are at least useful for corralling the evacuees and finding temporary homes for them farther from the morphing shadow deluge."

"Is there definitely a problem, then?" grumbles Gnash, one of the academy's administrators. "So the humans have a few new dark spots on their maps. They'll survive. The shadowkind creatures will keep them on their toes. They've gotten pretty complacent."

His colleague Shanty glowers at him. "You don't really mean that. If all humans get it into their heads that they've got monsters to fight, they'll come for us too."

"That is one major concern," Rollick agrees. "Another is the fact that I don't think even the current state of affairs is secure. I've gotten reports of signs of instability at many other regular rifts around the world."

Another chill washes over me, sharper than if Hail had flung a blizzard my way. "What if they all collapse?"

"I'd rather not find that out. So we need to work together to find ways to shove the shadows—and all the creatures coming with them—back where they belong. Which would be easier if we had more of an idea why they spilled out in the first place."

A dazed looking guy off to one side of the room grunts. "Maybe the shadow realm got too big. It's overflowing, like a bathtub."

"With very aggressive bath toys!" someone else pipes up with a giggle.

One of Sorsha's other men, the incubus whose voice always comes out smooth as chocolate, offers a wry grin. "Is another powerful higher shadowkind trying to take over the world again? That seems to be their favorite hobby these days."

Rollick grimaces. "I'd prefer an explanation that easy, but no one's noticed any odd activity other than the rifts themselves—and I've had people on the lookout ever since we found the first strange rift months ago. It'd be difficult to create a problem this big while keeping all evidence imperceptively small."

I find myself raising my hand—tentatively, half expecting most of the room to laugh.

Gloss's friend does snicker, and I think I catch a guffaw from elsewhere in the group of my one-time classmates, but Fen gives my other arm another approving squeeze.

Rollick's expression stays thoughtful. "What is it, Peri?"

"I've been thinking about it," I say. "Seeing all the strange ways the new shadowkind are behaving, and remembering the things Viscera said while she was tearing up the city… It seems like the warped beings have the impression that they're supposed to merge with the mortal realm somehow. That there's a place for them, and they just can't find it. A lot of them are trying in very physical ways."

"Yes, I've seen some of that behavior myself. And?"

I clasp my hands together. "What if… What if after all the back and forth, all the times shadowkind have affected the mortal realm and mortals have affected shadowkind… the barrier between the realms *is* starting to merge? So that there isn't really a barrier anymore. Everything's starting to get literally muddled together."

Someone else snorts, but the sound echoes out into deathly silence. I think I'd prefer laughter, actually.

"That does make a certain kind of sense," Sorsha says after a moment, but I can't say she looks happy about it either.

Mirage shivers where he's standing near me. "But what would that mean? If the shadows all mix with the sunshine… There's no sunshine left."

Rollick drags in a breath. "We don't know if that's what's happening yet. And if it is, we may be able to keep the effect contained. Let's all keep that theory in mind while we continue to investigate. And if anyone finds any power or action that makes the situation better rather than worse, let me know."

Raze touches my shoulder. When I look up at him, he tips his chin toward Rollick.

An image wavers up from my memory of the beams of light I shot out that one time yesterday—and the way the mass of shadow seemed to lighten as it absorbed them.

But that change didn't really *help* anything. I have no idea if I could do anything even that small again.

The demon goes on with a motion toward Jonah. "The new sorcerer I was bringing in to assist us has finally arrived. Let's have the two of you talk, and maybe you can find a strategy for talking most of the warped creatures into heading home. The rest of you, you have your assigned duties for the rest of the day."

Jonah follows Rollick out of the trailer first. My human lover at least looks steadier on his feet than he did in the middle of the fray yesterday. By the time I found him again, he insisted he'd only gotten momentarily overwhelmed.

With all the chaotic emotions that were whirling around me in the moment, I couldn't even tell if he was lying.

My other marked men head out of the trailer with me on foot. Technically we've been ordered to rest after the long hours we put into evacuating the city over the past two days. We'll recover better in the shadows. But too much uncomfortable energy is wriggling under my skin for me to want to lounge around and ignore the problems literally looming over us.

The second my feet hit the ground with a faint pang of old pain, Falkor scuttles out from under the trailer and winds around one of my ankles. He gives a warbled arf and peers up at me with his puppyish eyes.

Hail's lips curl in distaste. "That thing is still clinging to you?"

I thought the shadowkind creature that seems to have adopted me got bored of my company, but apparently he just had other temporary business to take care of.

"He's allowed to cling." I bend down to give Falkor a

scratch under his chin, which results in the entire back half of his serpentine body wagging behind his two paws. "That's a good boy."

"And here I thought it was bad having to share your attention with this lug." Hail's gaze slides to Raze. He keeps his tone dry, but the basilisk shifter growls at him anyway.

"You both need to behave," I tell them, moving to rubbing the puppy-snake's neck. "Maybe then I'll call you two good boys."

Oh. From the flare of hot-cocoa desire that floods me at my remark, both of them approve of that idea quite a lot.

Mirage spins around on the patchy grass with a swirl of his tail. "But you're the good-est of all girls."

Hmm, it does feel tingly-nice when someone says that. I grin at him. "Thank you!"

My gaze slides toward the mass of darkness in the near distance. "It doesn't feel right to be standing around when the rift could vomit up more shadows at any moment, does it?"

Raze slides his arm around me. "We won't be able to help anyone if we run ourselves totally ragged. That goes for you too."

"I know. I just—"

As we spoke, Falkor unwound from my leg. He's squirming off toward a grasshopper jumping between patches of grass when a knee-high, ridged spidery creature comes scrambling from around the side of the trailer.

The warped shadowkind lets out a whistly sort of shriek at the sight of my self-appointed pet and launches itself forward.

I yelp, but Falkor manages to wriggle away even faster. He shoots between my feet and coils behind my heels, quivering.

The armored spider jerks to a halt a few paces away from

me. Its legs twitch. Its feet dig into the dirt beneath them, scraping back and forth in little hitches.

Raze has tensed to pounce. "Is it still looking to attack?"

The emotions spiking off the creature taste as prickly as horseradish, with a searing thread of aggression winding through. My own emotions surge up with the urge to blast it away.

I catch myself, remembering how our bonds wobbled when I lashed out defensively yesterday. I deflected that other attack in a more peaceful way. "Wait. Maybe I can…"

I summon all the sympathy and affection I drew on before.

No matter how creepy this crawly thing looks, it's a shadowkind just like me. It didn't ask to be here or to be so confused.

Even while it simmers with fierceness, it's trying to meld itself with the ground.

"We'll help you find a place," I tell it, holding out my hands. "If you want to belong here, there has to be a way to make it happen."

A teal glow spills out from my hands. It washes over the creature.

The hitching of its many feet stills. It sinks down on the dirt and stretches out its legs as if it's decided it'd rather sunbathe than skirmish.

The acidic emotions that were jabbing into me smooth out into a gentle lemon cream.

Around it, my men are gaping.

Hail chokes on a laugh. "I hope you're not making offers you're going to go back on."

I raise my chin. "I'm not. Any being that wants to live here should be able to. We'll figure it out. We just… we just have to make sure that *here* stays here and doesn't become some warped part of the shadow realm."

Raze hums low in his chest. "Peri, I think this power of yours might be the key to that. If you can calm down the creatures and make them feel like they've already settled in… We should see what it can do on the rift when you really try."

I look at the swell of roiling shadow that cloaks the city, and my throat closes up. I can soothe a creature here and there, but… Does a cream puff like me really stand a chance at fixing a problem that huge?

I guess there's only one way to find out.

"Come on," I say. "We'd better find Rollick."

8

Raze

The overflowing rift doesn't look any prettier at its back end. The thick, dark atmosphere still drapes over the nearby buildings—big houses on bigger lawns in this apparently more upscale suburb—like a haze of watery mud.

Peri wipes her hands together and glances around. There's no one else in sight except for one of Rollick's assistants who came along to monitor her experiment. That's why we trekked all the way around the city to conduct it.

The demon figured it'd be better for her to make the attempt far away from the human refugee camp and the soldiers now marching among them.

He phrased it as if he was concerned about how their presence might distract her. I can't help wondering if he's also a little worried about her powers going haywire the way they used to and blasting a whole bunch of the mortal beings we've been trying to save.

Peri's control has gotten so much better, but the collapsed rift has thrown us all for a loop. I can't totally blame Rollick for wanting to be careful.

From the quivers of nervousness mixed with the aura of hope Peri gives off, she's picked up on his other possible reasons too. She sucks her lower lip under her teeth and then drags in a breath, setting her shoulders in a determined stance that makes my heart twinge with affection.

She might be short and soft, but my Glowbug is a force to be reckoned with.

She walks right up to the misty edge of the rift's deluge. No living beings show on the other side either, not even the warped creatures that've spilled out of the rift from the shadow realm. But I'm here if any of them decide they want to take a piece out of the woman I love.

My hands flex at my sides, ready to release my claws.

"All right," Peri says with even more than her usual good cheer. "Let's do this!"

She holds out her hands toward the shadowy haze. A gentle smile curves her lips, tugging at my heart even more.

Her voice comes out as soft as the rest of her. "We're glad you want to be part of this world. We'd like to be able to work together. You have so much power and passion. It could be a really great partnership."

Rollick's assistant arches her eyebrows. She flicks her gaze toward me. "Is she trying to clean the rift up or take it on a date?"

I scowl back at the shadowkind woman. "This is how her power works. She has to focus on how much she cares."

The assistant's expression remains skeptical, but thankfully her hushed comment doesn't appear to have rattled Peri. The turquoise glow that's now the usual color of her power has lit up on her palms.

She holds her hands out farther, and the glow expands. It washes into the mass of shadows, wavering and glittering as if caught in currents we couldn't see before.

I watch the edges of the mass, checking whether it's eased back or retracted at all. If Peri can convince the rift to suck all this noxious darkness back inside, to commune with the mortal world in some less harmful way, the catastrophe could be over just like that.

I don't see the border of its deluge budge at all, though.

Peri inhales again with a little shakiness to the sound. She pours out even more of her turquoise glow, but sweat has started to bead on her forehead. A tremor runs through her stance.

My claws pop out even though this isn't a threat I can tackle with brute force. I grit my teeth against the urge to tell her to stop.

I shouldn't distract her. She can tell when she's worn herself out.

That doesn't mean I like seeing it, though.

Peri appears to make a conscious effort to loosen her posture before her body can tense up. The glow emanating off her starts to ebb all the same. It dwindles and contracts, both fading away and absorbing back into her form.

A sigh tumbles over her lips. She cocks her head, examining the haze in front of her. "It hasn't moved one bit. I guess it's really stuck on this spot."

She lets out a short giggle, but I can't feel any real amusement in the connection between us.

I step closer to join her. "It does look different, though."

With the afterburn of the glow lingering in my eyes, it's hard to compare the patch of shadowy stuff in front of us to how it looked before. But it's definitely not quite as muddy looking as I remember—as if it's been watered down even more. A patch maybe fifty feet across and long has a much paler quality than the sludgy darkness farther out around it. Like the way she thinned the mess before, except on a somewhat larger scale.

Peri gives a more genuine laugh. "I brightened its day. I guess that's a start. I think… Does it seem calmer to you too?"

I study the patch in front of us and then the thicker darkness I can make out beyond it. There is a sort of stillness to the nearby area that contrasts with the sense of drifting fog I get from the rest of the mess.

"Brightened it up and brought it peace," I say, giving her shoulder an encouraging squeeze.

"It's still *here*, though," Rollick's assistant mutters. She stalks up to the border and pokes a pen at the haze as if she thinks she can prod the filmy atmosphere. "I don't think the humans are going to be satisfied with just having their home not quite so swallowed in shadows."

Peri lifts her chin. "It was a start. Maybe I can settle the shadows down completely if I keep trying."

I nod. "That's right. It's only her first attempt."

At the same time, I can't help taking in the immense sprawl of the city before us. How many attempts will Peri have to make if she's going to clean up even one neighborhood? Will her peacemaking effect last or will the thicker shadows creep back in while she recovers her energy?

Why is this ridiculous rift so intent on melding with the mortal realm anyway? Maybe we can convince it that everything it's heard was false advertising. Start up a smear campaign. *The mortal realm sucks. Burning sun, chaotic plants —who needs all that? Shadows rule! Let's stick to our own side.*

Somehow I don't think it'll be that easy.

I give Peri a gentle tug as I turn away from the mass of

shadows. "We should get back to Rollick and give our report. Maybe he'll have other—"

I stall in my tracks, my muscles going rigid.

Maybe a dozen humans are standing farther down the street behind us, pressed close together and watching with alternately wide or narrowed eyes. Several are holding splintered boards, baseball bats, or golf clubs.

It takes me a second to recognize that they're not looking to play some strange game of sports merged with construction. They're holding the objects like weapons.

My defensive instincts kick in with a jolt of adrenaline. I loom taller, my shoulders flexing.

The humans are pointing at Peri. One waves his golf club our way. "It's one of those aliens! All glowing like she's about to go nuclear. We've got to stop them before they fuck up our city even more."

Aliens? Rollick's assistant doesn't look surprised. I guess we did start talking about the supposed terrorists being from outer space. But we didn't mean *us*.

Maybe Rollick's been encouraging the otherworldly part of the story among the humans who don't already know what we are.

Does the demon really believe we can still contain the knowledge of our existence? What, is he going to wipe out the entire army regiment once they've finished relocating the refugees?

Actually, knowing him, I could almost believe he will.

But how is it better for the humans to think we're aliens than to see us as monsters? Other than, I guess, they're more used to the idea of aliens potentially coming and leaving in peace.

Peri holds up her no-longer-glowing hands. "Everything's okay! I'm trying to fix the problem, not make it worse."

"That's just what an invading alien force would say," another human snaps, wielding her baseball bat.

With those words, the humans surge toward us, eyes flashing, weapons raised. I can sense the violence in every angle of their bodies.

A rush of red blazes through my mind. No thoughts remain but the impulse to protect the woman I love at all costs.

With a snarl, I leap in front of her. My lips pull back to bare my teeth, where my reptilian fangs now jut from my gums. It's only because of a faint twinge of shame and the distant knowledge that Peri would be upset if I massacred these people that I keep my shielding contacts in place over my deadly irises.

"Holy shit!" a man barks, drawing up short. "It's a fucking invasion, all right. We can't let them take what's ours!"

My intent, as much as I had one, was to scare them off. Instead, they hurtle forward even more aggressively—just this time the aggression is directed at me rather than Peri.

That's a small step up, but it triggers the animalistic side of my brain even harder.

One human is hurling his broken board at my head. Another swings his bat at my ribs. My limbs lash out, my elbow sending an attacker flying across a nearby lawn, my clenched hand pummeling another in the gut so he doubles over.

"Raze!" Peri cries out. "Let's just go!"

Her anxiety swirls into my panicked rage, sending my own emotions spiking higher. More of the humans are aiming their makeshift weapons at me, looking to batter me as if I'm a birthday pinata and they've forgotten how to take turns.

My claws slash across one woman's face before she can

break my nose with her golf club. Another figure flings himself onto my back, and my nerves go completely haywire.

With a snarl, I hurl him onto the ground and gouge straight through his throat. I whirl around, my contacts disintegrating, ready to sear all the rest of them.

A voice breaks through my rage. "No! They're going to stop now, Raze. You can stop too."

Peri's plea and the gush of blood starkly scarlet against the asphalt jolt me back to the present. The meaty iron scent saturates the air, but there's nothing appealing about it even to my carnivorous appetites.

That man wasn't a meal. He was just a scared, misinformed mortal trying to protect his home.

Shrieks and yelps are reverberating from the few humans in the bunch still standing. They're stumbling backward, a couple of them ducking to help their injured companions scramble away.

"He killed Wayne! Tore him right open."

I sway on my feet, guilt and fury colliding inside me like I've been walloped over the head with a frying pan. A small hand slips around my arm.

Peri tugs me away. "You can't help him now. Let's move into the shadows."

Yes. That's what I should have done to begin with. Why did I go on the attack instead of just escaping?

I dive with Peri into the nearest patch of darkness. As we rush around the edge of the city, Rollick's assistant keeps up a persistent muttering behind us. "He's not going to like this. Oh, no, not at all."

My shame burns hotter. Peri's presence sidles close to me, exuding reassurance even though I can detect some distress underneath.

"They attacked you first. You were defending yourself. Anyone would have reacted like that."

But she didn't. She hates even upsetting people. Killing them?

The only reason she'll forgive me is because she hates feeling my pain over it.

How many more humans would I have killed if she hadn't been here to break through my furious stupor? Did I even really protect *her* when I've probably just made human-monster relations a thousand times worse?

If she's the only thing stopping me from going off the rails… can I really say I'm anything more than a monster?

9

Periwinkle

Colonel Hueber gazes around the table in the trailer, radiating so much disdain I think even a human could taste the burnt-broccoli flavor. "These are the… the *things* you have helping you run the show? No wonder it's all going to hell."

I clasp my hands in front of me, trying to look ever so responsible and ready to solve all our problems. Next to me, Raze shifts his weight, his head drooping low.

Where he's standing between us and the several other beings who've gathered for this conference, Rollick's eyes narrow just a smidge. If the military figures on the other side of the table could pick up on his demonic energy right now, they'd be ducking. It crackles through my senses.

He manages to speak in a deceptively even voice. "We've kept the situation much more under control than it would have been without our intervention. I don't think you'd want to see what would happen if we leave."

Hueber huffs. "Is that a threat?"

Rollick looks as if he's exerting immense effort not to roll his eyes. Interestingly, I get a similar impression from the slim, black-haired man standing next to the colonel. Major Yin's lips give a slight twitch like he's bitten his tongue, possibly literally.

All right, I think I like that one.

"It's simply a statement of fact," Rollick goes on in the same steady tone. "We're living in unprecedented times at the moment. You can't know what it would look like without us pitching in, because nothing like this has ever happened before. In any case, I don't believe any of *your* people were harmed in the incident."

Hueber's eyes narrow. "All the people around here are my people. The human ones, not whatever exactly you are. We came to protect them, and apparently you're here to tear them to shreds if the mood strikes you."

His gaze flicks to Raze, whose shoulders slump even more as if he's trying to fold his tall, sinewy frame in on itself into monstrous origami.

The salty-sour shame flowing out of my lover sparks my temper. I match Rollick's calm, but I'm not going to keep quiet. "He was protecting us. None of us want to hurt humans, but those humans ran at us with weapons. They were out to kill us! Don't you have laws about self-defense and standing ground and all that?" I feel like at least one of those terms was thrown around by a police officer in some movie I watched.

Hueber purses his lips. "We only have your word on that."

Major Yin clears his throat and motions for the colonel

to lower his head so he can convey something quietly. At whatever he whispers, Hueber's face tenses.

The colonel jerks straight again with a prickle of irritation as if it's his colleague's fault he needed to be corrected. "Fine. A few *human* witnesses confirm your story, so it seems you had some provocation. All the same, I can't imagine a human ripping any of you apart the way this monster did." He waves his hand toward Raze. "I don't want him anywhere near my troops."

Rollick ticks one eyebrow upward. "Not even if it's either Raze charges in to protect them or some new warped monster from the city joins the tearing-apart game? He's saved a lot more of you humans than he's harmed, you know."

Hueber glowers at the demon, seething even more bitterly on the inside. I'm a little worried he's going to hurl his tank-like body right at the table in an attempt to take us all down with it.

"I don't want to set eyes on him," he growls. "You have all those shadowy powers. If I can't see him, then I don't have to think about him. But if there are any more deaths on my watch—"

Rollick holds up his hands. "Message received, loud and clear. I don't suppose your investigations around the city have turned up anything useful?"

Yin speaks up at a hurried clip. "We've been busy making arrangements for as many of the refugees as possible to be moved to proper shelter in the nearby towns. I'm sure once we've had more of a chance to examine the situation—"

"It's fucking mad, that's what it is," Hueber breaks in. "I thought you all were the experts. Have *you* come up with any answers to why the sky is literally falling on our heads?"

I'd point out that the rift is not part of the sky, and it'd be pretty depressing if a piece of sky *was* always that dark, but I don't think either of those observations would be helpful.

Rollick offers a tense smile. "We've had time to conduct our own experiments. I believe we've made progress in making the city more livable, but it'll be a long process."

To my relief, he doesn't glance at me, even though it's my powers he's talking about. I need the colonel breathing down my neck about scrubbing the city clean of darkness like I need gravel in my pie.

If I had a pie.

Note to self: see if we can get some pies around here. Pie makes almost everyone happier.

Hueber could definitely use some blueberry or maybe a comforting apple right now. His thick eyebrows draw together. "I don't want it just *better*. We need the city back to the way it was. Hundreds of thousands of people have been forced out of their homes. Maybe you're happy lounging around in that murky crap, but we've got higher standards here on Earth."

Has he forgotten that we're not actually aliens from another planet? I take a breath to correct the misinformation I was a major force in spreading, but Jonah touches my arm at my other side.

"We're doing our best to get everyone back in their homes the way they were before," he says. "But this is an environmental disaster on the level of a tidal wave or a tornado. It wouldn't make sense for everything to be able to snap back to normal without any repairs."

Hueber snorts. "Show me how to repair a bunch of darkness and we're talking. And beef up your patrols! If you don't want us shooting at the crazy creatures that keep launching themselves out of that mess, you need to be there to catch them before they bring out the claws."

He spins on his heel with a forceful air as if he thinks he's made some impressive point. I'd like to tell him to put his own claws away.

Hueber, Yin, and the several soldiers they brought with them so they could feel like they weren't outnumbered—even though they totally were by all the shadowkind who've stuck to the shadows—stalk out of the trailer. As they pass through the doorway, a small form darts past Hueber's ankles. He lets out a grunt of disgust and kicks his foot toward the furry serpent, but thankfully Falkor is pretty quick even with only two paws.

My strange pet wriggles across the floor and winds up my leg. As the door thumps shut behind the soldiers, I detach the puppyish snake just long enough to tuck him around my waist rather than my knee. He coils the end of his tail behind his head to hold himself in place like a living belt, resting on my ample hips.

Rollick eyes the shadowkind creature. "You do attract some strange company, my glowing friend."

"At least he isn't one of those weird warping shadowkind," I point out. A pet like that would be about as good an addition to someone's happy home as an oven with a leaky gas line.

Raze swipes his hand across his face. "I'm sorry. It doesn't matter what the humans were doing—I know I shouldn't have lost control like that."

Hail shrugs. "You slaughter totally innocent animals all the time. Why not switch to humans who deserve it?"

His gaze darts toward Rollick with a flicker of wariness. "Er. But preferably somewhere Colonel Stuffed Shirt won't find out about it."

Rollick aims a chiding look at the winter fae. "Preferably we don't go around slaughtering humans, period. It's bad enough that some of this bunch has ended up with a whole new set of ideas about 'monsters' in their head. *That's* going to be at least as much of a clean-up job as the damn rift."

His words send a jolt of shock through me. I stare at him, knitting my brow. "After all this, you're still going to try to convince humans that we don't exist after all?"

Sorsha lets out a soft laugh from where she's leaning against the wall at Rollick's other side. "Yeah, Rollick, I think that ship has not just sailed but sunk to the bottom of the ocean."

Rollick waves off the phoenix shifter's wry remark, focusing on me. "*We* are going to convince the humans that we don't exist. It's still only a very small portion of them who've seen us. Once the city is cleared of the rift and the other odd rifts are contained, people will no longer have a permanent reminder. They'll want to go back to thinking things that go bump in the night are only imaginary, if we can point their minds in the right direction."

Even Mirage is frowning, an expression that doesn't sit right on his golden-brown face. "What if we can't make the rifts go away completely? Peri can brighten them up, but blasting them doesn't make them let go. They're stickier than cement."

The demon sighs. "It isn't as if we have any other options. We'd better sort this mess out, or we'll be in an even bigger one soon enough."

I raise my hand tentatively.

Rollick motions for me to speak, and I give a little cough, abruptly nervous. "I mean… we do have another option. We could just accept that some people know about us, and focus on telling and showing them what we're really like instead of burying them in a bunch of lies. If they understood us better, maybe they could make more progress in helping with—"

The demon is already shaking his head, his expression gone hard. "No. I realize you mean well, Peri, but so many humans don't. Even if they'd accept the shadowkind who can pass for human like most of us here, they're still going to look at your furry companion there and scream. And even the first part is an incredibly big if."

Riva speaks up in a cautious tone. "Yeah. I wish it could be that easy, but I've seen firsthand how hostile regular humans can get about even people like me and my guys who are half like them. And I don't think we want to encourage more of their scientists to start meddling with shadow stuff."

"They got away with what they were doing to you because of all the secrets," I have to point out. "If everyone knew, if we could keep an eye on things openly instead of always sneaking around, we'd have a lot more of a say."

Hail lifts his chin. "We should have a say, shouldn't we? We're part of this world too."

That's not exactly what I was trying to get at, but I'm glad to have someone's support.

Hesitation wavers through my connection with Raze—he's probably thinking about whether he'd be more likely to hurt humans if he was around them more. Jonah is balking inside too. I don't think he likes disagreeing with Rollick, even if the demon isn't his boss anymore.

Mirage—well, Mirage is full of flares of gumdrop delight. I think he's imagining all the tricks he could play with people if they wouldn't be as afraid of his illusions. I guess that's a note for the plus column too.

Rollick promptly stomps all over the gumdrops. "That kind of thinking is only going to lead us into a bunch of battles you won't want to fight. The more we put ourselves out there, the harder it's going to be to pull back. It's *already* going to be just shy of impossible. So forget about that, and let's focus on sorting out this rift so we can get on with the rest."

Get on with erasing our presence from the records and

reports. Get on with deluding the humans who've encountered us into believing we were only figments of their imagination.

I can see the reasoning in every word he says, but something about his decision doesn't feel quite right.

Maybe because under all his firm words, the vibe seeping off Rollick isn't calm certainty but a fishy tang of fear.

IO

Periwinkle

It'd be a lot easier to avoid humans if they weren't so curious all the time. When they came up with that saying about curiosity killing cats, I think they must have been projecting.

Raze, Hail, Mirage, and I purposefully went to the quietest edge of the city we could find so I could aim more loving vibes at the shadow sludge. We were hoping no one would be around to notice me glowing up the place and the three shadowkind men dealing with any strange beasts that pop out of the darkness while we're here.

But I've barely managed to summon enough tender concern to bring a soft glow to my palms when a voice rings out from behind me.

"Hey, what are you guys doing?"

Raze very smoothly rolls behind a trash bin with the snarling creature he'd just pounced on. Hail jerks the angle of his hand casting out an icy bolt at another beast in front of him so his power won't be visible to our new audience. When the scaly hippo whose legs he froze topples over, Mirage leaps in and leans casually against it as if it's actually a modern art fixture, not a living being.

I will my glow back under my skin and turn around.

A couple of teenaged humans are sauntering over to us, the guy with his hands shoved in the pockets of his baggy jeans and the girl nibbling on the tip of her long braid.

Does she have tasty hair? That's a meal I have trouble imagining as appealing.

She keeps nibbling as they come to a stop. The boy cocks his head to one side. "You really think you should be messing with that stuff? It makes things pretty freaky."

They believe we're humans like them, not monsters. We're still okay!

I smile brightly. "We're just surveying the problem. We're, ah, professional surveyors. It's totally safe. For us—you should be careful not to get too close to the shadowy areas."

"Yes!" Mirage adds in a cheerful tone. "Gotta have the knowhow to make sure the shadows don't gulp you down!"

Raze straightens up from where the creature he tackled is now a haze of essence wisping away into the air and scowls at Mirage. I'm not sure talking that way is going to set the humans at ease.

The girl removes her braid from her mouth long enough to ask, "If you're professionals, shouldn't you be wearing, like, uniforms or something?"

I can come up with an answer to that. "Well, you see, to survey properly, we can't disturb the natural environment too much. So we need to look like any regular person passing by."

That makes sense, doesn't it? The teens still look skeptical, but neither of them tells me I'm wrong.

Unfortunately, a two-legged lizard as tall as I am chooses that moment to burst out of the gloom and screech at the humans.

The girl nearly chokes on her braid before shrieking. The boy grabs her—I can't tell whether to protect her or to use her as a human shield.

"There really are monsters! Fuck!" He scrambles backward, dragging her with him. "What are we going to do?"

The lizard tilts its head in a birdlike way, which seems fitting because right then I notice the line of feathers poking out along its spine all the way down its back. It opens its mouth to reveal double rows of impressive fangs, but it doesn't charge forward.

I think this one might be friendly. Is that expression supposed to be a grin?

I wave to the retreating teens. "It's okay! It doesn't seem angry. If it gets dangerous, we can deal with it!"

The boy just sputters out a longer string of curses. Panic rolls off both him and the girl in a stomach-turningly briny wave.

The urge wells up inside me to comfort them—to summon the fond light I know I can gather within me and show them that not everything that comes out of the shadows is scary.

But what if Rollick's right? What if I only scare them more with my powers rather than reassuring them?

In a matter of seconds, it doesn't matter anyway. The two teens bolt off between the scattered houses of the fringes. The pounding of their footsteps fades away.

The feathered lizard blinks and then trots back into the shadows. Apparently it was only looking for a quick glimpse of the world outside.

Raze offers me a crooked smile. "I guess you might as well get back to work?"

Well, there's no one around to freak out about my glow now.

I reach for the affectionate feelings inside me again, but it's harder to unearth them from beneath the new heap of discomfort and uncertainty. As I concentrate on welcoming the shadows and encouraging them to settle down, my men stalk along the edge of the gloom around me.

They each dispatch one more creature while I work. Most of the warped beasts still have rampaging on the mind.

My glow spreads into the murky haze. The murkiness retreats, leaving only filmier shadows. But they're still shadowy, not the full sunlight that's beaming down on me here just a few steps away.

Why can't I convince the gloom to let go completely? Why is it so convinced it needs to be here?

What's so amazing about this city anyway that even the shadow realm itself wants a piece?

I extend my supernatural light as far as I can until my legs wobble under me. The old aches splinter up through my ankles. When I adjust my stance, my head swims with dizziness.

Mirage grasps my shoulder. "Hey, Rainbow. No crashing on us."

"She's tired," Raze says, and slashes through a flying horned beetle that's about ten times bigger than any insect has a right to be. "She's putting all her energy into calming the shadows. So many of these warped creatures are still coming through, though."

Hail peers past the lightened patch of city to the thicker sludge beyond. "You'd think the rift would run out eventually."

"Not if it's making more." My stomach knots, and I draw myself up straighter. "I can keep going."

Raze pushes right in front of me with a fierce expression. "No, you can't. You're going to collapse if you push yourself any harder. You need a break before you do any more work."

The winter fae scowls. "If this stuff wasn't so tough to budge…"

In his frustration, he whips out a lance of ice aimed at nothing but the clotted shadows. It pierces through the darkness—and my bonds with my men shudder.

My posture goes rigid. "What was that? Did you all feel it?"

All three of the men around me are frowning now. Hail looks down at his hands. "I didn't know—I didn't mean to do anything that would hurt us."

I peer into the murk. "We don't want it to attack us. I guess we'd better not attack it either. Something about doing that rattles our own powers." Or at least whatever power binds us together.

We felt similar effects before—when one or another of us reacted to the rift's energies in a more aggressive way. It doesn't like being forcefully rejected, and the backlash shakes us up too.

The growl of an engine distracts me from my pondering with a hitch of my nerves, but the vehicle that pulls into view is familiar. Jonah parks the van at the curb and gets out, taking in our stances—and my emotional state through our connection. "Is Peri all right?"

"I'm just a little tired," I mutter, though his concern sends a warm flutter through my belly. "Are you finished working with the other sorcerer?"

Jonah's grimace matches the grapefruit-sour tang of his emotions. "Yes. Today's meeting wasn't all that productive, but… hopefully we'll get somewhere eventually."

He doesn't really want to talk about it, which maybe Mirage can pick up too even though he isn't tied to Jonah directly. The fox shifter bounds toward the van. "This is perfect! We can all take a ride. Peri needs a mini vacation."

Hail's eyes gleam. "Didn't you mention you found a nice spot nearby in case we wanted some privacy?"

Mirage laughs. "Yes. It'll be perfect!"

"Wait," I protest. "We can't go off vacationing when the city is still such a mess."

Raze gives me a firm look. "You can't fix the mess when you're exhausted. You've been doing more than anyone." He pauses, and his expression turns slightly sly. "If you let us pamper you, maybe you'll recover faster."

He does know how to make an argument.

As I waver, Mirage tugs me toward the van. "You need to take care of yourself first. Put on your bicycle helmet before securing anyone else's, isn't that what they say?"

Jonah chuckles. "The saying is for oxygen masks, not bike helmets, but the principle is the same. Come on, Peri. I'd like to see this special place Mirage found."

"Oh, all right."

I let them escort me into the van. I end up cuddled up on the bench between Raze and Hail while Mirage gives directions to Jonah from the front passenger seat. "Turn left here. No, more left."

"That's not a road, Mirage."

"It'll take longer following the roads. But if we have to…"

It doesn't feel like very long before we pull to a stop near a patch of forest bordered by farmer's fields. The nearest buildings are at least a mile distant.

With a spring in his step, Mirage leads the way between the trees. He points out the babbling stream and the flowers blooming on bushes here and there in the underbrush. Then he stops at the edge of a grassy clearing that borders the stream with a wall of densely packed saplings all around it.

He spreads his arms. "Look at it. Like a room just for us."

Jonah considers the scene. "Very comfortable. And I think we can make it even more so. Just a minute…"

He lopes back to the van and returns with a rolled blanket that he spreads on the ground. "So our mate doesn't get her clothes dirty."

As I sit in the middle of the blanket, a giggle slips out of me. Jonah knows perfectly well that if the dress and leather jacket I'm wearing did get mussed, I could fix them as easily as blinking in and out of the shadows. But there's something sweet about being taken care of this way all the same.

Raze hums. "She could use a foot and ankle massage. All those sore spots she shouldn't have to deal with." A hint of a growl comes into his voice with the reference to my former captor's torments.

Hail smirks and sinks down by my feet. "I think I should handle that honor. A little chill can help chase the aches away."

I let him slide off my ballet flats because it's more fun than vanishing them away. As he applies his thumbs to the arch of my foot, I lean back on my hands with a sigh. "Maybe the aches and pains aren't so bad if it means I get treated like this to make up for them."

The winter fae makes a dismissive sound. "You should get the princess treatment without needing to suffer for it, Cream Puff."

"And there should always be plenty of color for our Rainbow too." Mirage waves his hand, and illusions spring up around the clearing. Vibrant flowers bloom from vines that wrap around tree trunks, filling my nose with a perfume it's hard to believe is imaginary. Butterflies with pearlescent wings flutter through the air. The water of the stream sparkles like it's made of liquid diamond.

My next giggle comes out breathless. Raze adjusts his stance, gazing down at me.

"You shouldn't need to hold up any weight at all," he declares, and plants his massive frame behind me so I can lean against his chest instead.

As I settle against the warmth of his body, Jonah reaches into his pockets. "I brought one more thing that might make the pampering complete. How'd you like a snack to regain some of that energy, Peri? One of the shadowbloods picked up some pretty fantastic chocolate on a supply run."

My mouth is watering just at those words. "Yes, please."

Jonah sits next to me, retrieving the bar of chocolatey deliciousness. He starts to hand it to me and then stops, a sly smile crossing his lips. "Even better…"

He opens the wrapper and breaks off a bite-size square. When he offers it to me, I open my mouth so he can pop it right onto my tongue.

The semi-dark chocolate melts in my mouth with a delectable mix of sweet, bitter, and creaminess. A shiver of delight ripples through me.

An answering tingle echoes into me from each of my men. I glance around to find them all watching me avidly, their heartbeats kicked up a notch. An even more intoxicating flavor laces the emotions that pass between us.

Hail moves to my other foot, caressing the sole between deeper digs of his thumbs. "I think our mate might need a different sort of pampering."

Is that the first time he's called me his *mate*? I like that phrasing even more than being called a good girl.

A rumble reverberates from Raze's chest. He dips his head, and I turn mine to meet his kiss.

The lingering chocolate in my mouth spikes his desire

even hotter. He kisses me deeply, his tongue teasing over mine. Hail's massage travels to my ankle, one hand stroking higher up my calf.

Tasting their desire gets me all kinds of heated up too. My thighs press together against the growing pressure.

Mirage kneels next to me and nuzzles my neck before teasing his fingers across my breasts. "We're all going to take care of you."

He trails his hand right down to my hip but then glances at Jonah with a mischievous glint in his eyes. "Is our sorcerer the only one who hasn't gotten to taste *you* yet?"

A sharper pulse of need throbs between my legs. Jonah's gaze smolders into mine. "It sounds that way. But I'd love to fix that oversight right now."

Raze rumbles again in apparent agreement and sweeps aside my hair to nip the lobe of my ear. As I ease my legs apart in anticipation, Mirage tugs the skirt of my dress upward between caresses.

Even Hail willingly moves to the side to make room for Jonah to bend down between my knees. I lean into Raze, eagerness buzzing through my veins.

The sorcerer's smile comes with an even headier flavor of emotion than the chocolate he offered. He bows his head.

The first swipe of Jonah's tongue has me gasping. The second provokes a full-out moan. I clutch at Raze's arm, at Hail's shirt where he's tucked himself closer to me, already melting with pleasure. And incredibly glad that no one lives near this patch of forest.

Jonah grasps my hips, massaging my ass as he laps at me. Every flick of his tongue sets off another jolt of bliss. I rock into his mouth, quivering and crying out when he teases the edge of his teeth across my clit.

It only takes a deeper suck of his mouth and a dip of his

fingers between my folds to tip me over the edge. I jerk in Raze's hold, swept up in the rush of pleasure.

Satisfaction emanates from Jonah into me. As I come down from my own ecstatic high, I find I want nothing more than to spread it around.

"I'd like to return the pampering," I say, and push up on my knees so I can lean over Jonah's lap.

"Fuck, Peri," he mutters as I yank at the fly of his slacks. It's definitely not a protest. His hips cant upward so I can ease his pants down, and his cock springs from his boxers, all eagerness.

I take his shaft into my mouth, drinking in the salty muskiness of him, and swirl my tongue around him as if he's the best kind of popsicle. Jonah's groan mingles with another ragged "Fuck!"

I'm vaguely aware of my other men moving around me. Mirage's playful voice comes from right behind me next. "We can't neglect our Rainbow even when she's in a sharing mood."

He delves his nimble fingers between my thighs and plunges them into the wetness of my pussy. The shock of pleasure sets off a moan that vibrates from my mouth into Jonah in turn.

As Jonah tangles his fingers in my hair, Mirage vanishes his clothing. The head of his cock slides teasingly along my slit. Then he presses into me, filling me in that giddy way I'll never get tired of.

I gasp and suck Jonah harder, wanting to pay back the pleasure offered to me in every possible way. Mirage sinks deeper, and his desire radiates into me alongside the pleasure blooming from my core.

Raze slips his hand around me to fondle my breasts, sparking even more bliss. Hail teases tingles of cold and warm breaths over my neck and shoulder.

I sway with Mirage's thrusts and bob up and down over Jonah's cock, feeling as if we've all melded together into a single mass of pleasure.

Perhaps we have. Just as my second orgasm crackles through me, Jonah's breath breaks. He comes in my mouth in a hot spurt in time with the jerk of Mirage's hips behind me.

I soar toward the sky on the whirlwind of their pleasure mixing with my own and glide back to Earth surrounded by my mates' loving warmth.

Because that's what they are, the best way to describe them. We're bound to each other in our hearts and souls, and we wouldn't have it any other way.

Hail lets out a light laugh and kisses my shoulder. "Never thought I'd get off more from feeling people who *aren't* me having sex than doing the pumping myself."

I give him a gentle swat. "You were part of it. You all mattered."

Raze strokes his fingers over my hair. "And so do you, Glowbug. Always."

A different sort of satisfaction wells up inside me. We've come so far together. We started out wary and hurting and in some cases seeing each other as the enemy, and now we make each other so happy.

Because we understand each other. We opened up to one another and discovered how much common ground we truly share.

My thoughts drift back to yesterday's conversation with Rollick, and my throat constricts.

The demon has been alive for a long time, yes. But that also means he has millennia of his own hang-ups and trauma clouding his vision.

He wants to let go of the chance to get true acceptance for shadowkind in the human world because of his fears based on the past. In the last few months, I've seen just how important it is to move beyond old pains to get to a better place.

My mates and I have accomplished so much. And this one thing feels so right.

The rift even showed us again today, didn't it? When we work with it, it lightens up.

When we treat it like an enemy, that force echoes right back into our bond.

How much farther could we get with humans if we weren't always treating them like enemies?

Jonah trails his fingers down my arm in a tender caress. "What are you thinking about, Peri? You've gotten all determined."

I open my mouth and hesitate. This is so big. So scary.

So let's meet that fear head-on.

"I think we should reveal the truth to all the humans," I say. "Even if we have to go behind Rollick's back."

11

Periwinkle

I set my hands on my hips and look around at my companions. "All right. Are we all clear on what we're doing today?"

My mates and I have assembled a collection of the allies we feel are least likely to betray our plans to Rollick. A *small* collection, since the demon holds an awful lot of sway over both his colleagues and the academy students who've come to the city to pitch in.

Fen nods with an air of determination that's only slightly diminished by the nervous drips of water trickling off her hands. Next to her, Brine—our selkie friend—draws her plump frame up taller.

Jonah picked out a couple of other shadowkind students who he knows have always wanted to show off their natures to the rest of the world and who are pretty good at following instructions. Right now, the two level four students are poised with one perched on the other's shoulders, bobbing energetically like they're about to launch into an acrobatic show.

Which works well for us, since we're planning to make as much of a spectacle as we can manage.

Hail has roped in a couple of his former fangirls… Well, I suppose they're *still* fangirls from the glances they keep shooting at him through their eyelashes. But when they turned up, he made a point of sauntering over to me and slinging his arm around my waist. The two he picked aren't so hostile they've bothered to glare at me. They've just preened harder.

And then, of course, there's Falkor the snake-puppy, who's squirming along the ground around my feet in his weird mix of bounding and slithering. With the way his tongue is flopping with his eager panting, he might be the most excited out of all of us.

It feels a little strange having everyone's attention on me. Jonah is the only one here who's had any real authority over us, even if Rollick stripped him of his title as teacher, and Raze is definitely the most intimidating, even if he's a sweetie under his hulking exterior.

But this is my plan. I insisted that we need to take action. My men have let me take the lead and handle things my way.

That's how much they trust me.

Everyone here is trusting me right now.

I take a deep breath, resolving that I'm not going to let them down in that trust, and clap my hands. "Let's get to it, then! You know where the cameras are. Take your positions and wait for my signal."

Fen grins, one of Hail's fangirls primps her hair, and our allies vanish into the shadows.

Mirage sidles closer to me and ruffles my hair. "Are *you* ready, Rainbow?"

I square my shoulders. "Absolutely. We're going to make history!"

Hopefully the good kind that people celebrate with holidays in the future, not the kind where they set up horrifying museums to warn people to never do it again.

"I'll set everything in motion," Jonah says. His expression is tense, I think because he has the most trouble going against Rollick, but he's giving this mission his all anyway. "Once the cameras are recording, you need to show up as quickly as possible."

"When it's time to play, we won't delay!" Mirage declares, the rhyme sounding more joyful than he has all week.

Raze gives a grunt of agreement, Hail rolls his shoulders, and the four of us shadowkind slip into the nearby patches of darkness as well.

We all ripple and leap around the edges of the camp to the area where several news vans have set up shop. It's like a food truck alley, except they're serving a lot of talk instead of delicious eats.

A few of the vans have no activity around them, their inhabitants either gone off to interview more survivors of the odd disaster or holed up inside poking buttons, staring at screens, and whatever else humans do when deciding what images to project to everyone's TVs.

In a few minutes, if this works, most of them will be projecting images of us.

Reporters and camera crews hang around outside the other vans, chatting and drinking coffee, which as far as I've observed is their main source of fuel. And also decoration, based on the various disposable cups scattered around the vans.

Jonah strides into the middle of the area, picking a span of the patchy grass where he's in clear view of all the vans. A few of the news workers glance over at him, but most continue their conversations. I guess he doesn't look all that different from the hundreds of refugees still milling around the temporary camp.

Then he clears his throat and starts speaking. "Who here wants a real story? I bet you've heard some unusual things from the people you've interviewed. I'm about to prove that the tall tales are all real, so you'd better get those cameras rolling!"

That sends all the humans into a flurry, whirling toward him. Several snatch up their cameras; the reporters scramble for their microphones and headsets.

Questions fly through the air toward Jonah, but he simply takes a step back. The moment I can see that most of the cameras are on, I leap out of the shadows.

"Hi, humans!" I grin and wave. "We've got a bit of a mess on our hands here with shadow floods and rampaging creatures. But I'm glad to tell you that lots of beings who live in the shadows want to help you, not hurt you. We're not gangsters or aliens, just people with some unusual powers who came from a realm next to yours to enjoy all the wonderful things here. I care so much about seeing everyone happy that it makes me literally glow!"

I focus on all the fondness I feel for the bewildered humans in front of me, all my hopes that they'll come out of this mess all right. A familiar turquoise light streams from my palms and flickers in my hair.

I gesture to my right the way I've seen presenters do on game shows. "We call ourselves 'shadowkind,' not 'monsters.' Some of us do look scary, but we'll only put that might to protecting you. And we can do that in more than one form."

Raze emerges from the shadows next, in his human-esque appearance, which is plenty imposing all on its own. He flexes his sinewy muscles before the cameras, his jaw clenching with his nerves, and then shifts abruptly into basilisk form.

One of the reporters shrieks at the sudden sight of a gigantic lizard in their midst. "What the fuck?" someone else mutters.

We can't risk losing momentum. I step to Raze's side and wrap my arms around his reptilian neck, still shining with my loving glow. "Look, he's nothing to be afraid of. He changes so he can take care of all of us better when the actual threats come charging in."

Raze gamely nuzzles my cheek with a flick of his forked tongue.

Hail pops into being behind us, provoking another round of gasps. He speaks up in his typical nonchalant tone. "Some of us prefer to keep our good looks while we're pitching in. But we have all kinds of ways to keep you safe."

"If you deserve it," he murmurs under his breath so only I can hear the words, and holds up his hands like a magician presenting a show.

Snow whirls down over us. Icicles sprout from the ground. In a matter of seconds, we've got our own little winter wonderland, population three.

And then four, when Mirage springs in to join us. He flips onto his hands and spins on one finger while releasing all five of his foxy tails alongside his ruddy ears.

I sweep my arm toward him. "And when you're not in trouble, lots of us shadowkind like to play. We can brighten your lives in all sorts of ways."

Mirage shoots me a thumbs up at my rhyme and leaps back onto his feet. He swirls his tails in full view of the cameras before giving them a quick fluffing. "I wish all we needed to do with humans is have fun. It's the demented beasts from that murky mess who are spoiling our good times."

"We're doing everything we can to clear up the darkness that's spilled out of our home realm," I say, standing as tall as my frame allows, my legs spread in what I think of as a super-hero pose. I aim my hand toward the sky. "We'll defend all of you with whatever it takes. Shadowkind have always been here, living among humans. Most of us have always been on your side, but we stayed hidden in case we scared you. Now there's something scarier to deal with, so we want you to know we have your backs."

At my flourish, the rest of our allies materialize from the shadows.

Fen sends a spurt of water arcing over our heads and gives a little bow, her scaly arms on display and her deep brown skin shifted into its more natural green naiad tone. Brine whips her pelt of a cape around her shoulders to show off her seal form, rolls over, and re-emerges as a tawny-haired woman.

Jonah's two would-be acrobats prance around us, one of them shooting off sparks into the air like miniature fireworks. The other transforms into an impish form with dragonfly wings and soars between the bursts of light.

Hail's fangirls flank us with vaguely bored expressions, as if they can't bring themselves to act anything other than too cool for the rest of us even now. But one of them brings out her horsey centaur haunches with a swish of her long tail, and the other conjures a cloud of butterflies out of nowhere to flutter through our audience.

Mirage beams at the growing crowd. "We shadowkind just want to live near you and keep this world healthy and happy for all of us! We're going to beat the messed-up shadows back to where they belong."

Supernatural power thrums in his words. He's generating an illusion to encourage friendly feelings in the reporters.

That may be the only reason none of them have run away

screaming so far. Little dabs of anxiety reach me, but the strongest flavor is buttercream-icing-sweet awe.

A dozen cameras are now pointed our way, with as many reporters' voices gabbing to their distant audiences. I see a couple of signs lit up that say *LIVE*—does that mean humans all around the world are seeing us already?

All those mortal beings are finding out that monsters exist—and that we're not so monstrous after all.

The thought brings a fresh glow to my skin. I aim my hands toward the camera crews and let the shine wash over them, thin enough that they can still see the rest of our performance through it.

Mirage resumes his spinning and flipping. Raze shifts into a form mostly human but still with his basilisk scales, and even lets one of the reporters walk close enough for her to touch them. Hail twirls a delicate ice sculpture over his curled fingers.

And an authoritative voice rings through the commotion: "What exactly is going on here, Peri?"

I sense the thrum of Rollick's power before I see him.

As I whip around, my skin prickles uneasily. Fen chokes back a yelp, a stream of water dappling the ground beneath her hands. I taste her tang of fear alongside my own.

The demon is standing behind our little gathering, his arms folded over his chest and his gaze smoldering like he might start setting us all on fire if we're not careful. My heart hiccups with the thought that he might send all those cameras up in flames and end our show in an epic meltdown.

I scramble over to him and dare to grasp his forearm. "Look! The humans know, and it's okay. They aren't freaking out. We can work together and solve this problem faster instead of constantly worrying about how much to give away."

Rollick's expression tightens. He pitches his voice low but

ominous. "I specifically told you we couldn't take this step. You have no idea what people are thinking on the other side of those cameras. Now I need to clean up another mess—whatever it takes."

"No!" I yelp, and yank on his arm to bring his attention back to me. Thankfully no cameras—or humans—have ignited so far. "They've already seen plenty. We can't take it back now, can we? We have to go ahead and watch what happens. If you storm in there and act all upset about it, *that* will make them think we're a threat, not anything the rest of us have done."

The demon scowls at me. "If you'd listened in the first place—" He cuts himself off with a short growl and motions to Mirage. "You can take care of this. Send some illusions through the video. Convince them all it was only a bunch of special effects."

Mirage pauses in his play to meet our headmaster's eyes. His thick red hair ruffles as if with a breeze and his eyes widen with a jolt of grapefruit-sour nervousness, but his stance goes rigid in defiance. "No. I'm here for Peri, and I'm staying for Peri. I don't want to keep hiding."

Rollick looks as if he's restraining a snarl. He jerks toward the one human in our midst. "Jonah? You went along with this scheme? After all the responsibilities I've given you—"

Jonah stiffens, but he holds his former boss's gaze unflinchingly. "I think it's time we tried this. Imagine how many more shadowkind we could help if we didn't have to keep everything so secret."

"Imagine how many more might be hurt!"

I swallow hard. "I think a lot of them were getting hurt already because of all the ways humans don't understand us."

"Excuse me!"

A reporter with flushed cheeks is hustling around the still-performing shadowkind to where we're standing, her camerawoman hurrying behind her. She thrusts her microphone toward Rollick. "Are you part of this coalition of supernatural beings too? What's your role in the group? Can you say who's responsible for the damage being done to Jackson City?"

Rollick's eyes narrow. I tighten my grip on his arm, tasting the acrid emotions rolling off him like fetid salsa.

But I recognize the flavor of them. They don't taste like anger or revulsion, not really.

Like I tasted with Raze that first day I stumbled into my dorm room and found myself face to face with him—Rollick isn't furious. *He's* scared. He's not sure we're wrong, only afraid of what will become of all the beings he's tried to shelter if we are.

I nudge a wave of my determined affection over him. "We can make them see. This is the best chance we're ever going to get, isn't it?"

Rollick sucks in a breath. Then, to my immense relief, he puts on one of his charming smiles as he turns fully toward the reporter. "Until recently, I thought of myself as something of a leader in this group. But I may have overestimated my own importance."

12

Hail

Peri's plan is going well. Humans mill all around us, babbling to and about us, shoving their cameras in our faces. Gaping as if they've never seen a snowflake before.

Which, all right, fine, they probably *haven't* this far south in the middle of summer, but that doesn't mean they have to look like such dopes about it.

My Cream Puff's mission appears to be a massive success, and I hate everything that makes it one. All those staring mortal eyes. All the gasps of astonishment and anxious murmurs.

If they'd opened their eyes properly centuries ago, we wouldn't have needed to make ourselves into a sideshow act to prove we're no more harmful than clowns.

Of course, an awful lot of humans are afraid of those too.

They really are so easily terrorized. I don't see how it was ever our fault.

Still, because Peri is beaming in her beautiful, joyful way and even Rollick is deigning to speak to a couple of the humans, I keep up my end of the deal. I bring down another brief shower of snow and then summon a tower of ice crystals to provoke more oohs and aahs. I paste a smile on my face and turn so the cameras get my best angles.

I mean, if I have to be on TV screens all around the world anyway, I might as well give them a good look. They should know that Peri deserved the best possible mates. And that our human audience is lucky we're even bothering to show ourselves to them.

More humans have drifted over from the refugee camp we're on the outskirts of. I think some of the news people must have called in colleagues as well, because a few additional vans sporting satellite dishes roar up.

As the newcomers spill out, one of them hollers to his colleagues loud enough for me to hear. "What's the big fuss? Looks like a bunch of Halloween tricks and costumes to me."

My teeth grit behind my determined smile.

He thinks so, does he? Peri went to all this effort to present us to the beings who've threatened us across all of history, and he's going to spit in her face?

I might not like that we're courting their favor, but if that's what she wants, I'm going to make sure this show hits all the right notes. She deserves *that*.

She deserves their respect.

Reaching inside myself, I summon more of my wintry power.

Spires of gleaming ice shoot up from the ground all around our makeshift stage, close enough for the reporters surrounding us to touch them. Let them feel the chill and try to tell us it's all smoke and mirrors.

Peri beams out a little more light. The humans farther back are craning their necks to watch—I'm not sure they can even see her.

We need a bigger stage. And even more shadowkind to make her point.

I turn my head toward the shadows around us where I can feel other beings are lurking, drawn by the spectacle but afraid of emerging. What can they really be scared of now that even Rollick is talking with the reporters like a diplomat rather than a demon?

"Come on, you wimps!" I shout to them. "Let's really give them something to talk about. They need to see just how amazing shadowkind can be."

And how many of us there are. I won't deny a small part of me wants these humans to recognize they could be outnumbered.

Why shouldn't they feel a tiny bit intimidated by us? We do have more power in our pinkies than they've got in their entire bodies.

Isn't it generous of us to extend that power on their behalf?

A few higher beings pop into view, and then a few more. Peri makes a coaxing sound with her tongue, and her weird furry snake pet tumbles out of the shadows to wind around her legs.

I think the reporters look more horrified than awed by that creature, but it doesn't appear to mind. They should be glad it isn't interested in gnawing on their intestines like the warped beasts that keep surging out of the bloated rift.

As the newer shadowkind shift forms and toss around the most obvious aspects of their powers, I focus my attention on expanding our stage. All eyes should be on Peri, right in the center, with the rest of us around her proving her point.

I've always wanted to build something for shadowkind,

haven't I? I pictured it as a sprawling structure far away from human habitation, where all beings could be themselves without worrying about who they'd freak out. But this could be a decent start.

We *are* being ourselves, and the mortals will just have to deal with it.

I summon more ice, urging it to rise in a flat plane beneath our feet, rippling it with small ridges so it doesn't become too slippery. Peri glances down and then shoots a grin over her shoulder at me that lights me up almost as much as she is.

Yeah, I'll glow for her if she wants me to. She'd do anything to help me reach my own dreams, so I'm damn well going to make hers happen.

The layers of ice continue to stretch and thicken beneath us. We rise off the ground, first just a few inches, then a foot, then a few feet, until we're peering down at the reporters.

But a flat plane hardly feels impressive enough. I build one chunk higher here, another there, elevating Peri with her glow and Mirage with his acrobatic tricks so they're visible from even farther around.

The reporter who made his idiotic comment of disbelief is staring, his jaw hanging open. He reaches out to touch the edge of my conjured platform and jerks his fingers back as if the chill of the ice has burned him.

Oh, yeah, that's a real freeze, you dimwit. Look at what we're capable of and shake in your boxers.

Okay, maybe that's more hostile an attitude than we're supposed to be taking here, but a little attitude is fine if I keep those thoughts to myself.

The imp produces a pair of glittering skates and glides around the edges of the platform. I raise up an ice sculpture like a fearsome bear in front of Raze, and he arches an eyebrow at me before taking on his basilisk form and pummeling it into shards with his brutal strength.

Peri's drippy naiad friend peers down at the frozen water beneath her. I conjure two delicate goblets beneath her hands to catch the last few trickles of water that stream off her hands before she laughs in delight. Then she makes the water arc between the two cups, doing a loop-de-loop in the middle like a liquid roller coaster.

A lemur shifter shrinks into animal form, and I sprout a crystalline tree where he can leap from branch to branch. When a troll lumbers forward, I turn the surfaces around him extra smooth to reflect his blue-ish skin and tusk-like fangs.

Through it all, Peri keeps glowing her vibrant blue-green light. Gazing up at her, my heart skips a beat.

"Peri!" I call out. "Light up the ice!"

Even as I speak, I'm hollowing channels all through the stage to reflect the beams she can emit. When she casts her glow farther, the entire massive ice structure echoes her glow, highlighting every being standing on it.

A joint gasp ripples through the crowd below.

Oh, yes. Watch in amazement. You've never seen anything like this.

A glance behind shows Rollick eyeing me from the base of the stage. I didn't dare send the demon hurtling up off the ground without permission. He cocks his head, but his skeptical gaze doesn't feel deadly, so I think I'm safe from demonic vengeance for now.

I conjure a few more intricate spires here and there, just for the hell of it. And then some dolt who barely fits in his plaid shirt comes lumbering toward my creation.

"How the fuck is she doing it?" he hollers, pointing the soda can he's clutching at Peri. "She's got to have some kind of bulbs on her."

As if he thinks he can prove as much by hurling his sugar-saturated beverage at her, he wheels back his arm to pitch the can.

All the animosity I've been holding back rushes to the surface. Something like a roar erupts from my throat. I step forward with a snap of my hand.

Only the slightest shred of self-control—fueled by the image of how Peri would look at me if I fuck up—and all the practice I've been doing at strategically freezing rampaging creatures stops me from transforming the jerk into a gigantic ice cube.

As it is, his arms turn blue from fingertips to elbow and lock in place. He yelps, teetering backward, waving his partly frigid limbs as if he can shake the frostbite off them.

Rollick's muttered curse reaches my ears from behind. The reporters' voices rise in an anxious warble, several of them converging around the man I can already hear them saying I "attacked."

My skin tightens. Every instinct in my body screams to either lash out more or dive into the shadows away from them.

The icy gleam of the stage around me flickers before my eyes, merging with memories of a snow-draped forest, of my fae mentor slumped amid pooling blood, the human hunters shouting and stabbing him—

A pulse of warmth washes over me through my bond with Peri. I yank my gaze to her.

She's smiling down at me, a bit sad but just as fond as always.

She knows I was only trying to protect her.

I'm not going to make a disaster of this moment the way Raze did with the idiots who charged at us the other day. I've got more control than that brute, don't I?

I set my jaw and force myself to step forward to the edge

of the stage. I haven't done a good enough job of taking care of the woman I love if I let her spectacle devolve into panicked chaos. It's on me to fix it.

"I'm sorry!" I force myself to say over the clamor. "I was only trying to protect my mate. If I remove the ice quickly, he'll be perfectly fine."

As disappointing as that fact might be.

I keep the rancor to myself and leach the frigid cold from the man's arms before anyone needs to respond. The man shudders and drops the pop can he nearly turned into a projectile weapon. He gropes at one hand with the other, confirming that his fingers still move.

The nervous energy of the crowd diminishes, but it doesn't fade away completely. Many of the eyes that gazed as us with awe before have sharpened with wariness.

Fuck.

Did I completely screw up what Peri was trying to accomplish? Is it just not possible for me to interact with humans without wanting to freeze-dry them?

Peri believes the shadow realm wants to merge with the mortal one, that we need to find some kind of balance where the two can co-exist. But what if I'm simply not capable of playing nice?

13

Periwinkle

I know I'm in trouble when Rollick materializes next to me while I'm enjoying my first ever iced frappuccino. I got it from this wonderful woman who works at a coffee shop down the highway, who brought it along with dozens of other drinks for the refugees. When she grinned at me with a twirl of her multi-colored hair that might be even more impressive than mine—without the glow—and told me, "I saw you on TV! You were amazing!" my spirits lifted pretty high.

Rollick's expression deflates them in an instant.

I gulp down the dregs of the frozen bitter-sweetness faster than anyone really should and wince. "Brain freeze."

But worth it in case he was going to tell me I've lost edible treats privileges.

The glower hasn't left his eyes since last night's initial

scolding after our TV performance. It's out in full force right now.

He beckons me to join him in the shadows. "I think there's something you should see, my glowing rebel."

I *would* like to get back in the headmaster's good graces, and not just because the ominous wafts of his demonic energy set off alarm bells all through my nerves. I put on my brightest voice. "Absolutely! Lead the way!"

Rollick's eyes narrow. As he melds into the nearest patch of darkness with me trailing behind, I think I hear him muttering something under his breath about how cursed he is with mutinous underlings and what gods he offended to deserve it.

I didn't *exactly* stage a mutiny. I just… didn't follow one little order that he gave.

Okay, maybe it was a big order. But still. I followed lots of others to the letter. It should balance out.

And I have to believe that revealing our presence to the world—or as much as the world watches the evening news—was a good thing in the long run.

I follow Rollick's unnerving essence through the shadows to the area at the edge of the refugee camp where the army has hunkered down. They have their own tents and even a few temporary cabins they erected quickly, everything a dun brown that blends into the earth between the patchy grass.

No wonder they're so grouchy all the time if that's the kind of atmosphere they're surrounded by.

Rollick draws to a stop by the cabin that I assume belongs to Colonel Hueber, because he's standing right outside, with Major Yin and a few other soldiers poised rigidly nearby. A few humans not in uniform—but not as scruffy as most of the evacuees are by now—are facing them, one talking with broad gestures of his hands.

The demon's essence nudges mine. "I've reminded you before how humans typically react to the knowledge of our existence. Along with everyone you hoped to win over, your demonstration reached the ones who already have it in for us."

What sense of a stomach I have in this state sinks. I ease closer to the cluster of humans, staying hidden in the darkness.

"This is a bigger bunch than we've seen all together before," says the man who's talking as much with his hands as his voice. "But the same techniques should work. We can fill you in on all their weaknesses and the best ways to protect yourselves. For starters, you'll all want to be wearing one of these. They won't protect you from a physical attack, but they block most mind-altering powers from affecting you."

He hands out a couple of circular metal patches that look like silver brooches. The colonel frowns at the one he accepts but pins it to his chest.

The moment he does, the mild awareness I had of his mingled interest and consternation vanishes.

My heart lurches. I stare at Hueber, just in case he's somehow kicked the bucket without me noticing and that's why he's not experiencing any more emotions. He's standing steadily on his feet, tugging his shirt straight and blinking before he opens his mouth to respond to the brooch-gifting man.

I'm pretty sure no corpse is capable of all those things.

"Of course we'll be happy to consider any tips you might have from your experiences," he says, but I'm too distracted to keep following their conversation.

"What *are* those things?" I ask Rollick.

"Badges made of combined silver and iron. He's right that they don't protect the humans physically—I could still punch him or disintegrate him just fine—and they can't ward off hybrid powers, but they cut off any talents that involve the wearer's mental state."

I squirm uneasily. The man who offered that badge said it was for blocking powers that *altered* minds. I usually just read minds—and only the squishy feelings-y parts of them, not actual thoughts.

Why would people need to protect themselves from that? How can I figure out how to make our new neighbors trust us if I can't pick up on their emotions?

I suspect Rollick doesn't have the answers to those questions, and that's exactly why he brought me here: so I could see the new problems my performance created.

I ball my essence tighter and ask the next most obvious question. "Who are those people?"

"Most likely, hunters." Rollick's tone has turned resigned. "They have a pretty cohesive network. It'd only have taken a few of them catching your stunt for word to spread to all of them. Now they're offering their shadowkind-wrangling skills to the humans on the front lines of what they no doubt consider a war."

A chill ripples through my being. "But *we're* not trying to hurt them. We've been helping them!"

"That's not how they'll see it, and it's not how the soldiers wanted to see it when they showed up. Now they've got confirmation of their natural inclinations." Rollick turns away. "I'd imagine hunters are speaking to people in power all across the world now, filling in governments and corporations on how to deal with this new shadowkind 'threat'."

I'm struck by a deeper shiver. "Does that mean—are they going to bring out those nets, and the whips Gnash talked about?"

"And anything else they've invented more recently."

As Rollick drifts away, I hurry after him. For all my

nerves are jittering, I can't give in to despair. "But they're just a small group of humans. *Lots* of humans will have seen us on their TVs. Mirage worked his powers to make them feel friendly to us. They won't all want to attack us."

"It doesn't take very many on the hunt to create a catastrophe," Rollick mutters, but he pauses when we're close to the trailer that serves as our base of operations. "But we can't put the cat back in the bag, so you and your team need to be on your best behavior today. I want you going out there and working on cleaning up this city again, without *any* aggression whatsoever. Not that you're so inclined, but you can keep your mates in check, can't you?"

I have the sense of him raising an eyebrow.

I give him my most emphatically chipper voice. "Yes! Yes, I'm sure we can manage that."

"Good. Jonah's been working out strategies with that new sorcerer I called in—it's time for them to put those into practice. Let's see if between the bunch of you and our other associates we can't put a real dent in this problem before we've got dozens more hunters and sorcerers with less cooperative intentions on our doorstep. If you don't want me seeing your actions as a catastrophe, prove they weren't."

At his last words, Jonah and the woman I've gathered is the new sorcerer step out of the trailer.

Lilah only looks a little older than Jonah, maybe in her early 30s, as well as I can judge human age. She's half a foot taller than me, with dips and curves in all the places humans seem to think are best and ripples of auburn hair streaming down her shoulders.

I might be a little jealous of her intruding on my mate to work so closely with him if the too-garlicky-pickle flavor of discomfort didn't waft off Jonah so strongly. He shoots her a tight smile, his stance equally tense. "Well, I guess it's time to see how that theory works in real life."

He's always been uneasy about using his powers even when it's absolutely necessary, worrying about the effects on the shadowkind he has to manipulate for their own good. Which is just one of the many reasons this particular sorcerer is so loveable.

I slip out of the shadows right next to him and grab his hand. "You managed to turn away a few of the strange creatures before. I'm sure you can do even more now that you have help!"

His brighter smile for me lights me up in turn. "We'll do our best. Why don't we see if we can expand one of the patches you worked on before?"

"That sounds like a perfect idea."

My other marked men waver into being around us. Raze flexes his shoulders with controlled might, ready to go but clearly determined to keep his more aggressive instincts in check. Mirage spins around and claps his hands to set off a burst of encouraging but illusionary cheers.

Hail stands stiffly a little apart from us, his mouth slanting. "Tame the beasts rather than tear them apart. That's the MO, right?"

Raze shoots him a stern look with a hidden dollop of guilt. "It always is. And the same to the humans."

The corner of Hail's mouth dips even farther.

As if determined not to be left behind, Falkor bursts out of the shadows too. The snake-puppy wriggle-bounds around my feet with a wag of his tongue.

I bend down to scratch his head. "You can be lookout. Bark if you see anything scary!"

He lets out a soft woof as if agreeing.

As we set off toward the edge of the city, I sidle over to Hail and tuck my arm around his. "Don't feel bad about last night. The man you froze started it."

Hail snorts. "Somehow I don't think the news stories

played up that fact over my 'monstrous' behavior." He pauses, and a thread of curdled shame winds through his general stale-peanut-brittle mood. "I'm sorry I ruined your big show."

I tap my elbow against his side. "It wasn't ruined." My mind slides back to the hunters who were advising Colonel Hueber. "Maybe it's a good thing for the humans to realize we *will* defend ourselves if they get monstrous themselves. They need to respect us as well as like us, right? Anyway, I know you only wanted to defend me. It was sweet."

Hail looks chagrinned, but the blush that touches his pale cheeks and the sudden splash of delight I drink in tell me that he doesn't actually mind the compliment. I bob up to give him a quick peck, and he tucks his arm around me with a low murmur. "As long as you're happy, that's what matters most."

Unfortunately, I think all the people waiting to get back to their homes in the swallowed city would disagree. They'd much prefer we make this wacky rift happy so it'll suck up all its shadows and go home.

As we come up on the vast swath of murk with its small lightened patch where I cast my glow the other day, I notice a couple of news crews trailing several paces behind us. When I glance over at them, the humans freeze as if they're afraid I might tackle them with some kind of glowy attack.

Instead, my good mood returns. I give them a wave. "Hello, humans! We're going to try to clean up some more of this mess and make sure no more rampaging creatures come out while we're doing it. You're welcome to watch."

Hail grumbles under his breath, but whatever he says is too quiet for even me to hear, so I let it pass. He steps apart from me so he can scan the filmy darkness for approaching shadowkind.

Raze stations himself at my other side. Mirage grasps my

shoulders to plant a kiss on the back of my head and then bounds a little closer to our mortal audience with a whirl of his bushy tails. His joy at being able to show off bits of his foxy form resonates into me, rich as toffee.

"This show won't be quite as spectacular as last night's," he informs them cheerfully, "but great things can come in small packages." He winks at me.

Jonah smiles crookedly and moves with Lilah to stand a little farther down the border. The two sorcerers murmur a few of those odd syllables that shiver across my skin, as if testing their magic out.

There's no sign of any unnerving beasts yet. I focus on the shadows right in front of me, several paces to the left of the previous spot I brightened, and summon the swell of affection I've relied on before.

"Hey, you great big blob of darkness! Welcome to the mortal realm. Let's see if we can get you more settled in. We'd really like to make sure everyone's as comfortable as they can be."

Let's make this a home—for everyone who needs it. All this strange rift seems to want is to make friends. Such a generous goal, even if its methods have been misguided. I'm sure we can find a way to accomplish it without putting humans out of their homes much longer.

As I focus on those thoughts, the turquoise glow exudes from my hands. I pour it into the murk with all the gentleness and compassion I can offer.

Behind me, one of the humans sucks in a breath with a tingle of awe. I'm not even doing anything all that amazing.

My efforts seem to be drawing even more attention than usual from the shadow side of things, though. Through the glow I'm pouring ahead of me, I become aware of maybe a dozen creatures of various shapes and sizes slinking out from behind buildings, through doorways, and over window ledges.

Mirage chuckles. "Everyone wants to see Peri work her magic."

Falkor's yip suggests he's less convinced of their good intentions.

Jonah and Lilah lift their voices in unison, presumably to urge the creatures away from our gathering. I tune out their sorcery as well as I can, but a hint of it prickles through my senses.

As their voices rise, I don't notice any of the creatures even hesitating. They keep prowling closer through the area my glow has touched.

Jonah lets out a huff of frustration. He swipes his hand across his mouth, his gaze fixed on the approaching creatures. His shoulders twitch alongside a splash of juniper-sharp anxiety.

His sudden fear sparks my own worries. My light falters in their wake.

As I inhale deeply, gathering myself for another attempt, Raze hums. "They… they don't seem like they want to attack us this time. I'm not getting predatory impressions from them."

I pause and study the creatures—who, it's true, have come to a stop in a scattered line a few feet away from me rather than stalking closer. Some sprawl out as if they're lounging on the pavement. A few simply sit placidly.

One dog-shaped creature stretches its legs like it's begging to play, and Falkor appears to have given up his earlier concerns. He slither-bounds away from my ankles to join it.

Are the creatures emerging from this rift actually… calming down?

I cock my head, extending my emotional awareness toward the beasts. The flow of sensations I pick up from them still has an odd edge to it I'm not used to from other shadowkind, but it's nowhere near as frazzled as most warped creatures are. While I watch, none of them show any sign of abruptly morphing into some new form.

Hail lets out a low whistle. "It looks like you might have chilled out the flood in more ways than one, Cream Puff."

I calmed down a few creatures before, but only when I was directly focusing on them, and I've never tried so many at the same time. Could the light I've cast into the murk really have that much of an effect?

My gaze slides past the loafing creatures to the thicker darkness beyond. I only brightened maybe another hundred square feet this time, and it's still *dark*, just not as dreary as it was before.

There has to be more we can do.

Even as that thought passes through my head, an engine roars behind us. My head jerks around.

An SUV grinds to a stop on the road near the news crews. The humans I saw talking with the colonel emerge. Silver-and-iron badges glint on all their shirts.

The one who seems to be the leader folds his arms over his chest, his jaw clenched. "Stop what you're doing right now."

14

Mirage

The humans stand still while they stare at us, but every bit of my essence prickles like my body wants to scatter into pieces and run away in different directions. Which these people might actually approve of.

A few of them have instruments holstered at their hips that I think are those shiny whip things that can sear right through our beings. A couple hold bundles of glinting strands that I know are the hunters' preferred type of net.

What will they do if we don't listen to them? Will they bundle us off into cages to poke and prod—

The memories of my past captivity rise up in a surge of icy panic. The air around us wavers, a metallic sheen glinting onto every surface. Spikes sprout from the SUV's windshield; war bugles go off in the distance.

Oh. Those aren't real transformations. I'm projecting illusions unconsciously.

The news crews stare at them, one of the camera men taking a step back, but the hunters don't react. Even as I yank my powers back inside, my gaze catches on the shiny metal circles pinned to their shirts and jackets.

Right. Those trinkets stop my powers from reaching their minds. When they're wearing them, they can't see my illusions.

I'm not sure that's a good thing. The odd gleam and the imaginary sights and sounds vanish as quickly as they appeared, but I kind of wish I'd unsettled the more aggressive people we're facing.

Peri sets her hands on her hips, unfazed by my slip or the hostile humans glaring at us. "Why are you interrupting us? We were helping the city."

I hope she can feel the rush of affection and awe that fills me as I watch her. She's half a foot shorter than even the smallest of the hunters and so much softer looking, but so strong she faces them head-on, no shying away or shivering.

The leader of the hunters flicks his gaze toward the darkness behind us, taking in the thinned area where Peri's been working her powers and the sludgier shadows beyond it. His stance tenses, maybe because of the audience of warped shadowkind creatures who are staring right back at him and his colleagues from the murk.

A couple of the creatures have gotten to their feet, tensing in turn. Even the ones still lolling on the pavement have lifted their heads with sharper alertness.

Are they picking up on the hostile atmosphere and giving in to the usual aggressive impulses after all?

I don't think a sudden rampage is going to help this situation.

I aim a subtle illusion toward the beasts, making them imagine soothing lights and cozy surfaces around them. If I can lull them right into sleep, even better.

One with a cheetah-like head gives a jaw-cracking yawn. That might be a good start, although one of the hunters flinches at the movement.

The lead hunter jerks his attention back to us. "It doesn't look very helped."

Jonah steps forward, the new sorcerer he's been trying to work with at his heels—hanging back as if she thinks she might want to hide behind him. More uneasy frustration skitters through my nerves.

We only want to make everyone happy. That's all Peri has *ever* tried to do. Why can't the humans just let us?

Why do they always have to boss everyone around, no matter who it hurts?

Jonah holds up his hands in a placating gesture. "Dealing with a mess this big takes time. Like Peri said, we're working on it—doing what we can to clean up the city. I'm as human as you are, and so is she." He indicates the other sorcerer. "Would you really want us to stop?"

The leader of the hunters narrows his eyes. "Do you really think the monsters are going to fix things instead of breaking them more? I hear dozens of humans have already gotten hurt."

Raze's jaw tightens as if he's suppressed a wince.

Hail's hands clench at his sides, but he flexes his fingers out of the fists and lifts his chin. "We aren't a hive mind. Some of the creatures are running wild, and the rest of us are doing our best to rein them in. And doing a pretty good job of it." He points to the creatures which have gone back to looking more sleepy than scary in the grips of my illusion.

One of the hunters snorts.

The leader lets out a cold laugh. "I've dealt with hundreds of you fiends in my time. There's nothing natural or safe about any of you. Get away from the city, or we'll make sure you do."

Jonah frowns. "Does Colonel Hueber know that you're going around threatening beings he's approved to pitch in?"

The other man sneers. "Mr. Military Big Shot welcomed us and said he was happy to have more people around who can 'control' the monsters. It didn't sound like he liked having any of them on the loose. He didn't lay down any rules about where we could step in."

I'm guessing the colonel didn't even think about the fact that some of us shadowkind are actively working to protect the city and the people who fled it. He seems to have tried as much as possible to pretend we don't exist.

Maybe he thinks the hunters would do a better job cleaning up the city anyway. He might have not mentioned there were some beings they shouldn't hassle hoping that they'd run us off and he wouldn't have to worry about us anymore.

Raze's posture has slumped, but he speaks up in a low voice. "We want the same things you do—to keep the humans around here safe. To get them back to their homes."

"Well, forgive me for not believing that," the leader says in a tone that's not at all apologetic, and gestures to his colleagues.

Those with whips unfurl the gleaming lengths like slashes of light—light I know will sear right into my being if one hits my body, even in my ephemeral state if I move into the shadows. The two with nets shake them looser, ready to throw.

The leader glowers at us. "Get out of here, *now*, or you'll regret it."

Peri pipes up with her unshakeable good cheer, though little trickles of fear tingle into me through our bond. "Now, hold on. There's no need to make this a fight. Why don't we all go talk to Colonel Hueber again, and he'll—"

"I told you to *go,*" the hunter snaps, and with those words, his colleagues barge toward us.

I'm not totally sure why I react so swiftly. Maybe it's the signs of distress in my friends—Raze stiffening his limbs rather than bracing to spring, Hail shoving his hands downward rather than raising them to cast out his icy magic.

They don't want to prove these humans right by hurting any of them like they have before.

I can't let the humans hurt any of us either. Not like the scientists with their iron chains and silver blades. Not like the men and women who yanked me around and dizzied me with pain.

But I have to make sure my powers can reach them.

"Hail," I say in a sharp whisper. "Can you freeze the metals off them?"

He stares at me for just an instant before resolve hardens his features. His fingers twitch at his sides.

Little snowballs erupt right beneath the silver-and-iron trinkets—and snap their pins off the fabric they're attached to. As the protective brooches clink against the asphalt, I hurl my illusions forward.

A whirlwind of chaotic images flies up around the hunters. Shadowy shapes soar past them, snapping razor teeth and pinning them with glowing red eyes. Thorny brambles shoot from the road and the sidewalks as if to pen them in.

They could walk right through the illusions if they tried, but the visuals look real enough that they stall in their tracks.

A heavy rumbling like incoming thunder sounds overhead, then a rattling as if an earthquake is shaking the nearby buildings. I give the hunters the impression that the ground is lurching beneath their feet for good measure.

I have to make *them* want to go away. Make them run so

far they'll never bother us again, never touch any of us with those whips or nets.

The panicked urgency propels more of my power out of me. The brambles twine and grow, sprouting sharper thorns that glint a poisonous purple hue. A fearsome roar reverberates down the street. Scarlet lights flash right before the hunters' eyes where only they can see, tinting everything the shade of blood.

Just a little more, and I can open up the thicket behind them so they'll dash away.

Even as I think that, a gentle hand comes to rest on my forearm. Peri's concern and love seeps through her warm touch.

"Mirage," she murmurs, with another caress of her soothing emotions, "this isn't how we make things better. The creatures are getting riled up. And I don't think it's good for you either. You always want to make people laugh, to play with them, don't you? What if we played with the hunters too?"

My immediate instinct is to balk. Play with these pricks? We should tell them to suck their own dicks!

But her encouragement has twined through my essence enough to produce that rhyme, to bring a smile to my lips at the rhythm of it—if also a little at the picture it presents.

She is right. I don't really want anyone feeling as trapped and anguished as I did in the scientists' cage.

The hunters are being ridiculous. Calling us monsters when we've done more to look after the humans here than any of their fellow humans have. Let's show them that absurdity.

The resolve has barely clicked in my head before my illusionary barrage shimmers in a new direction. The roar gives way to bright, childish giggles. The ground steadies and cushions the hunters' feet as if they're standing on a vast, cozy mattress.

The thicket's vicious thorns sprout a rainbow of flowers giving off an upliftingly tangy scent. They stir in a soft breeze, and the brambles contract so rosy sunlight can drift across the figures within.

Bluebirds chirp and flit merrily overhead, one and then another flipping in a loop-de-loop. A couple of them tuck their wings together and spin in a little dance that I don't think any real birds could manage, but it looks like fun.

The hunters shuffle backward, poised shoulder to shoulder. Their expressions look more befuddled than frightened now. I make one of the flowers form a face that blows a raspberry at them and then grins, and a couple of the humans actually chuckle.

The leader's head jerks around as if he's offended by the sound. I send a few of the illusionary bluebirds leapfrogging past him in a bouncy chain, and he pauses as if in a daze.

The sunlight I conjured spreads into a rainbow of colors, glowing vibrantly over the street in Peri's honor. She squeezes my arm with a waft of affection.

Finally, the leader swipes his hand through the flowers around him—and realizes his body passes straight through the image. He waves his arm around some more as if trying to dispel it like a puff of mist. "What the fuck is the point of all this? Get it out of our way!"

"It's not really in your way," Peri points out. "You can walk right through it."

He glares at her. "And we will. If you think your crazy games are going to change anything—"

Several more figures stride forward at the edge of my vision. The reporters and their camerapeople come to a stop just a few feet away from the group of hunters.

I was so focused on our potential attackers, I'd forgotten

the other humans were even here. Have they been filming this whole scene?

Is that a good thing or a bad thing?

One of the reporters has planted herself right in front of the lead hunter. She raises her microphone to her lips. "We've just seen a vivid display of how unsettling exteriors can turn out to be deceiving. Who doesn't need more flowers and rainbows in their life? Sir, do you have any evidence that these specific… shadowkind, I believe they call themselves… have caused any harm in or around the city?"

The leader grimaces. "Well, I— You can't go by the powers they throw around. They're trying to deceive you."

Another reporter pushes in. "It sounds like you're the one dodging questions. We've been watching these so-called 'monsters' at work, and they really have been lightening the darkness that's fallen over the city and calming down the violent creatures inside. Look at how they settled down the monsters over there right now."

I glance over my shoulder. The warped creatures have returned to their lounging, their expressions relaxed rather than fierce. A smile tugs at my lips.

My ferocity riled them up… but my playfulness chilled them back out again.

Another of the hunters barrels into the conversation, her voice harsh. "You can't believe anything these *things* say or do. They're lulling us into a false sense of security so we won't be ready to defend ourselves."

The first reporter lets out a skeptical cough. "I don't know. I think it's already been proven that we *couldn't* defend ourselves from whatever this onslaught is. If these supernatural beings wanted to hurt us, we couldn't be more vulnerable. Everything I've seen has shown that they're trying to prop us back up. And that we could use that help."

The third reporter jabs his microphone in the lead

hunter's face. "So tell us: are you and your colleagues going to be part of the solution or only add to the problem?"

As the leader opens his mouth and closes it again, struggling with his words, the other hunters seem to deflate.

Peri shoots me a flash of a smile, and my spirits settle back to their normally breezy state.

There could be more battles up ahead, but we've won this one—with dancing birds and cheeky flowers.

15

Periwinkle

I thought doing one big presentation in front of the humans' video cameras would set the record straight. But it seems people like to hear and see the same things over and over again before they totally believe them.

So here I am sitting on a wobbly chair on a makeshift set while yet another reporter smiles her blindingly white teeth at me and asks me questions as if off a checklist.

"And you've been traveling to our world for how long?"

I smile gamely and try to answer in a way that will make sense to her and anyone watching this interview through the TV. "I don't exactly know. We don't have clocks or calendars in the shadow realm, and I wasn't paying much attention to that sort of thing when I first arrived! But I think it's been a while. When I first came through, those phones you like to carry around were usually bigger, and a lot of them would bend in the middle. And you had to press buttons instead of tapping on the screen, which I guess was less convenient."

The woman nods, looking a bit thrown. "Oh. Yes! I remember my mother having one like that when I was a kid. So I suppose…" She hesitates with a sour tremor of anxiety that I think might be because she doesn't want to give away how old she is. The amount of cream and powder smeared on her face suggests she's covering it up as well as she can. "At least a couple of decades."

"That sounds about right!" I agree cheerfully.

"I gather the 'shadow realm' is awfully dark. Do you find it difficult being here in the sun? You must need a lot of sunscreen."

A laugh tumbles out of me. "Oh, no, not at all, actually. We don't get hurt by the same things humans do—well, not all the same things. It was a little strange being somewhere so bright at first, but also wonderful."

The reporter hums thoughtfully. "And what did you typically do on your trips? Before you had strange floods of darkness to deal with, I mean."

It's my turn to hesitate, because it wouldn't be a good idea to mention that one of my main activities was blasting my own darkness at innocent people under duress by the sorcerer who used to hold me captive. The whole point is to make humans feel *more* safe around me, not less.

But I've enjoyed lots of more pleasant activities too. "I like to visit the places where people feel happiest. Parks, playgrounds, entertainment complexes—anywhere they go to relax and have fun. As I mentioned before, I get nourishment from absorbing emotions, and it's a lot more satisfying when they're positive feelings."

A frown crosses the reporter's face. "And does your 'feeding' affect the humans whose emotions you 'eat'?"

I wave my hands emphatically. "Oh, no, not at all. You'd

never even know I'm doing it! It's like, your emotions give off this energy into the air whether anyone's around to notice or not. And I just pick up on what's already come out of you. I don't do anything to you at all."

Well, other than the fact that I've learned I can push my own emotions onto people. And blast them away if I get too emotional in any given direction.

Other facts I suspect it's better I keep quiet about for now.

The reporter's apprehension has simmered down. "Well, how wonderful that something we don't need can keep you fed. I hope you've found the people you've encountered here are welcoming."

Has she not noticed the hunters prowling around, or the soldiers with their rifles?

"Um, well, it would be nice if no one was coming at us with guns or nets or whatever. But most people have been very nice, like you!" I beam at her and then at the camera. "The shadowkind who come to this world would like to live among you totally peacefully—and we can. We want a lot of the same things humans want. It bothers us to see you in trouble, which is why we're trying so hard to sort out the mess here. I really think we can fix this problem if we all work together."

"Cheers to that." The reporter aims her own smile at the camera. "You've just heard from Periwinkle, one of the so-called 'shadowkind' who are attempting to clean up a strange atmospheric condition that's uprooted all the inhabitants of Jackson City from their homes."

As she chatters on to her unseen viewers, one of the TV staff people ushers me out of my seat. A little girl who can apparently juggle hamsters is waiting to go on next.

I guess the humans think my glowing is a similar trick? At least my super power doesn't involve flinging harmless rodents around. I send a trickle of soothing energy toward the three furry creatures in the cage she's holding.

When I step away from the recording tent, my own furry companion squirms over to join me. I bend down to rub Falkor's long belly and grin as he wriggles off again. A few of the humans have turned to stare.

"He's friendly!" I assure them. "No chomping or slashing."

They don't look particularly convinced.

At least the vibe around the evacuee camp seems to have mellowed out since the hunters showed up two days ago. The figures with their whips and nets are still stalking around the edges of the city, claiming they're just looking to subdue any hostile creatures we miss while continuing to glare at us every chance they get, but they haven't pointed anything at us worse than the evil eye.

Rollick had a long talk with Colonel Hueber after the reporters who saw our initial confrontation broadcast it all over the country. Luckily the hunters came across looking more monstrous than us, so most of the reporters played up the drama of big bad bullies harassing the city's saviors.

That means I've been able to make a little more progress. An achy sensation still grips my limbs from the day's second session of sweet-talking the murky deluge early this afternoon. Maybe twice in one day was a little much even for me.

But from here, I can't see any difference at all to the shadows cloaking the city. How can what I'm doing be enough if it's going to take a million years before the city's habitable again?

I'm pretty sure the people who call it home would like to move back in before they die.

I'll just keep working on it and finding new tricks. The process might speed up once I've made more progress. Or maybe we'll come across other beings with similar powers to mine who can pitch in too.

A salted-herring pang of loneliness passes into me through my bonds. I turn toward the sensation, tasting the different threads of flavor woven together.

It's Mirage, bored and itching to pull a prank or invigorate the atmosphere but worried that he might disrupt people who won't take kindly to it.

Playing isn't more important than making sure the humans still want us around, he told me the other day after he befuddled the hunters. *I'm not good at telling when I've gone too far.*

A renewed smile touches my lips. He doesn't have to fret about overwhelming me. A little play might be just what I need to revive my own energy.

I dive into the shadows and wind through the patches of darkness that stretch across the camp to where I can sense Mirage's presence.

He's slipped into one of the factories that border the city —one that escaped the deluge of murk and that's been shut down for a while. I ease through a cracked window and glide along a dusty floor amid machinery that looks awfully bored too.

Mirage is bounding around on the second floor that only covers half of the vast open room below, entertaining himself alone as well as he can. He darts along the railing on his human-like feet, bounds into the air while transforming into fox form, spirals through a few flips, bounces off the wall, and spins around to land on his renewed hands. Illusionary applause echoes through the dim space.

He doesn't appear to have noticed my approach yet. Perfect.

Holding my emotions in as tightly as I can—a practice that doesn't come naturally to me—I slink up to the second floor and position myself behind him. When the fox shifter pauses for a moment to roll his shoulders, I pounce.

I fling myself out of the shadows and into physical form at the same instant, tackling Mirage like I expect him to give me a piggyback ride. Adrenaline spikes from him to me as I glom on to his back, but he laughs at the same moment and whirls us around.

"You decided to catch *me* by surprise for once! My sneaky Rainbow."

I kiss the crook of his jaw just below his earlobe. "I didn't think you should have to play alone."

"But I'm never really alone now that we're connected." He peers around at me with a joyful gleam in his bright brown eyes that makes my arrival worth it.

The gleam glimmers slyer. "Catch me if you can?"

Mirage vanishes beneath me, leaving me tumbling for a split-second before I shoot after him into the shadows.

A laugh bubbles through my essence. I whip after my foxy mate, tracing the citrus-sharp sweetness of his exhilaration across the abandoned factory floor.

I do catch him under one of the vacant tables, twining my being around his. Mirage yanks us both into physical form to roll around and toss me back onto my feet. "Your turn!"

With a jolt of my own excitement, I dash away from him. It only takes a few steps before a prickle spreads up my ankles, and I spring into the shadows instead. Past the shelves, around the sagging stack of boxes, over and under more tables…

I've almost returned to the railing when Mirage wraps around me, and we both tumble into physical form. He twists as we fall so I'm cushioned by his lean body, toppling into him with my legs splayed on either side.

Our hips press together, and sudden desire that's much headier than the previous thrill floods us both.

Mirage pushes up to catch my lips as I lean down to meet him. Our shared delight at the kiss beams around us in the pinkish glow of my hair.

The fox shifter runs his hands down my curvy body, nothing but satisfaction emanating from him as he traces the soft slopes of my breasts, my stomach, my thighs. An urgent noise works from his throat.

"I like it when we're all taking care of you together… but sometimes I want you just to myself, Rainbow. I want to savor every bit of you just for me."

I bow lower, my hair falling forward to frame his face as well as mine, the tip of my nose grazing his. Love swells through my chest, so fast and breathless I know he must feel it too.

Words seem necessary anyway. "I want times when it's just me and you too. There's something special when it's all of us, and something different that's special when it's only the two of us. You can make me so happy all on your own. You know that, right?"

He grins at me, so bright my heart skips a beat. "I do now."

He kisses me again, his hands skimming back up my body to cup my breasts. In this moment, the layers of fabric between us feel like nothing but an annoyance.

I kiss him harder and then blink in and out of the shadows to dispel my jacket, dress, and underclothes all at once.

Mirage chuckles raggedly and performs the same trick beneath me, so fast I barely feel the loss of him. The glow of his mark beams from his chest to mingle with the light from my own.

Then his cock is pressing between my legs, the hard shaft

sliding against my clit with just enough friction to make me sigh.

"No matter what those humans do, no matter what happens with the city, I'll always be here to brighten you up if you get down," he promises, teasing his fingers into my still-glowing hair. "You're my treasure, Peri. Better than any gem, any heap of gold."

I rock my hips against him, drawing a groan from both our chests. "And I'll be here to do the same for you."

He flips us over in one smooth movement and plunges right into me. The shock of the motion turns the jolt of pleasure even giddier.

I raise my knees to welcome him in and urge him on, every inch of my body tingling. As he thrusts deeper, he teases his fangs along my neck, sparking even more thrills.

The rhythm of our collision is all elation. I sway to meet him, trailing my hands over his compact muscles, kissing him until we're both panting for breath.

Mirage slides a hand beneath my ass and tilts me at an angle that brings him even deeper into me. I gasp with a quiver of pleasure so intense it's electric.

It only takes a few more thrusts before I'm crying out and clutching him as ecstasy washes through me. My body shudders with the force of my orgasm.

Mirage growls and fills me again, and again. Then he follows me with a rasped inhalation and a rush of heat inside.

He rolls us onto our sides and wraps me in his arms and the joyful warmth of his adoration.

"Did you get what you were looking for, Rainbow?" he asks in a mischievous tone.

I bump my nose against his. "I'm always happier after I've been with you. Did you?"

"I didn't even know what I was craving until you came to

give me exactly what I needed. That's just how perfect you are."

Unfortunately, the abandoned factory isn't all that atmospheric a setting for romantic interludes. When we've caught our breaths, Mirage pulls me into one last lingering kiss, and we dip into the shadows to make our way outside.

We're just emerging from the big brick building when a tremor ripples through the air. My heart lurches.

I spin around in time to see a thicker gush of shadow spilling from the rift overhead.

16

Jonah

A volley of shouts brings me running to the trailer door. The group of shadowkind I was discussing strategy with hustle over behind me.

Outside, people are running through the paths between the trailers and tents—away from the city. My heart is already lurching as I scramble down the steps and whirl to get a better view.

A thick black torrent of shadow is spewing from the vast rift high above the buildings. It mingles with the gray haze below like a stream branching into trickles as it gushes down a mountainside.

It's happening again? This mess is getting even worse?

As my legs lock in my first jolt of shock, someone swears behind me. Shadowkind flit into the darkness. Hollered voices with a military-precise edge reach my ears from farther afield.

Riva and Zian jog up beside me, skirting the panicked refugees who are hurrying farther away. Riva's expression is tight, Zian's eyes wide.

"What the fuck is happening?" the big guy demands.

I shake my head, needing a moment to locate my words. "I—I don't know. I guess the same thing as before?"

Riva lets out a disbelieving sputter. "Like it wasn't bad enough already. We'd better get over there and see what we can do."

Yes. Right. Because we're the ones who are supposed to have a handle on the problem. The experts in this situation.

Someone needs to convince my brain of that before it spirals into total panic.

The shadowbloods race off toward the city. I spur myself into similar action, tuning out the frantic thrum of my pulse as well as I can. With each hurried footstep, I gulp deep breaths to offset the lightheadedness that's creeping over me.

There's got to be something I can do. That's why I'm here.

I'm sure as hell not going to help anyone if I fall apart again. I'm not a little kid anymore. This isn't that old catastrophe.

Nope. It's one much more immense.

As I pick up my pace, dodging the frantic humans, Peri and Mirage pop out of the shadows alongside me. Peri stares at the new deluge of shadow with a twist of her lips. "Why would it happen now? Did the soldiers do something? Or the hunters?"

"Not that I noticed," I say. "But I wasn't even outside when it started, so I wouldn't have seen. I guess that's possible."

Of course, the soldiers and the hunters were nowhere around the first few times the strange rift started spewing. It seems a little unfair to blame them for the current bout, as many other complaints as we could raise.

A trace of a blush colors Peri's cheeks. She glances at Mirage, and a twinge of emotion that's both guilt and pleasure passes through our bond. "You don't think— It happened right after—"

Mirage laughs, though the sound is more halting than his usual buoyant humor. "The rift didn't mind when we all took care of you before. How could just the two of us having fun set it off?"

Having fun? Oh, they were— I did pick up on some wafts of desire and delight not that long ago, but they were distant enough that I could ignore them.

Despite the awfulness of the situation, the corner of my mouth kicks upward. I tease my fingers through Peri's hair. "I'm sure getting it on didn't set the rift off."

She rubs her forehead. "I guess maybe nothing did. As far as we know, it was totally random all the other times, wasn't it?"

"As far as we know." I don't like to consider how much we *don't* know.

Given Rollick's inability to find any specific culprit, it seems likely that my previous worries were only panic-driven paranoia. Peri's theory about the borders between the realms thinning makes more sense than anything else. But we're not much closer to figuring out how to fix that problem.

We jar to a stop at the edge of the evacuee camp, where the temporary shelters give way to the last short span of scruffy grass before the first factory buildings rise from the earth. A few dozen soldiers have already marched into some kind of formation nearby, but they're gaping at the scene looking just as dazed as I feel.

The thicker darkness pouring from the rift isn't just

streaming down now. It's… churning, swirling into the lighter murk as if someone's stirring it with a giant spoon.

All the things Peri's suggested about how part of the shadow realm might be trying to merge with the mortal world come back to me.

I glance over at her. "Are you picking up any emotions from the creatures in the city? Does this *feel* different from before?"

She frowns, an uneasy orange glow flickering through her hair. "A little… Bits and pieces… Restlessness. Impatience. They're tired of waiting."

The churning of the haze seems to echo those emotions. I can almost taste the tension in its spiraling movement myself, winding tighter into the atmosphere, seeking something it's not finding.

A shiver runs over my skin.

Mirage's posture stiffens. "Here they come."

A few incongruous creatures are shuffling into view out of the murk. They weave back and forth with no clear sign of direction, scratching at the earth and bumping against the nearby buildings, but agitation shows in every twitch that wracks their warped bodies.

One of the soldiers shouts, and they all level their guns. I open my mouth instinctively, the sorcerous syllables that've become an innate part of my being flowing off my tongue.

Go back. Go home.

I toss out the command as firmly as I can, but only one of the creatures even sways in its steps. It veers to the side before straightening out its path again.

The soldiers open fire.

As their bullets tear holes through the creature's body that send even more dark smoke into the air, Raze and Hail appear behind us.

"What fresh hell is this?" the winter fae mutters.

"I don't know." Peri pushes forward with an air of determination. "But we need to get closer. See if we can settle things down, keep the creatures from barging out before they get into range of those guns."

An image passes through my head of a whole horde of the creatures charging toward us. My legs lock for a few seconds before I can force them to follow her.

We rush past the nearest factory building and slow as we come up on the edge of the deluge. Here, I can't make out the darker current whirling into it from above, but the haze trembles with minor eddies.

More creatures are prowling back and forth on the streets within. One's quills rattle with its shudder, while another makes a high-pitched keening sound that quavers through my nerves.

A scaled form looms high on two legs, its other stubby, clawed appendages grasping at the air. My mind flashes back to the coiled form of the leviathan as he glowered down at my three-year-old self with serrated teeth flashing.

My breath hitches. A flood of cold sweeps through me alongside the stuttering of my heart.

Peri's hand squeezes around mine. The warmth of her touch alongside the concerned affection coursing from her into me brings me back to earth, back to the present.

She peers at me, worry shining in her bright blue eyes. "Where did you go?"

Before I can find the words to tell her, more voices ring out from farther along the murky area. Voices speaking in sounds that belong to no human language but that I recognize down to my soul.

Sorcerers. And not just Lilah, if she's even among them— there must be several chanting together.

My companions tense up. They've all been held in the grips of sorcery before for cruel ends.

"You try to help things here," I blurt out. "I'll go see what's happening."

I lope off around a shed and along a fence. A cluster of people comes into view beyond the next factory, maybe ten of them facing the shadowy haze and calling out their sorcerous syllables.

At least a few hunters lurk beyond them, whips and nets at the ready—I suppose in case the sorcery doesn't work. Or maybe to subdue the creatures if the sorcerers decide to draw them out rather than urging them back in?

The meaning of the magical chanting seeps into my awareness. They're telling the shadowkind to stay away from humans—and to lash out at each other.

My throat constricts. Are they hoping they can get the beasts to destroy each other?

I guess that is one way of dealing with the threat, even if the idea sends a lurch of nausea through my gut.

Whatever their plan, it doesn't appear to be working all that well, even with their numbers. More creatures have swarmed into the streets here too, but they're prowling toward us without any sign of hostility toward each other.

The sorcerers' faces are going taut with frustration. One of them breaks off the chant with a curse under his breath. "Why aren't they fucking listening?"

I clear my throat, and more of the voices falter. Sorcerers and hunters alike jerk their gazes toward me.

I stride over, willing down the apprehension pricking at my skin. "Sorcery doesn't take hold on the creatures from these warped rifts, at least not very well."

The man who complained scowls at me. "You would know, wouldn't you? You're one of us, but you've been slumming it with the monsters as if they're your *friends*. I saw you on the news."

The good news is Peri's efforts are obviously making the

rounds on screens everywhere. The bad news is apparently those efforts also drew these pricks here.

I size the group up as they do me. It isn't surprising, really, that sorcerers would show up to offer their "services" in controlling the shadowkind just like the hunters did. They'd want the ego boost of being able to put their power on full display.

Would they ever reveal to the rest of humanity how they developed those powers? The stories Quinn told me float up through my head: the training center she visited where the acolytes slaughtered shadowkind creatures to drink in their essence.

It's only by mixing a little of what shadowkind are made of into our own bodies that we can gain power over them. The talent can be passed on genetically, but mine wasn't all that strong until my shadowkind guardians voluntarily donated bits of their essence to support my training.

Somehow, based on the sneers and glares showing on the faces before me, I don't think asking permission occurred to anyone in this bunch.

How many shadowkind have they killed to absorb the smoky haze of their lives? How many more have they enslaved for God knows what purposes?

"I'd imagine I know a lot more about the shadowkind—and everything they're capable of—than you do," I say evenly. "I *definitely* know more about what's happening here, considering I've been monitoring this rift since before it even expanded, and you only just showed up."

Another of the sorcerers lets out a scoffing sound. "You've been brainwashed. You're probably under the control of one of those mind-altering fiends." She waves her hand toward the murk. "This is what they're made of. This is where they come from. Look at what it's doing to our world. And you're going to help them take over our home?"

Even though I automatically balk at the lie in her final question, her other points stir up memories of walking through the shadowed city. The twisted buildings, the mutilated bodies, the deranged creatures. My pulse hiccups.

I've seen what happens when shadowkind get too much power. I barely survived the last attempted invasion.

I set my jaw firmly against the wobble in my nerves. "I'm helping them stop the problem from getting worse. None of the beings I work with"—and do other things with that I'm not going to mention in this company—"want the shadow realm collapsing into this one. They like the mortal realm as it is."

The first sorcerer snorts. "Right. They like it to be easy pickings. But now that option is off the table, so they're going to swarm us all if they get the chance. I don't believe for one second you don't know they're capable of it, no matter how hard you're pretending."

The image of the leviathan wavers through my mind again. My mouth goes dry.

The sorcerers turn away from me to murmur amongst themselves.

"We've got to find some way of getting a handle on these freakish things," one grumbles.

"Imagine if this immunity spreads? If we can't get a grip on any of them…"

"We'll alter our techniques, learn to adapt just like they are. We can't let them get the upper hand."

The first man glances over into the haze and braces himself. "They're coming."

The creatures are prowling nearer, most of them now focused specifically on the humans beyond the murk. Their eerie eyes—some smoldering, some glinting, some multi-faceted panes like an insect's—raise the hairs on the back of my neck when their gazes pass over me.

A tiny voice wakes up in the back of my mind, niggling through my thoughts. *Why are you going along with all this? What if this is your chance to put an end to it—find a way to stop the shadowkind from breaking into this world at all?*

For a second, the idea knocks the breath from my lungs. It's brought a smack of horror, yes, but also an uneasy surge of exhilaration.

I could protect the entire mortal world. I could put an end to all the conflicts and the pain.

If I worked with the humans here rather than the shadowkind, with everything I know— Even if we can't order around the warped creatures, we could bring the regular beings under our sway and call on them to fight back more avidly—

There's an odd sort of comfort in those thoughts, and that's what turns my reaction completely sour. I recoil within myself, swallowing hard.

Sure, it'd be nice never to have my awful memories triggered again. Never to live through that old panic. But that's *my* problem to deal with. None of the shadowkind I know now had anything to do with it.

And how can I say the shadowkind were the only problem, even back then? The ones who killed my parents and kidnapped me were using sorcerer powers they stole by devouring humans who'd enslaved and murdered shadowkind first.

Here I was imagining commanding the beings who *are* my friends, my colleagues. Doesn't that make me a monster too?

Just like them, I can make the choice not to be one.

My voice comes out ringing with conviction. "We should be able to affect the creatures if we all focus on the same intention. Don't try to push against their natural inclinations so much. They don't want to fight each other. They do want to feel safe. Tell them to run deeper into the shadows and seek shelter."

As the other sorcerers peer over at me, their brows knitting and heads cocking, I swivel toward the approaching creatures and take my own advice, even though I know it won't do much good on my own.

I summon all of the sorcerous energy I can instinctively sense deep within me and channel it into my message. *Run away. Flee into the shadows where it's safer. Stay far away from humans, from danger.*

A burst of gunfire from back where the soldiers were stationed punctuates my orders, but the creatures only stare at me. A couple of them slink closer.

My heart thumps harder. I repeat the syllables that spring to my lips, tamping down my despair—

And another voice rises to join mine. Lilah's, from my other side where she must have joined us without me noticing.

Then another, and another, as the newcomers must decide my suggestion is worth giving a try. Our magic-laced words with their odd sounds wash across the urban terrain.

A few of the smaller creatures quiver and turn around. Two scamper right off, vanishing into the darkness as they do.

I repeat my command again, this time with a whole chorus chanting alongside me. More of the beasts peel away from the pack. The largest two pause with grunts and discomforted shakes of their heads.

Again. Again.

One and then the other fades into the shadows. I don't know how far away they retreat, but they're at least not poised to pounce on us any longer.

I let out my breath in a rush, holding my body back from

sagging with the release. The other sorcerers chatter eagerly with each other over our temporary victory.

My own sense of satisfaction is tempered by the fact that I don't trust this bunch not to start spouting their anti-monster garbage all over again. No matter how much panic jangles through me, I know down to the center of my being that the shadowkind deserve their place in this world just as much as we do.

One sorcerer glances my way again and goes rigid. "What's *she* doing here?"

In the moment before my head turns, I think he's talking about Lilah, which doesn't even make sense. Then I catch the gleam of teal hair.

Peri has appeared next to me. She twines her fingers with mine like she did when I almost slid into a panic attack earlier, but the vibe emanating off her is all urgency now.

"Can you come?" she asks quietly. "I think I need your help."

17

Periwinkle

Jonah hustles after me without hesitation, back to where I left my other mates.

We found a spot away from the soldiers, where we wouldn't have to worry about stray bullets tearing through us. Raze stands braced at the edge of the murky area, ready to swipe down any rampaging creatures that make a break for it. Hail is poised in a similar stance, his hands raised and glittering with an icy sheen. Mirage's usually cheerful face has hardened with concentration as he attempts to lull both the shadowkind within the deluge and the humans in the camp behind us into some kind of calm.

I stop between them, my breath coming shaky. Their tension reverberates into me alongside my own—and alongside the discontented vibes churning all through the flood of darkness.

The new shadowy spew is stirring everything up again

after it'd started to settle down. If we can't soothe the atmosphere again…

I don't want to think about what kind of messed-up meal it'll make out of us.

The impulse that brought me racing to Jonah is still thrumming through my veins. I close my hand tight around his and extend the other toward Mirage. "I want us to make a circle of light like we did around Viscera. Maybe I can reassure the rift and the creatures coming out of it better if my powers have that extra oomph."

I'm not sure if "oomph" is the correct technical term for what we're attempting, but even thinking about combining forces with my men brings a fuller swell of love into my chest. The sensation echoes back to me from all four of my mates, melting the sharpest edges off their fears.

Jonah nods and squeezes my fingers. Mirage extends his arm toward me and to Hail at his other side. The winter fae pulls his slim frame straighter and holds his hands out at either side.

Raze completes our circle, his eyes smoldering with concern. "You don't want to push yourself too far."

"Don't worry about that," I tell him. "Just focus on how much we want to solve this problem. How much we're hoping we can find a balance between the mortal and shadow realms and bring happiness rather than destruction for all the beings in both."

Twinges of that hope waft through our bond. I stare up at the rippling mass of darkness and call on all the tender feelings of my own I've been able to turn to before.

Let's be friends, I think at the flood of murk, the whirling bits of thicker darkness and all. *There's a place for you here. We can find it if we work together, like I'm working with my mates right now. See how easy it can be? We want to help you.*

The turquoise light I've aimed toward the deluge before

streams from the bond mark in the middle of my chest, bright enough to shine through my shirt. The matching marks glow on my men's chests.

A current of loving light flows between us until it forms a solid circle. Jonah lets out an awed laugh.

We've only ever done this once before. I wasn't totally sure it'd work—maybe he wasn't either.

Now let's see if I can put our giant mood ring to good use.

I train my attention on the emotions coursing through our glow—the fondness and exhilaration and longing to set things right. The awareness of those sensations quivers through every particle of my body.

Inhaling deeply, I will the light to surge out from our circle like a smaller version of the rift's flood. Out and up and over there, in a glowing teal wave.

It washes over the road and shimmers against the murky edge of the deluge. One beam and another streaks through the darkness.

Somewhere nearby, a creature that was charging our way pauses in mid-snarl, its anger simmering down. The darker eddies that trickled this far waver and dissipate in the wake of the glow.

As I nudge the bright energies farther, the light thins. Can I spread it all the way to the thickest currents spilling from the rift before our glow vanishes completely?

I summon even more compassion from my body and channel it into my light.

No, we haven't been able to orchestrate a merging of worlds in a matter of days, but that doesn't mean we've turned our backs on the shadows. We're right here, doing our best. Patience is a virtue and all that.

The rift should be patient with us, just like we're being

patient about the whole rampaging-creatures-and-warping-city thing.

I can't tell how much the murk has thinned, but I have the sense that the new deluge of darkness is ebbing. The shadowy haze is chilling out. I'd offer to buy it a drink if bar-hopping was a thing huge masses of shadows did.

A smile crosses my lips. I exude another wash of light—

And a body slams into me from the side.

I tumble to the ground, my hand breaking from Jonah's grasp. Yells career all around us, cut through with a roar I know is Raze's.

"Where's the— Didn't you have the thing?"

"Here!"

Tendrils of fabric smack into my body with a searing burn. My essence seizes with recognition.

I'm caught in one of the hunters' nets, woven with silver and iron. Someone's thrown it around me.

"Just take this one! The power was coming out of her."

"Come on!"

The humans who've barged into our midst swarm around me. At least a few pairs of hands wrench me off the ground and shove me into the back of a van I hadn't heard approaching.

The pain dizzies me so much my vision blurs.

"Wait!" I cry out. "What are you—"

I'm not sure if my words were even clear in my muddled state. The van's doors clang shut, and the engine revs. The vehicle lurches forward.

Panic and anguish rush through my chest from my connection with my men. They feel… stuck, as if the people who nabbed me harmed them as well.

No! I have to get back to them—I have to make sure my mates are all right.

Another roar fades into the distance. My pulse starts to

stutter. If these people drag me too far from my marked men, we'll all be in another kind of agony. I doubt my attackers even realize that.

They also might not realize that my mates should be able to track me down by following their impressions of my emotions. They'll come after me as soon as they can. It'll be okay.

As long as wherever I'm being taken isn't even worse than what's already happened.

Are they going to throw us in cages? Bend our minds to sorcerous commands?

Why did they come after me right now? I was trying to fix the rift—I don't even know if they ruined whatever progress the five of us managed to make together.

The fraught uncertainty overwhelms me, and my thoughts scatter again with the throbbing of pain all through my body. The net burns everywhere it touches my skin, but I can't shed that skin and slip into the shadows while the noxious metals are grounding my essence so forcefully.

The van bumps over uneven ground. I roll from one side of the cargo area to the other, smacking against the wall. Apparently my captors are trying to turn me into tenderized shadowkind.

I grit my teeth against the pain and try to think of what to do. It's pretty tricky when I don't seem to be capable of doing *anything* at the moment.

Abruptly, the van screeches to a halt. More voices holler back and forth outside.

The usual prickling of discomfort at distance from my mates hasn't started up. We haven't experimented with getting farther apart since we confirmed our love for one another. Maybe our bonds have settled down with our acceptance of them?

One small plus in a big heap of minuses.

The van's back doors swing open. I'm lying on my side partly facing them, so I have an awkward view of the several humans standing stiffly outside, staring at me as if they expect me to erupt into vengeful flames.

As far as I know, that's more Sorsha's area. Maybe they got the two of us confused, just looking for a shadowkind with some sort of vibrant hair?

I manage to speak, though my voice comes out reedy. "Why did you take me?"

One of the humans makes a scoffing sound. "You're one of those monsters. You were messing around with the shadows. As if things aren't bad enough already."

I swallow against the pain. "I was… trying to make it better. Calm down the flood. Stop the real monsters."

Another of my captors snorts. "Why would you want that? You're getting what you want, aren't you? Taking over the world?"

Taking over the world? My mind spins, and a response I haven't totally thought through spills out. "That sounds like… too much work."

Then I blank out completely.

I WAKE up sitting in a folding lawn chair with my skin no longer crisscrossed with net webbing. That should be an improvement, but a deep throbbing around my arms and legs tells me I'm not exactly home free.

Shiny cords that must be woven with silver and iron gleam around my wrists and elbows, restraining me to the chair's arms. From the gnawing sensation across my lower legs, there are more tying my calves to the aluminum base.

The plasticky fabric against my butt and back feels awfully flimsy. I'm not sure my captors have given their current plan the most in-depth consideration. It's not as if the chair would hold me back if I decided to throw myself at them.

I am still stuck to it and in my physical form, though. They're just lucky I'm not the havoc-wreaking type.

My impressions of my men have dulled with the distance, but I can still tell none of them are currently overjoyed. Pain and fear trickle through me.

I need to get back to them—so they know I'm okay. So I know *they're* okay.

A few humans are sitting in similar chairs across from me. When one of them gives a shout that my eyes have opened, ten more come hurrying over.

The woman in the middle chair stands up. A silver-and-iron badge glints on her shirt, and something long and sinewy glints as it streams from her hand.

It's one of those shiny whips of light the hunters also use. These people don't look like the hunters I've seen before, much more nervous and jittery rather than grim and jaded, but they've stocked up on all the tools of the trade.

I can't taste the woman's emotions while she's wearing that protective badge, but I'm familiar enough with human interior states that I don't buy the toughness she's attempting to exude. She's hiding her nerves pretty well on the outside, but a faint tremor ripples through her voice when she speaks.

"You're the one who made a big deal on TV about being here. You're mixed up in this disaster the most. You're going to tell us what you really want, or I'm going to make you."

She lifts the whip threateningly.

What I really want is to get out of this chair, wave good-bye, and hightail it back to the city. Somehow I don't think that's what she means, though.

It's not as if my broader intentions are particularly horrifying either. "I want to get all that murk off the city so the people who lived there can go home safely. And to figure out why it came out of the rift in the first place so we can make sure no one's hurt the same way again."

The humans all peer at me so blankly that I start to wonder if I accidentally spoke in a language they don't know. Did the pain rewire my brain so I'm accidentally using French or Cantonese or Klingon?

The woman who's leading the interrogation waggles the whip. "Then why were you over there sending your weird powers into it?"

Okay, so she did understand my explanation. They just don't believe it.

I exude as much reassuring warmth as I can summon when I feel like my limbs are about to burn off, which I'll admit isn't a whole lot. "My powers—which I really don't think are all that weird; you should see what this squid shifter I met can do—seem to lighten up the darkness. I've been thinning out the murk for a few days now. When more darkness was spewing out, I got my mates to help me in the hopes that we could stop the situation from getting worse."

A man who's still sitting in one of the chairs folds his arms over his chest. "Then why did the darkness *stop* spewing after we tackled you?"

My spirits lift. "We must have had enough of an effect before then. That's great!"

Everyone looks taken aback by my chipper response. Did they expect me to wail and gnash my teeth?

Given that they seem to think I have an evil plan I'm hiding, possibly yes.

The woman opens her mouth, but I decide that it should be my turn to ask a question or two. That's only fair, right?

"Where did you all come from? I haven't seen you around the evacuee camp."

And while they might not have the hunter vibe, they

don't look like the city's refugees either—clothes too clean, hair too neat.

The woman grimaces. "We're concerned citizens who arrived to see what we could do to help. If everyone stands back and lets monsters take over, we're all screwed."

I beam at her. "But that's why I came too—to see how I can help! I was trying to help even before the rift vomited all its shadows over the city."

One of the people hanging back jabs his hand toward me. "You admit it, then! You came and set off this whole mess."

I knit my brow. "No, that's not what I said. We just noticed something strange was going on and came to investigate. We never expected it to get *this* strange. That shadowy stuff hurts us too if we're in it for too long, you know. It's not good for any of us. So of course we all want to—"

"That's enough!" the woman snaps, and motions for her companions to follow her as she stalks out of hearing distance.

I peer after them, my heart lurching in my chest. Is there anything I can say that they'll believe?

What if Rollick was right about most humans after all?

18

Raze

The metal-laced cords bite into my flesh, sending pain sizzling through my nerves. I thrash and snap my teeth, but everywhere I move my limbs, there seems to be more of the noxious stuff.

A basilisk caught in a net like a fish. And the indignity is only the smallest part of the crime.

Another roar bursts from my throat. A tugging sensation in my chest tells me that Peri is still being dragged farther away, radiating distress.

What are those demented humans going to do to her? Why did they take her at all?

If they hurt her even as much as they've already hurt me…

Snarling, I shove harder at the burning strands, but I only seem to tangle myself farther. Nearby, Hail is cursing up a storm, bringing out swear words I've never even heard before. Mirage emits a continuous growl alongside a frantic rustling. They must both be caught up too.

Where's Jonah? The human in our group shouldn't be affected by silver and iron. Why isn't he helping us?

At that thought, I force myself to go still. It'd be awfully hard for Jonah *to* help us while we're flailing around with fangs and claws gnashing. I might have been preventing my own rescue in my furor.

A slight but horrible miscalculation.

When I take in the scene around me, though, it's clear our sorcerer isn't going to be leaping to our rescue even when he won't risk getting torn limb from limb. He's sprawled by a telephone pole at the side of the road, engaged in a wrestling match of his own.

It takes me a moment to figure out what he's struggling against. Then my jaw clenches.

One of those blazing whip-things is looped around his arms and chest, binding them to the pole. It might not sear into his skin the way it would ours, but apparently it works well enough as a makeshift rope.

All four of Peri's mates trussed up like the rodeo came through, while she's suffering through who knows what. When I get my claws into those wretches…

My muscles flex to resume my thrashing, but my momentary stillness has made me more alert to the exact angles of my bindings. I think I can make out one edge of the net down by my feet…

Carefully rather than frantically, I shuffle my legs back and forth. The friction of the cords sends more pain lancing through my flesh, but I manage to shift the net off one foot and then the other.

Gritting my teeth, I keep up the ridiculous squirming. Thankfully, there's no one to see me wriggling around like a tadpole rather than a giant, lethal lizard.

Bit by bit, I work my lower body out from under the interlaced strands. My essence is still too weakened from the contact with the metals for me to manage to stand—my legs are wobbling just lying on the ground—but with a few forceful heaves, I manage to wrench the rest of my body free.

Air floods my lungs which can now expand to full capacity rather than squeezing tight against the ache. After several deep breaths, I shake off the lingering jabs of pain and sway upright. I nearly fall over again when one last surge of agony sweeps through my body.

I clutch at a nearby fire hydrant and catch my balance. With the metals off me, the pain quickly retreats. My essence knits itself back into proper health.

Hail and Mirage are still fighting with their own nets, sprawled farther down the sidewalk. My hands flex at my sides, but I don't think I'd have the strength to yank the material off them once it starts burning me again.

Jonah, though…

I sprint over to the pole he's bound to and wrench at the whip. Jonah pauses his struggles to let me work.

My strength can't seem to dislodge the stream of light. It's folded over on itself somehow, as if it's melded right together in a way no regular strip of material could. And when I grasp any part of it for more than a few seconds, my fingers start to burn.

I bare my teeth at the weapon that's managing to foil me even when it's not in a hunter's hands. "I don't know how to get it off you."

A sharp twinge of pain radiates through my connection with Peri, followed by a trickle of fear. My head jerks toward the direction those sensations are coming from.

I can feel them so much more vividly now that my own distress isn't overwhelming my senses… or maybe she's feeling significantly worse than she was a few minutes ago.

Jonah must be picking up on her emotional state too. He gazes up at me with widened eyes. "Get to Peri. If you have the chance to alert Rollick or any of his people, do it, but— we can't let anything happen to her."

We're on the same page there. I nod and hurtle into the shadows without another word.

I've only run down a few streets, veering to one side and the other as I track the impressions I'm getting from Peri, before frustration nips at my heels. Even racing through the shadows, I can't move as quickly as an army jeep that rumbles past me.

The asshole humans threw my mate into a van. They sped off far faster than I'm moving now. Every second I'm away from her is another second they could be tormenting her.

How hard could it be to operate one of those hunks of metal anyway? I've watched Jonah do it plenty of times.

Cars, trucks, and vans are parked here and there between the makeshift shelters of the camp. I steer away from anything with the blotchy army coloring, leaping from vehicle to vehicle in search of one with the key or fob that'll turn on the engine.

There! Someone's left their car running, the door cracked open while they must have run off to grab something. They'll just have to excuse me grabbing their ride for a short while.

I dive into the driver's seat while yanking myself into physical form. My spine jars against a seat pressed a little too close to the steering wheel for comfort, but I don't have time to fiddle with the controls. Someone's already shouting in alarm from behind me.

I tug the door all the way closed and step on the pedal that makes the car go.

The engine groans, but the vehicle doesn't move. I peer at the stick next to my seat and remember that it's supposed to be next to D for drive. P for park is getting me nowhere.

Footsteps pound toward me. I yank the stick and slam my foot on the gas again.

The car lurches forward at a speed I wasn't prepared for. I jerk at the wheel to stop it from careening right into a tent and then in the other direction so I don't run over a shadowkind being who was crossing the street.

The figure I nearly crashed into blinks at me and then leaps into the shadows. Well, I guess I've probably just informed Rollick that there's a problem, one way or another.

I aim the car away from the mass of tents and people until there are a lot fewer obstacles on either side of me that I could slam into. Peri's off to my left. I haul on the wheel again, and the car bounces off the road across the packed dirt of the nearby terrain.

I'm getting closer. When I find them, they're going to regret ever setting their hands on my mate.

My anger brings my fangs to my gums and my claws poking from my fingertips even in my human-like form. I itch to stretch into my full basilisk body, but I suspect directing the car as a giant lizard will be quite a bit harder than it already is as a sort-of man.

As pebbles rattle against the undercarriage, another waft of emotion reaches me. It's still twined with anxiety, but there's a warm glow of affection mixed in.

For me, because Peri can tell I'm coming?

The sensation spreads through my nerves, and a knot forms in my gut.

I jumped in to protect her from attackers before… and ended up nearly causing a total disaster in human-shadowkind relations. We know a lot of people are scared of us. Charging in there and slaughtering all of them the way I'm craving is only going to make the rest more frightened.

What will the army people do if they find out I eviscerated a dozen humans this time? Will they send their new hunter and sorcerer friends against us and all our other allies?

My hands squeeze around the wheel so tightly my claws gouge the material covering it.

I *have* to defend my mate. I have to make them pay…

But what if there are better ways of making them pay that don't come back to hurt us even more? That's what Peri would want, isn't it?

She's the one who taught me I could be more than just a killer. That my power doesn't have to be completely brutal.

My gut stays knotted, but a spot of warmth blooms in my chest alongside the stream of her love. I want to protect my mate *and* make her proud.

My sense of her presence grows stronger by the second. I swerve around a stand of trees, wincing at the screech of a branch I didn't quite avoid scraping the roof.

A cluster of human figures comes into view up ahead next to a familiar van.

As I hit the brakes, the humans startle and scramble apart. I spot Peri's vibrant turquoise hair in their midst where she's sitting in a chair. Her head ticks toward me, but it looks like her arms and legs are tied in place.

A growl slips from my lips. I spring into the open air through the shadows, not bothering with the door.

A few of the humans are running toward me rather than away, holding more of their nets and whips. I'm ready for them this time.

Before they get within ten feet of me, I narrow my eyes and let just the thinnest punch of poison exude from my basilisk gaze.

One and then another figure goes rigid and topples over on the ground. More of their companions charge over, having grabbed weapons of their own, but they hesitate after seeing how quickly I took down their colleagues.

I don't care if they're having second thoughts. I'm not leaving anyone willing to fling those toxic things at me conscious while I free my mate.

A renewed flare of rage hazes my vision. I suck in a breath and shut my eyes for long enough to quell the worst of my fury.

I will not let their monstrousness make me more of a monster.

With rigid control, I glance from one to the next of our attackers. They drop like flies in a gust of insect spray, but they're not dead.

A few others remain, huddled by the van empty-handed. I stride toward them and Peri, letting my voice come out harsh. "Do I need to knock you out too?"

"No! No, please, no! Don't kill us!" One of the men cowers with his hands raised in appeal.

I grimace at him. "I didn't kill anyone. They'll wake up in a couple of hours—when my mate and I are far away from you. *I* don't hurt people when I don't need to."

"That's right," Peri says, her voice as bright as the sun.

When I look at her, her beaming smile lights me up the way nothing else can. I hustle the rest of the way to her, eyeing the glinting ropes wrapped around her limbs—

And a roar that's not mine reverberates over the low hill several paces away from us.

As I brace in reaction, a tiger-like creature with talons protruding from its paws—and too many other places as well —crashes down the slope. It barrels toward the van and the three humans now frozen in fear there.

I have to admit that my first instinct is to let it have them. Why should I extend myself to shield three beings who held my mate prisoner?

But in that first instant, it's obvious that if I *don't* intervene, the warped shadowkind will kill them. And I can't convince myself that's particularly better than if I had murdered them.

Restraining a sigh of resignation, I spring into the creature's path.

I don't kill it either. It deserves the chance for Peri's joyful energy to work her magic and simmer down its temper, if this being is capable of chilling out. Like with the humans, I only aim a portion of my gaze's power at the creature.

At first, it merely stumbles. Shadowkind aren't quite as fragile as mortal beings. When I glower at it with a little more intensity, it stiffens up. It flops over on its side with a *whoomph* and a spray of dust.

The humans stare at the creature that nearly mowed them down, their jaws slack. I will my contacts back into my eyes and glower at them in the non-basilisk way. "You're welcome. Now how about you untie my mate?"

Two of them just gape at me too, but the third rushes over to pry at Peri's bindings.

"Thank you," my mate says, sweet as anything, as if this prick wasn't one of the people who took her captive in the first place.

Maybe someday I'll be able to see as much good in other beings as she always can.

As I spin toward her, I realize our skirmish has an audience. A couple of news vans pulled up while I was distracted by my need to rescue my mate. The camerapeople are recording nervously from beside their vehicles.

One reporter backs up a step and hollers at me from across the distance. "Please, don't hurt anyone else."

I frown, but before I can answer, one of his colleagues takes a cautious step forward instead. "I don't think—That car I saw you steal. Did you need to get here to help your friend? What have you done to the people who took her?"

I will my fangs to retract into my gums and smooth as much gruffness out of my voice as I can. She's asking questions rather than making accusations. That seems like a good sign.

"They kidnapped my mate and tied her up," I say. "For no reason! She was trying to help the city. I know a lot of you are scared, but…" I inhale deeply. "I used my powers to knock these people unconscious. They're still alive. You can check them to make sure. *We* can treat humans fairly. I wish they'd do the same for us."

To my surprise, an awed expression crosses the woman's face. "They grabbed your… your mate, and you still saved them from the creature that was coming at them?"

I shrug. "More beings dead doesn't help anyone. I do what I can."

As those words leave my mouth, it occurs to me with a pang in my chest just how true they are… and just how much I *can* do when I keep control of myself.

Maybe being a monster isn't so bad if it means I can accomplish as much as I did here today.

Peri dashes over and wraps her arms around my waist. "Raze saves people whenever he has the chance. And we're going to keep doing that as long as you let us."

19

Periwinkle

It takes a long time for my heartbeat to level out and my mind to stop its frantic scrambling. We're well into the evacuee camp before I realize that Raze's driving strategy is more "keep swerving to avoid whatever object you're about to drive into" than "continue down the road." He stares at the street ahead, looking a little frantic himself, his tawny knuckles paling as he jerks on the wheel again.

He drove like this all the way out into the wilderness to find me—because he was so worried about me it mattered more than how worried he was about crashing a car. I can't help beaming at him even as I jolt against the seatbelt again.

I'd ask if we really need to drive, but he said that when he left my other men, they were still restrained. From the smacks of irritation and discomfort that keep hitting me, I'm guessing no one else has found them.

We need to free them as quickly as possible, no matter how much rubber we burn getting there.

With another faint squeal of the tires, Raze peers around him, his jaw tight. "I—I was going to give the car back, leave it where I found it. I don't remember what tents it was near."

I pat his arm. "We'll park it and make an announcement, and the owner will find it. I'm sure they won't mind when they hear what a noble use you had." A wave of fondness rolls off me to soften his agitation. "You were amazing with the humans. You rescued me without hurting any of them."

He manages to aim a quick smile at me alongside a waft of his own affection before he yanks his gaze back to the trash bin we need to dodge. "You showed me how."

The joy of that knowledge stays with me until we come up on the looming, shadow-drenched city.

As Raze navigates around the now-abandoned factory buildings, my awareness of my other mates' emotions thickens into an unpalatable slop. Acidic fear mingles with bitter frustration, like the most gag-worthy of cough syrups.

My pulse hiccups. "I've got to get to them," I say to Raze, and dive out through the strip of darkness around the car door without waiting for him to park.

I dart through the shadows along a few more buildings before I reach the patch of thinned murk where I was casting my powers not long ago—and see the men trapped there.

Hail is lying on his back, a silver-and-iron net tangled all around him, his chest heaving with pained breaths. Mirage squirms within similar bindings, flinches, and goes still for a moment.

They're both too lost in agony to notice my arrival, but Jonah perks up where he's been lashed to a telephone pole with one of those glowy whips. Sweat has beaded on his forehead, but relief shines from his face. "You're all right."

The strain in his voice combined with all the distress

emanating from my mates makes my hands clench into fists. I can't do anything about the nets, since they'd burn my hands the moment I touch them, but I hustle over to Jonah to see if I can loosen the whip.

Why were the humans so cruel? We were brightening the darkness, not adding more. Isn't that what they want?

Jonah isn't even shadowkind. They can't claim *he's* a monster.

They tied him up like this and left him helpless just because he's on our side.

My anguish brings a prickling sensation into my chest. I start to tamp down the swell of unpleasant emotions automatically—and then realize they might be just what I need.

Taking a deep breath to steady myself, I hold out my hands toward the side of the whip where it's taut against the pole—not Jonah himself. With careful control, I release a spurt of the dark energy inside me.

My concentrated jab cuts right through the searing light. The rest of the whip sputters out, and the handle clatters to the pavement.

Jonah scrambles up with a ragged inhalation. "I'll get Hail and Mirage."

I can only watch as our sorcerer rushes to peel the nets off my other mates. As I stand there, mired in my own frustration, a slim dark figure wavers out of the shadows.

"Peri!" Fen cries, with a swivel of her head as she takes in the scene. Drips of distress trickle off her fingers and patter on the pavement. "I was going to see if I could pitch in at all here, but... What happened? Is everyone okay?"

"Some humans attacked us," I tell her through the tightness in my throat. "Not hunters, I don't think, just regular people who got some of their weapons. They grabbed me and tried to get me to 'admit' that we have a conspiracy against humans or something like that. They think we wanted this to happen!" I wave my hand toward the deluge of shadows cloaking the city.

Fen blinks at me, her brow knitting. "What? Why would anyone want that?"

"I don't know! That's why it's so ridiculous."

But no matter what I said, the humans didn't believe me. They probably still think they were right—as much as they're thinking at all right now before Raze's paralyzing power wears off.

A shudder runs through the naiad's slender frame. Her face tenses with determination. "I can go find Rollick and—"

I grasp her forearm. "No. I… I'm not sure I want to talk to him about this. At least not yet."

He warned me things like this would happen, didn't he? That most humans would never trust us.

It was only that small group. It doesn't have to mean anything.

Except more and more "small groups" keep popping up. At what point do I have to acknowledge that they've become a big group?

Jonah heaves the untangled net off Hail, and I dart over to throw my arms around the winter fae. His ebbing pain gives way to a rush of honey-sweet adoration. "There's my Cream Puff. I hope you gave them a piece of your mind."

His voice is so ragged my throat completely closes up. It takes a moment before I can speak, with tears burning in the back of my eyes. "I tried to. They weren't very good at listening."

The winter fae tucks his head next to mine as if I'm a balm on his wounds, and I'm happy to offer that if I can. Then his gaze drops, and a spurt of jalapeno-sharp anger radiates from him. "They left scars!"

I follow his gaze to my wrists where the sleeves of my

leather jacket have ridden up slightly. Faint pink lines mark my pale skin where my captor's metal-twined ropes bit into them. A bit of an ache lingers too.

I grimace. "I'm sure those will fade. They didn't have me tied up for very long."

A few ruddy streaks cross his face and hands too where the metals of the net burned him. I hate to think how the rest of his body might have suffered through his clothes.

Before I can say as much, Hail lets out a growl Raze would be proud of. "They shouldn't have tied you up at all. Those fuckers."

Any further angry ranting is cut off by Mirage springing free. He bounds over and flings his arms around both of us, to Hail's sputtered indignation that's flavored with a dollop of amusement.

After a moment, Mirage slumps. His time wrapped in the net has sapped most of his usual energy. He has his own temporary scars etched across his flesh.

Even though I know his and Hail's will heal as quickly as mine, my gut twists at the sight.

I tuck my hand around his neck to draw him into a kiss and then help both of my men to their feet. Raze hurries over to support Mirage, but Hail waves off Jonah when he attempts to offer the same.

"We'll just go through the shadows," he says. "We'll recover faster there anyway."

Jonah nods. "We should get back to the center of operations and find out what else has been going on."

My stomach sinks. I slip after my three shadowkind mates into the patches of darkness.

The journey back through the camp in our shadow forms is much more sedate than my trip by car. Which means I have more time to take note of the human refugees around us.

Everywhere I look, my gaze catches on metallic gray glints on people's chests. I think at least half of the humans we pass have the badges the hunters showed off pinned to their shirts.

We're the ones who got these people out of the city before it could warp them to death. Are they really so scared of what else we might do?

Either because of that or for other reasons only the humans know about, a lot of them are packing up their meager remaining belongings. Buses parked at the edges of camp are taking in streams of passengers, I guess to bring them to other accommodations farther away from their original home.

Colonel Hueber did say they were planning on moving people elsewhere, but I didn't realize so many of them would be gone so quickly. The sprawl of tents already feels much more vacant than it did a few days ago.

In a few days more, will it only be us, the army people, and all the hunters and sorcerers who keep arriving? What will they try to do to us if the news crews leave too and there's no one to witness their hostility?

I'm trying to squash those uncomfortable worries when an imposing presence drifts over to us through the shadows.

I'm already braced for Rollick's words when his low drawl reaches me in the darkness. "I've been hearing a lot of... interesting reports from my sentries. Something about a stolen car?"

Raze's essence twitches. I jump in before he needs to explain. "It was only because—"

"—a rescue operation was in order," the demon supplies. "A couple of my people followed and determined that."

Raze's voice comes out gruff. "I left the car over by the factories. It didn't take any damage—at least, nothing major..."

Rollick chuckles. "I'd imagine we can arrange its reunion with the owner without too much trouble. Better they go without their car for a couple of hours than we go without our glowing friend here, hmm?"

He pauses, and I have the impression of him considering us with the full ominous weight of his demonic powers. When he speaks again, his tone is more somber. "Are *you* all undamaged? I suppose I didn't do enough to prepare you… I hadn't expected the situation to escalate quite this quickly."

The tang of his guilt slides across my tongue. It stirs my own conscience.

He tried to warn me. He tried to stop us from getting into this situation where more humans knew about our existence—and might decide to come after us.

And I didn't listen.

I hang my head, as much as I have a head in my current state. "I think we're all fine. I'm sorry. I had no idea—I didn't think they'd be *so* scared after everything I said on the TVs."

Why do so many of them hate us for what seems like no reason at all?

Rollick sighs. "It isn't your fault, Peri. Maybe we couldn't have helped word spreading farther, and your efforts have meant they aren't as unwelcoming as they would have been otherwise. I can understand wanting to believe in people. It's only that they don't often justify the faith, in my experience."

"Some of them have. But… so many of them think the worst of us without giving us a chance." My insides squirm. "What if it only gets harder? What if even more of them start attacking us?"

Rollick's presence halts at the edge of the camp, and we all stop alongside him. He's quiet for a moment, but his energy continues roiling.

"I've been considering what measures we could take," he

says, "if we decide it's gone too far, that we're dealing with an emergency. Do you know about Andreas's powers?"

Andreas—the shadowblood Riva usually calls "Drey." I haven't seen as much of him as some of the others.

I peer around us as if I might spot his dark, lanky frame. "No. Can he make humans like us more?"

The demon sounds as if he's stifled a guffaw. "No. His supernatural skills mainly have to do with memory. With some effort, he could make all the humans here forget they ever saw us. And since shadowbloods aren't affected by silver and iron like us, that includes the ones wearing badges."

Hail sounds skeptical. "The rift would still be here. And all the people who saw us on the news."

"We could continue working on the rift's issues more discreetly than we are at present," Rollick says. "As for our wider audience… Andreas has done some experimenting with using his powers at a distance. He may be able to broadcast them just like you did your little show."

The idea gives me a rush of relief. If we could hide back away that easily, escape all the animosity that's been aimed at us, pretend we were never here… *wouldn't* that be better after all? Has knowing about us actually helped anyone?

Even as the urge to tell Rollick to go for it full speed ahead wraps around me, other sorts of doubts rise up.

"Not everyone who saw us before will be watching TV at the same time. And what if the memory wipe doesn't work completely even though Andreas is a shadowblood? If the humans realize that we've tried to mess with their heads, they'll have a good reason to be afraid of us."

And then what? Will they declare war on us with their tanks and guns?

As if drawn by that thought, Colonel Hueber struts past us, unaware that we're watching from the shadows. He waves to a nearby cluster of his soldiers. "All clear on the east side?"

They salute him. "Yes, sir!"

"No more meddling from those crazy monsters?"

"Things have been very quiet, sir."

"Good riddance. Stay on your guard and keep your weapons ready."

I ball in tighter on myself. "He *knows* we've been doing our best to work with him."

"Not if he doesn't want to know it." Rollick's presence brushes closer to mine. "I'll call together a meeting. We can hash it out together. I wanted you to know that there are options."

As he veers off through the shadows, I notice another figure in military uniform standing by one of the temporary cabins. Major Yin is watching the colonel, his mouth slanted at a tight angle.

I'm so used to picking up on the emotions of everyone around me that I'm not surprised to taste his uneasiness, tart as pomegranate. Then a jolt ripples through my essence.

I *can't* pick up anything from Hueber or the other nearby soldiers. Unlike them, Yin isn't wearing a badge to ward me off.

He's not as scared of us as they are. Is it his boss making him uncomfortable, not the shadowkind who might be lurking around?

Mirage sidles over to me. "Come on, Rainbow. Let's get away from these grouches."

"I don't think they're all grouchy." I push myself forward. "I'm going to talk to Major Yin."

Raze and Hail both let out sounds of consternation, but they tag behind me as I slink over. I don't want to make a big production out of this conversation.

After a few minutes, the major heads into the cabin. I slip after him and note that he's alone in the compact space.

Perfect. Well, other than the fact that I'm going to look like a breaking-and-entering stalker.

I pop into physical form with an appeal already on my lips. "Hi! I'm sorry to barge in. I didn't think your boss would be happy if he saw me coming over."

Yin startles and takes a step back toward the wall as if he needs it to steady himself. He doesn't reach for the gun on his belt, though, which I think is a win.

His voice comes out carefully if a bit rough. "You're the shadowkind who caught the attention of all the news stations. Periwinkle? What do you want now?"

The question isn't exactly friendly, but I'm warmed by the fact that he remembers my name—and that he called me a shadowkind rather than a monster.

I back up to give him more personal space and clasp my hands in front of me. "I just… Things have gotten kind of tense in the camp for us shadowkind. You must have noticed. I wanted to find out… Do *you* want us to go away? Or for the hunters to get rid of us?"

If he has negative intentions, he could lie—but I'd be able to tell from the shifting of his emotional state.

Instead, the major hesitates, uncertainty and something with the cherry-tang of hope winding together inside him.

"I think you've been doing more than any of us have managed to mitigate the effects of the catastrophe," he says in a guarded tone. "What exactly *is* it you've been doing that's diminishing the dark areas over the city?"

Oh. Er.

"I'm not totally sure how it works," I admit. "When I focus on warm and friendly feelings, it seems like the rift's energies sort of… calm down, at least a little. I want to figure out how to cover more area faster so we can get all those people back home."

A flicker of a memory passes through my head—how I

managed to reach farther with my glow earlier today with my men helping.

What would happen if I had more beings focusing on those encouraging emotions with me? Would the collaboration even work with anyone other than my mates?

Yin's stance and his inner state relax more. "That's a goal we can all agree on, even if we have some differences of opinion about the methods." His gaze darts to the cabin's small window and back to me. "You know we have to look after our own. We can't place the needs of whatever exactly you are over humankind."

"Of course not." I smile at him. "But I do hope we can at least cooperate so we're all better off."

A hint of his own smile touches his lips. "I'd like that too, Periwinkle. I'm doing *my* best to see that we get there, for all our sakes."

At the rap of knuckles on the door, he stiffens again. Without needing an order, I duck into the shadows so whoever's calling on him won't find me there.

My shadowkind mates and Fen have been watching the whole conversation. I drift with them back into the center of the camp. Around us, other shadowkind are moving toward Rollick's trailer for the meeting he's called.

"What are you going to do?" Fen asks.

Hail lets out a humph. "One human who isn't totally awful isn't much in the grand scheme of things."

No, it's not. But when I think about Major Yin and the way he accepted my presence, his curiosity about my methods and his willingness to show his appreciation, the worries that've been jabbing at me soften.

It isn't just Yin. There are dozens of people who've spoken up for us right here in the camp. Who knows how many have all around the world?

How can we risk a full-out human-shadowkind war when there are still so many reasons to hope?

We enter the trailer to find Sorsha and her men as well as all six of the shadowbloods already there. A large assortment of Rollick's other shadowkind allies lurk around them, mostly sticking to the darkness.

Jonah comes through the door right after we arrive, and we materialize to stand around him. He shoots me a grateful smile. "I was starting to wonder how far you'd wandered off."

I squeeze his hand. "I had a chat with Rollick. And… someone else."

Rollick himself emerges from the shadows at the head of the table and claps his hands for attention. "All right, people. Let's get down to business. If we're going to attempt to return to our previous state of secrecy—"

I don't see any point in letting him go on. "No."

Rollick's gaze snaps to me. His tone turns dry. "You have an objection already, Peri?"

I lift my chin. "I got scared today, but that's on me. I don't want to take back what I've done, not unless we absolutely have to, and I don't think we're there yet. If we try, we could create a way bigger problem. We have humans hunting us, but we also have lots of them cheering us on. Aren't we just as bad as them if we dismiss them all because of a few horrible ones? Don't you criticize them for doing that to us?"

Rollick's glower makes me want to crawl back inside my skin. Have I driven my point home a little too hard?

But the words felt even more right coming out of my mouth than they did in my head. If we want humans to be better than they are, we have to show them how.

Before he can speak, Sorsha's tall, slim mate with the bright curls nods and speaks in an equally bright voice. "That sounds right to me. I have seen a lot of kind behavior from some of the humans around the camp."

Sorsha shoots him an affectionate glance. "You see the good in everyone almost as much as Peri does, Snap. But you do have a point." She turns to Rollick. "We've got to tread carefully. I don't see any reason to pull out the big guns yet."

Murmurs of agreement pass around the trailer.

Rollick's mouth twists. Before he can say anything else, another shadowkind bursts into physical form right by the door she must have ducked under.

"That bunch of hunters who've settled in outside of the camp," she says breathlessly. "They've captured a human! Because she came here asking to talk to the shadowkind—to talk to Peri. I think she said her name is Gracie."

20

Periwinkle

At the name "Gracie," my heart skips a beat. Memories flood my head of the girl who used to slip into her dad's basement to talk to me through the bars of my cage.

I haven't seen Gracie in years. Not since she defied her sorcerer father and arranged to free all his captive shadowkind from their cages. My *last* memory of her is hearing David Blaver ranting at her as I raced off through the shadows.

It has to be her, doesn't it? Who else with the same name would be asking for me?

Even as my heart squeezes tight at the thought, I push closer to the being who just popped into the trailer. "Are you sure that's her name? Why would the hunters capture a human?"

The gawky shadowkind woman stares at me, maybe

taken aback by my vehemence. I guess I'm not usually quite that forceful.

"I—I'm not totally sure," she admits. "One of the hunters asked her name, and that's what I thought I heard, but I wasn't all that close. I don't like hanging around their camp. Too much silver and iron." She shivers.

Rollick speaks up before I need to, in a more measured voice than I managed. "That's completely understandable. Did you get a sense of what the hunters want with her?"

The woman nods. "They seemed upset that she already knows at least one of the shadowkind here. They were saying she's a traitor to other humans, that she must be part of a conspiracy or something."

I let out a huff. "Where do they come up with these silly stories?"

I spin toward Rollick, my gaze sliding over my men as I move. "We have to help her. She's David Blaver's daughter— the one who saved me from his sorcery. She must have come here hoping she could help with this problem too."

The demon frowns. "Does she have powers you haven't mentioned? I can't see how one human would make much difference in the current catastrophe."

I fold my arms over my chest, daring to glower right back at him, though my pulse stutters while I do. "She might have some sorcerer ability that she inherited from her dad, but I don't know about that. What does it matter? She came because of us, so we should get her away from the hunters before they do anything even more awful."

Jonah weighs in with his even, teacherly tone. "We can't abandon a friend. And having more humans on our side is only going to be a good thing, right?"

The second part is clearly meant to appeal to Rollick's sense of practicality. Jonah does know his former boss well.

The demon sighs and waves his hand in a vague gesture.

"Fine. And I can't say I'd be sad to see the hunters lose out on whatever prize they think they've caught. But don't spend too much time on it, and don't make a bigger PR crisis than we've already got on our hands."

I nod with all the determination I can summon. "Right. We'll be ever so stealthy and whisk her away. Let's go!"

I dart out of the trailer through the shadows with my mates following behind me. Although Jonah has to use the door anyway, so I guess we could just as easily have walked.

As we gather in a cluster next to the room on wheels, a few other beings join us: Fen and Brine, the sparky shadowkind and the imp Jonah brought to our first TV appearance, and the centaur shifter who used to be Gloss's friend and seems to want to go wherever Hail does.

She isn't batting her eyelashes at my mate now but watching me with avid attention that she tries to hide behind a bored expression when I look at her. She twists a strand of her coppery hair around her finger and takes on a bland tone that doesn't fit the lemon-drop eagerness of her curiosity. "Are we really going to pull one over on the hunters?"

I beam at her. "I bet we can. They shouldn't think they can go bossing everyone around, right?"

A gleam lights in her eyes. She tosses back her hair. "Definitely not."

Who would have thought I'd end up bonding with anyone from Gloss's crew over sticking it to hunters?

Jonah rubs his hand over his mouth. "Should I stay back here? I can't sneak quite the way the rest of you can."

I shake my head. "No, we might need you to distract them. That's how heists work, right? Confusion and misdirection."

Mirage springs onto his hands and whirls around. "Enough tricks to make them sick!"

"Except your illusions don't affect them when they're

wearing their badges." I worry at my lower lip, wondering what we can do about that. The hunters will definitely notice if we start popping their badges off like Hail managed before.

The winter fae tilts his head toward the edge of camp where the hunters have set up their own exclusive mini-camp. "Why don't we get over there and see exactly what we're dealing with, and then we'll make plans? Our mortal dude can hang back until we're sure how we're using him." He aims a thin but not unfriendly smile at Jonah.

I clap my hands together. "Yes! Right. Stick to total stealth-mode. Let's go!"

Even if I didn't already know what spot the hunters had staked out, I'd be able to sense it from a distance. As we creep through the shadows toward it, the aura of noxious metals wriggles through my senses.

Their tents are strung with silver and iron beads. They have a caravan that I suspect is stuffed full of nets and other anti-shadowkind weapons, considering that just looking at it makes my skin crawl so badly I want to teleport myself to the other side of the world. And of course they're wearing their badges.

But despite all their precautions, they're no match for our shadowkind sneakiness. They show no sign that they realize we're lurking around the perimeter of their camp.

From the shade of a nearby sapling, we peer between the tents and trucks they've gathered. At least twice as many humans are roaming around the hunters' camp now than there were when they first barged in. More of them must be traveling out this way hoping to show off their shadowkind-wrangling skills.

They're not so great at wrangling anything else, as far as I can tell. The creature roasting on a spit over their large campfire looks like… a squirrel? Is that what they're having for dinner?

I don't even want to ask what's in the pot bubbling on a kerosene stove nearby. It smells like mildew and bad dreams.

Amid all the humans prowling around their camp with their narrowed eyes, tensed stances, and badges flashing on their chests, it's not hard to spot the one person who doesn't belong. A young woman is sitting cross-legged not far from the fire, the light glinting off her chestnut hair with its streaks of purple and pink.

I'd smile at Gracie's interest in vibrant hair coloring if the rest of her situation didn't wrench at my gut. The hunters have tied her wrists together behind her back in a position that looks very uncomfortable. Dirt smudges one of her cheeks as if it was pressed against the ground not long ago.

Two hunters stand over her like prison guards, their expressions extra somber. You'd think they'd caught her attempting to stage a mass murder rather than wanting to talk to little old me.

Anger prickles through my essence. I gather myself and will my emotions to settle down.

We're not going to rescue Gracie by charging in like a bunch of cowboys. This needs to be a spy film, not a western.

I have the sense of Raze cocking his head where his presence is crouched next to me. "It doesn't look as if her legs are bound. If they stopped watching her, she could probably get up and simply walk away."

Fen wrings her hands. "But they'd see her. There are so many hunters around. Where would she go?"

"We've got to get her back to our home base," I say. "And be fast about it. She can't jump into the shadows with us. Maybe if we brought around a car…?"

Hail snorts. "They'd notice anyone driving over this way and start keeping an eye on them. Especially if the driver's skills are anything like Raze's."

The basilisk shifter lets out a huff but can't exactly argue.

A glimmer of inspiration lights in my head. Maybe we should think like cowboys as well as spies.

I glance toward Gloss's friend—Sorrel, I think her name is. "Humans have other ways of getting around quickly. Would you be willing to let her ride on you, as a centaur?"

Sorrel shifts uneasily. "I've never had anyone on my back like that before. But…" She pauses. "The human doesn't look very big or heavy. I'm sure I'm strong enough. I'd be the getaway car!"

Her voice brightens with those last words.

I grin. "Exactly. They'll never see it coming."

"All right. I'm on board."

We just have to make sure that Gracie is. She won't be expecting rescue via centaur.

I study the mini-camp again. "Okay… So we divert some of their attention. Jonah can come and ask to speak with them, make a fuss so more of them go over. But that probably won't be enough."

Mirage's presence squirms in the shadow. "I'd use my illusions, but they won't be able to see those anyway."

Another lightbulb goes off. If this keeps up, my head will be blazing.

"They can't, but Gracie can," I say with a quiver of excitement. "You can let her know we're here and guide her to where we'll scoop her up without them having any clue!"

Hail chuckles. "I like the way you think, Cream Puff. I could conjure up something as an extra distraction—a sudden, condensed flurry, or icicles shooting up here and there."

"Hmm. I'm not sure that would have the right effect. They know we have someone with wintery powers, so they'll go more on guard trying to figure out where you are."

A soft *woof* emanates from the darkness near my feet. I

have the impression of a furry serpentine body pressing against my ankle.

I tickle the top of where I think Falkor's head approximately is. "Hey, boy. I don't think there's anything for you to do here."

The snake-puppy woofs again and squirms a little toward the edge of the shadows—toward the camp. Then I feel his attention turn back to me with an eager panting.

My stomach clenches. "You want to run in there? I guess that would be another distraction… But what if they catch *you*? They could really hurt you."

Falkor wriggles from side to side without any trace of concern. He seems to think it's all a big game.

I try again. "They have powerful weapons. They could stick you in a cage. It's not fun."

All at once, my self-declared pet wraps his presence around mine as if he's squeezing me in a hug. The vibe he gives off is all brave supportiveness.

The clenching sensation in my stomach rises to grip my throat. I think he's saying that he wants to pitch in just like the rest of us are.

I wouldn't have thought the strange shadowkind creature paid enough attention to the missions we've been on to realize we've even had missions. Apparently I underestimated him.

Like so many people do me, because of my perky and soft exterior.

I give Falkor another pat, stuffing down my worries. "Okay. If you want to be a part of the team, you can lend a hand. Or paw. Whatever." I turn my focus to my other companions around us. "Let's do this!"

~

Fifteen minutes later, Jonah is marching up to the hunter's camp in a bright red cape. It billows in the wind as if he's a superhero.

When the imp produced the garment, our sorcerer raised his eyebrows and asked, "Are you sure?" But I pointed out that it'll definitely catch the hunters' attention.

"They'll also assume I'm totally nuts," he muttered, and then laughed. "Which might work in our favor. Nuts and harmless."

Mirage grinned. "A little entertainment!"

It looks as if the hunters are more confused than entertained at the moment. Several of them walk over to meet Jonah at the edge of their camp, furrowed foreheads and puzzled frowns all around.

Unfortunately, the two watching over Gracie stay put.

Jonah sells the role awfully well, swishing his cape behind him and striking a gallant pose. "Who's in charge here? I have a lot to discuss with your leader."

Sputtered guffaws pass between the hunters. A couple more amble over to see what's going on.

Raze has come up with a way to add his power to the mix. He glares at the base of a tree at the far side of the camp —and the roots must shrivel up and die. The cedar topples over, smacking into the roof of a nearby truck.

As a bunch of the hunters whirl toward the sound, Jonah waves his hand in the air. "And look at that! You can't even take care of your own vehicles."

Before any of the hunters can recover from their growing bewilderment, Falkor recognizes his cue. He dashes out of the shadows straight toward the two hunters poised around Gracie.

With a burbled arf, he twines between their legs, nearly tripping both of them. Yelping and cursing, the hunters snatch at the whips on their belts. The snake-puppy slither-bounds away, and they take off after him.

Which leaves no one near Gracie.

Mirage wiggles his fingers, and a neon sign blinks in the air in front of her. *FOLLOW PATH TO PERI.*

A strip of the hard-packed ground lights up like a red carpet straight toward our tree.

Gracie gapes for a second, but thankfully she's been around supernatural beings enough not to be too thrown for a loop. She scrambles to her feet, swaying for balance, and dashes along the glowing path Mirage has conjured for her.

She makes it nearly to the edge of the camp before someone shouts, "The girl!"

Too late. Sorrel has already materialized in her centaur form. She bends her horsey legs while Hail slices a blade of ice through the bindings on Gracie's wrists. Gracie throws herself onto Sorrel's back, wrapping her arms around the centaur's human-like waist, and Sorrel gallops off toward the main camp.

"What the—" someone yells behind us.

I don't stick around to find out how they're going to react. We all dive into the shadows and dart away after Sorrel. Even Falkor manages to catch up with us, panting hard but exuding triumph.

The last thing I hear is Jonah saying, "You know, you're obviously way too disorganized to have a conversation about this right now. I'll return when you're ready."

Then we've left the hunters behind.

2I

Hail

After yesterday's epic rescue effort, I expected to see Peri beaming even more than usual. But when I find my mate drifting through the shadows under Rollick's trailer just after dawn, her mood is unusually deflated.

A jitter of the concern I'm not totally used to feeling ripples through my nerves. I sidle closer to her. "What's wrong?"

Peri gives herself a little shake. Through the mark constantly pulsing on my chest, I can feel her rousing her most upbeat spirits as well as she can—as if she thinks she has to put on that cheerful front for me when her heart isn't in it. My own heart squeezes.

"Nothing's wrong," she says. "So far. Rollick seems to think the hunters are going to retaliate against us somehow. And I haven't really been able to talk to Gracie yet. She was so exhausted and even a little dehydrated when we got her back... The hunters weren't very nice to her. Dominic healed her some, but he said we should give her time to rest."

I don't see why the shadowblood who doesn't appear to have been alive for more than three decades should be calling those shots, but Peri obviously took his request seriously.

I nudge her gently. "I bet she'll be awake and recovered soon."

"I know. But then we *will* have to talk." Peri's spirits droop again. "She helped me so much, and I ran off on her. I don't even know what her dad did to her after we left. He probably punished her. And then I *killed* her dad."

I would have thought the first part made the second part okay, but I'm still getting a handle on how much standards of morality can differ, especially when it comes to humans.

I do know this much. "*You* didn't kill him. You freed the shadowkind who killed him, but your hands are totally clean."

Peri gives a little huff. "I don't think both of those things can be true."

"Well, is she really going to be all that upset when her dad was such an asshole?"

"I don't know. I don't even know if she knows he's dead. How long would it take anyone to find that secret lair of his? Maybe he'll never be found. So I have to tell her."

"You could just... forget to mention it."

"No, I couldn't." Peri shudders. "I'd be an awful friend if I kept something like that from her. I do hope we can still be friends..."

I suspect my Cream Puff is worrying too much about other people's feelings the way she tends to do. *I'm* more worried about the other difficulty she mentioned. "Does Rollick think the hunters are going to attack us—or encourage the other humans who are playing at hunter to try to grab you again?"

"I'm not sure. I don't understand why they do any of the things they've been doing. I guess Jonah and Sorrel are the most likely to get in trouble, since they're the only ones the hunters saw."

Of course she'd be fretting about everyone other than herself. The tightness in my chest condenses into an ache.

I tuck my presence around her in a shadowy embrace. The ache creeps up to my throat. "I wish I could keep you safe from everything that could hurt you." Hunters, other marauding humans, former friends who might react badly to unexpected news.

That's all I've ever wanted, really. To protect as many shadowkind as I can from the harmful parts of the mortal realm.

Peri deserves that security even more than most beings.

The thought of my long-held dreams sends a shiver of exhilaration through me. Maybe I *can* shield her, at least for a little while.

I nudge her again. "Come with me."

She does, curiosity tingling through her more fraught emotions. I lead her through the camp and into the stretch of trees where Mirage found his pretty little clearing.

I don't need to go as far as the clearing. As soon as we're out of view of the human settlement, I emerge into physical form and reach for my powers.

Ice shoots up amid trunks. It shapes into a turret here, a staircase there.

The structure winds between the trees. With each wave of power I pull through my body, more and more crystalline surfaces glimmer into being. I cast them farther, higher, my pulse racing alongside the sensations.

Peri gasps, and I come back to myself. We're standing

before a castle like the ones I used to build in my dorm room at the academy, only bigger. Its spired roof rises nearly as high as the treetops.

An arched doorway stands open before us. I hold out my hand to Peri, taking on the chivalrous pose I imagine a knight would.

I never thought of myself as that kind of hero… but maybe for her, I could be.

Beaming now, Peri twines her fingers with mine. We step through the doorway into the castle's interior.

Intricate carvings decorate the icy walls. The building is only big enough for one grand if narrow room, but I made it as impressive as I could, with a soaring ceiling that lets in light through thin sections of ice and a spiral staircase leading up into the tight space of the turret.

Peering around at it, another urge tugs at me. I inhale deeply and release my grip on the humanesque form that's become an ever-present disguise.

I see the transformation shimmer over me in the reflections on the glossy ice. A snowy pallor spreads over all of my skin, with the stark blue veins that normally only show on my forearms rippling across my limbs and chest and up my neck. My eyes widen and drift farther apart.

Stag horns sprout from my skull, jutting off into the air like miniature tree branches. My pale hair turns shaggier and spreads down my back.

A soft noise escapes Peri. As I turn to face her, I brace myself, but her awe washes over me before I've even met her shining eyes.

"This is your true fae form?" she says. "You look even more handsome than usual."

I don't normally have any trouble accepting compliments, but a blush tingles over my cheeks.

"You should get to know every side of me." I pause. "I don't think I've ever seen your true form."

"It's, ah, kind of hard to see." Peri giggles and then shimmers. A glow courses over her skin—

No. The glow *is* her skin. It's all of her. In the space of a few seconds, her entire body has transformed into a shape made entirely of light, pure and bright as a spring afternoon's sunlight.

My breath catches at the back of my mouth. Of course this is what she'd look like. Of course she'd shine even brighter when she lets go of the trappings of humanity.

"You're amazing," I tell her. The word doesn't even come close to encapsulating what I feel.

It's hard to make out Peri's features in her glowing face, but I think she smiles. Her voice somehow comes out extra shiny too. "Maybe I should show the humans this side of me."

Every particle in my body balks. "No. We shouldn't give them any more reason to think we're strange."

They turn every bit of oddness into something to hate.

Peri's light contracts until she's in her regular humanesque form again—leather jacket, sundress, and all. She tips her head to the side as she considers me.

"You said you wanted to protect me. You know you can't just shut me away in a place like this to stop anything from hurting me, right?" She waves at the castle around us.

"Why not?" I can't help muttering.

Peri laughs and tucks her hand around my elbow. "I want to look after myself, but I need people too. To feed on their emotions, to learn more about their world, to find my own happiness… It's nice to take a break, but I want to be out there with them some of the time."

I already knew that. I don't think any part of me actually

believed I could keep her hidden away in this castle until the disaster is over.

That doesn't erase the longing to, though.

I open my mouth, searching for the words to convince her to at least spend the day in here until we know what the hunters will do next. Before I can, heavier footsteps tread up to the doorway.

I spin around, jerking back into my own humanesque appearance, just as Raze steps inside. He ducks to fit his hulking frame through the entrance.

All my nerves prickle with alarm—the lug is going to shatter apart all the beauty I built for our mate. I can just picture him crashing and smashing through the ice as he lumbers around.

Tart words to send him out again leap to my tongue, but they might be unfair. Because Raze eases farther inside gingerly, taking every care not to so much as brush against the intricate carvings.

He gazes all around and then catches my gaze with an awkward smile. "I was worried about Peri, so I came looking for her. You made this?"

"I did," I say, a little sharper than I intended.

Raze shows no sign of offense. His expression relaxes. "It's incredible. It's *art*. I've never seen anything like it—that's some talent you've got."

The compliment warms me more than I expected it to. I've given Raze a hard time more often than I can keep track of. I still don't like thinking about the creatures he slaughters in his hunger for blood.

But he's good for our mate. And apparently he appreciates creative expression. Who would have thought?

Peri has turned her smile on him. "I'm totally okay. Hail was just distracting me from my worries for a bit."

I guess my intentions were pretty transparent. That

doesn't mean I can't extend them. Tasting the waft of affection that's expanded with Raze's arrival, I can think of one simple yet very enjoyable way to keep Peri safe and secure for at least a little longer.

"I've only just made a start of that." I grin at Raze. "Do you want to put *your* talents to use helping me keep our mate busy while the humans are still snoozing?"

Raze catches on fast, with a flare of heat in his gaze. It's echoed from Peri through our bond.

Her cheeks flush, and a ruddy light dances through her hair. "Right here?"

"Where better? I can make it into an even more appropriate setting…"

I flick my fingers and conjure a bed frame of ice, topped with a snow-soft mattress.

Raze dips his head, and Peri bobs up on her toes to meet his kiss.

Watching their embrace doesn't spark the slightest flicker of jealousy in me anymore. Possibly because I know I can bring out that flare of passion in her just as well as he can.

And when we work together? Then we can really show our mate a good time.

My dick is already stiffening in my pants with a throb of desire. There isn't a single being in all my time and all the ways I played around who could stir this hunger in me.

My hands itch to chart every plane of her softly curvy body. I step up behind her and skim my fingers down her sides.

With a pleased hum, Peri turns to face me. She touches my jaw to draw me into a kiss of our own.

When I cup her well-rounded breasts, such a gorgeous more-than-a-handful, her lips part against my mouth with a tiny whimper. I drink in the sound and the brightly sweet taste of her.

Raze dips one hand between her legs, and a deeper moan reverberates from her throat. Peri rocks into his touch, her breath quickening in the most delicious way.

He reaches for her jacket and then pauses. "We don't want our Glowbug getting cold."

I make a dismissive sound. "I can take care of that."

With a push of my power, the chill of the icy walls contracts so it's pressed close to the frozen surfaces, leaving room for the warm air from outside to breeze in. It's hardly a furnace within my castle, but none of us will get frostbite.

Peri claims another kiss from me while Raze tugs off her jacket. As I ease up her dress, she yanks at my shirt.

I strip off both garments in turn. The caress of her hands over my bare chest sends the headiest of quivers through my nerves.

Her fingertips linger over the glowing spot on my sternum. It pulses with nothing but eagerness at her attention.

Raze kicks off his jeans and boxers before grabbing Peri's hand. "She shouldn't have to feel any of the chill."

He sprawls out on the snowy mattress, his massive frame indenting the cushiony material—offering Peri another surface to climb onto.

As she straddles him, I hustle over, tugging at my own pants. My cock aches, so rigid now I can barely think about anything other than pressing it inside her.

Peri sinks down onto Raze's admittedly impressive shaft with a little shudder and a gasp that shoots straight to my groin. I clamber onto my homemade bed behind her and trace my fingers along the cleft of her ass.

"Ready to be doubly filled?"

"Please," she says with so much wanting I almost explode on the spot.

I conjure a slippery substance that's only slightly chilly

and slick it over Peri's back opening. She bobs slowly over Raze's cock. At the swivel of his hands over her breasts, another moan spills out of her.

When I delve my fingers right inside her, she pushes into my touch. "More. Now."

A shaky laugh tumbles out of me. "I can't deny you that, Cream Puff."

Her tighter opening grips me in the most thrilling possible way. I bite back a groan, sliding in as far as I can go, inch by inch.

Peri holds still until she can feel we're fully joined. I slip my hand around her waist to finger her clit right above where she and Raze meet, and she hitches up with a mewling sound that heats me up twice as much.

I buck into her, slowly at first and then faster as Raze picks up his own pace beneath our mate. Peri sways between us. Every little sound that works from her lips is the most precious delicacy I've ever consumed.

It doesn't take long before I'm on the verge of bursting. I bow close, kissing her neck, her shoulder, and strumming her clit with all the skill I based my old reputation on.

Peri comes apart with a cry and a clench of her muscles around me. I can't hold myself back from spilling over in turn.

Raze groans a few seconds later and arches up to lock Peri in the fiercest of kisses.

Our mate's satisfaction radiates through me for my final few thrusts and our sagging together onto the bed. The mattress's chill doesn't nip at my wintery skin, but I force myself to press close to Raze so we can support Peri's body off the cool surface between us.

"Mmm," she says in a dreamy voice that almost makes me come all over again. "That was a good distraction."

She cuddles close to us for a few minutes longer before

she sighs. "We should be getting back. Gracie might already be awake."

I suppress my impulse to argue. I've given Peri what I could. The last thing she needs is me holding her back out of fear.

I kiss her one last time and help her off the bed. We blink through the shadows into our clothes and emerge at the edge of the camp.

When we come into view of our cluster of trailers, I halt in my tracks. Shadowkind are rushing here and there in an apparent panic.

My gut knots. I dive toward one who's slipping past us. "What's happening?"

The being whirls around. Her voice is taut. "This warped atmosphere… It's spreading on the shadow side too."

22

Periwinkle

By the time we've found Rollick, I still haven't wrapped my head around what we heard from his assistant.

"How can the shadow realm be warping?" I demand without preamble.

Rollick has a harried look that makes me suspect he wouldn't mind if all of us warped to some other plane of existence. He rubs his face and manages a crooked smile. "We didn't think the mortal realm could warp until these rifts started belching their shadows all over the place. All that matters is, they are."

Hail frowns. "So, what, on the shadow-realm side of the rifts, they're vomiting sunshine?"

It's hard for me to imagine how beaming daylight could be a bad thing, but Rollick shakes his head anyway. "Not exactly. The shadowy atmosphere is thinning, which makes sense if you assume some of those shadows are being poured into this realm. And what's left… is twisting. We're hearing about the aggressive, morphing creatures rampaging on the shadow side now too. Strands of darkness are wrapping around beings like murderous seaweed. And the regular shadowkind, if they stumble too close to those twisting areas, have had their bodies warped too. In the worst cases…"

He stops, looking sick. I've never seen the demon so unsettled he's lost his words.

"In the worst cases?" I prod tentatively.

His mouth tilts into a grimace. "We've gotten a few reports of beings actually *dying* in the shadow realm. Which shouldn't be possible. In all my millennia, I've never heard of it happening. I trust the people who reported their observations to me, though."

My heart stutters. "They're just… completely fading away? And not coming back?"

Yes, that is what dying normally means, but it's not something shadowkind normally *do*. The one benefit of the shadow realm compared to the mortal world has always been that our essence can't totally break apart when we're at home in the shadows.

If that advantage is off the table… We might be in just as dire circumstances as the humans who evacuated the city.

What's next—all the chocolate in the world turns into cow manure?

Rollick waves his hand dismissively, though his expression stays somber. "My associates are looking into the problem more closely. We may have more answers soon. The important takeaway is, we need to get those rifts closed as soon as possible." He fixes his gaze on me. "The sorcerer's daughter is awake and seems coherent. Why don't you find out what brought her out here searching for you?"

Does he think Gracie might know something about the strange rifts? I don't see how that's possible when none of us had any idea that they'd come or what they'd do, but it's hard not to hope.

Wouldn't it be nice if the answer to the biggest problems the world has ever faced dropped into our laps like a perfectly flung buttered croissant?

Okay, even I can tell that's optimism on overdrive.

Still, I weave through the cluster of trailers that we shadowkind and our associates have been using to the one set up as a sort of medical room. I peek inside to see a couple of shadowkind beings lying on the cots at one end of the room, one of them still seeping a little essence from his bandaged limbs, and a sort-of familiar human sitting up on her cot at the other side.

Only sort-of, because for all I recognized Gracie on sight, it's obviously been years since I last laid eyes on her. The final lingering childish chubbiness has faded from her face, which is still youthful but definitely a woman's now. The chestnut hair she used to wear in ponytails and braids has been cropped into a chin-length bob that's drooping after her trials.

But when her eyes light up at the sight of me, there's no denying she's the same Gracie I knew.

"Peri," she murmurs, as if she can't totally believe I'm here. "You look… You look good. You've been okay the past six years?"

Six years since I escaped. Having a number doesn't change anything about the blur of time spent huddling in the shadow realm and then creeping out into this one to feed.

A quiver of my old guilt runs through me to join all my current regrets.

I push my mouth into a smile. "I am now! I mean, other than the whole crazy rift spewing shadows into the mortal realm thing. Everything else is great!"

Gracie's lips twitch, probably because that statement

sounds absurd no matter how you cut it. "I always wondered… I was worried the things Dad did might have injured you permanently."

I see no need to mention the ache that prickles through my feet and ankles when I'm on them for too long. It's one small discomfort that barely matters compared to being out of that cage.

"Shadowkind are pretty tough." I ease closer to her, feeling oddly cautious, as if she might run away after all the hassle she went through to find me. "Have *you* been all right? I worried a lot… If I could have stayed and helped you… I heard how angry your dad was after you set us free."

Gracie's brief laugh is careless enough to soften the sharp edges of my guilt. At least, that particular patch of it. "The whole point was to get you out of there. I'd have had him angry at me for nothing if you'd stuck around and gotten captured again."

Her lips form a smile as crooked as Rollick's was minutes ago. "I won't say it was fun. He laid into me a lot, and for a whole year he wouldn't let me out of his sight except while I was in school. But then he got distracted by some new project—the second I got accepted into college, he shipped me off to the dorms and took off. He came back for a couple of Christmases like he was going through the motions, but I haven't seen him in almost… two years now."

The other gob of guilt sticks in my throat for a few seconds before I can speak. My voice comes out thin as if it's squeezed around the lump. "You aren't going to see him again."

Gracie's brow knits. "What do you mean? He doesn't have anything to do with all this, does he?" She motions vaguely to the city beyond the trailer walls.

She doesn't know anything specific about his research then.

I grope for the right words. "When we were first investigating the rifts—just us shadowkind—we found one off in the wilderness in Canada. Your dad was up there too. He must have noticed the unusual energy somehow, and he was studying the warped creatures, using them for his… usual sort of purposes."

Forcing them to attack people he wanted out of his way, mostly. David Blaver was the kind of guy who'd sooner choke you on a cupcake than offer it on a plate. And then be mad if you didn't thank him for the honor.

Gracie winces. "Oh. He barely talked with me about that part of his life after I 'screwed things up' for him. I had no idea."

"Yes. Well." I twist my hands in front of me. "We didn't want him to hurt any more people. We found the place where he was working and freed the shadowkind he'd caged there. And they… They killed him."

You can hardly blame them for holding a grudge against a guy who'd forced them to live surrounded by silver and iron, ordering them around day in and out, zapping them with his weird testing equipment when he was in the mood.

But, maybe you can blame them if you're the guy's only kid. That kind of relationship comes with special benefits.

Gracie stares at me for several seconds as if in a daze. Then she blinks and gives herself a little shake. "Oh. Oh my God."

Another laugh spills out of her, rougher than the last. "I guess I shouldn't be surprised. I started telling people he was dead just to avoid awkward conversations about what he was up to. I always wondered if he'd try to tackle the wrong monster someday."

She doesn't sound angry, but the word 'monster' ripples through my senses alongside a dollop of resentment as sharp as cactus skin. I don't know who that resentment is aimed at more, but I'm not sure I want to find out.

"I'm sorry," I say quickly. "I wish… I wish things could have been better."

Why couldn't David Blaver have been a more loving father? Or at least found a good mom to look after Gracie instead? I might not fully understand human family dynamics given that shadowkind come into being fully grown rather than starting as babies, but I don't think they get much more messed up than this.

"So do I." Gracie leans against the pillow propped on the head of the cot frame. Her gaze goes distant. "At least it's over now. I don't have to worry about him popping back into my life and screwing things up for *me*."

I swallow thickly. "What have you been up to? I mean—I guess you went to college— How did you even know to come looking for me?"

Gracie's next smile looks warmer, a splash of strawberry-sweet amusement coming with it. "I saw you on TV, silly—like most of the world did, as far as I can tell. The reporter said where you put on your little show. I know it's kind of dangerous being near this weird rift, but I wanted to see you again. I had vacation time at my job I needed to use…"

Her attention slides away from me. "I had no idea there'd be people here who'd have such a problem with that. What is the deal with those assholes who think wanting to talk to a shadowkind is a crime?"

I shudder. "They're hunters. Humans who know about shadowkind and have figured out how to capture us and kill us. I can't tell whether they're happy the whole world knows what they've been fighting or annoyed that now they have so much more competition for being the biggest jerks to us."

Gracie lets out a small snort. "Maybe some of both." She takes a deep breath. "Anyway, I also… Because of people like that—even if I didn't know they existed until now—and also people like my dad, I feel bad that I never did anything to make this world safer for you and your friends."

I gape at her. "What do you mean? You *saved* me and all the other beings your dad had locked up."

"I know. But after that… I went on with my life as if you didn't exist. As if everything was normal. While you still had to worry that some other sorcerer might come along, or these hunter guys, or whoever."

Gracie squares her shoulders. "There are a lot of voices talking about shadowkind now, some who think you deserve a chance, some who want you gone. I know what kinds of things you've had to endure to survive while still trying to help everyone. I know *you*. We need you so we can get through this mess, don't we, Peri?"

A strange sensation sweeps through me, as if I'm brightening up and cringing at the same time. She sees me as the hero here. That's a real honor.

But some tiny part of me was holding out hope that she was going to charge in and save the day one more time.

Nope. Looks like it's still up to me.

"Yeah," I say. "It seems that way. And I'm still not sure how I'm going to manage it. The progress I've made doesn't feel like enough."

Gracie holds out her hand. I let go of my tentativeness enough to walk the rest of the way over and wrap my fingers around hers.

She smiles at me with all the fondness and determination of the teenage girl who promised she'd get me out from behind those bars of silver and iron as soon as she had the chance. "Then this is where I should be. Here with you, figuring it out, pitching in however I can. We aren't going to let the shadows beat us, are we?"

"Of course not!"

I put a surge of enthusiasm into the words automatically, but deep inside, my gut has twisted.

I have one more person relying on me—a person who matters a lot to me.

One more person I might let down if I can't stop this rift and the others like it from belching more awfulness over both our realms.

Are there enough rainbows in all the world to put a bright side on that?

23

Mirage

As I stare up at the small rift, my skin twitches as if it wants to jump in the opposite direction.

I can't really blame it. Most of the rest of me would like to jump that way too.

I glance back at Peri and the rest of our little family, who've come along with Rollick to see me off. Mostly I focus on my shiny mate, who isn't all that shiny at the moment. "I don't need to do this. If you'd rather I stayed here, so you have nothing to fear…"

The rhyme touches a little too closely to my own mood for comfort, but Peri's grip on my arm calms my nerves a little. "*I'll* be fine. I didn't feel any strain at all when we tested out how far you could go in the shadow realm—I don't think our bonds are restricting us anywhere near as much as they used to. And if anyone can help the beings caught up in this disaster, it's you. You know how to guide the way. But if *you're* having second thoughts—"

I shake my head quickly. The determination that prompted me to agree to this plan in the first place expands inside me, buoying my resolve.

I've seen how hard my Rainbow has worked to help so many beings already. I'm not sure how much I've really contributed to the rescue efforts so far.

Long ago, when the humans with their scalpels and syringes held me in their cold metal cells, they tormented me into using my mind-altering magic to draw other shadowkind in. Remembering those days still leaves my stomach churning.

Now I have the chance to draw shadowkind who are in just as much danger to someplace safer, like I did for the humans days ago to get them out of the city. How can I refuse that opportunity just because I want to stay by my mate's side?

If we can't stop the destruction soon, we might be torn apart no matter what I do.

I give her and then Rollick a jaunty salute, drawing my body up straight like I'm one of those grouchy soldiers who are always marching around the evacuee camp. "I'm still on the team, prepared to do my duty. Let's see what this fox can fix!"

Peri's smile at my wordplay sets off a warmer glow inside me, echoing the affection that wafts through our bond. It's a sensation that's going to disappear the moment I slip into the rift, but I'm not going to let myself think about that fact.

She bobs up on her toes to offer a quick but sweet-as-ever kiss. "Don't get too close to the warped areas, and don't push yourself too hard. Come back as soon as you start feeling tired."

I touch her cheek. "You look after yourself too, Rainbow. We need you more than anyone else."

Rollick folds his arms over his chest, looking as if he's getting impatient with our goodbyes. Before he can make any snarky comments, I shoot him a thumbs up and spring into the rift.

It's a normal-sized one, no more than five feet across, floating over a hill just outside the city. Leaping through it as my physical body shifts into shadow form feels the same as it always has, like a gust of cool breeze rushing through my essence and then stillness settling all around me.

I turn in the portion of the shadow realm I've emerged into, absorbing the quiet and the dullness all around me. With no concrete objects in this place where we shadowkind come into being, there's nothing to see or smell or taste. It's all only drifting dark haze, the impressions of other beings whose essence we pass close to, and the occasional conversations we might take up if we're so inclined.

What is there to discuss? We don't even have any weather to make small talk about.

But this time, there is something remarkable about my original home. As I gather myself, tremors ripple through the atmosphere around me. They carry the same erratic energy the warped rifts give off.

My essence cringes in response, but I nudge myself toward the disturbance.

It's what I'm here for. No running away now.

I'm not on the move long before I notice the thinning of the shadows that Rollick mentioned his people had observed. Everything is still *dark*, but it starts to feel as if I'm moving through clear air rather than fog. Air that could barely fill my lungs if I tried to breathe it.

Cries and whimpers reverberate through the atmosphere alongside the growing tremors. They form a disjointed chorus—not at all the sort of symphony you'd want an orchestra to play.

Let's see if I can transform it into a happier tune.

I slow down, slinking closer through the filmier shadows. A being lurches out of them toward me, just as ephemeral as I am but with his essence roiling so forcefully it smacks against me as he squirms.

"Make it stop! Make it stop!" His presence jerks and shudders as if he's trying to lash out with his essence while jerking it back inside. I don't think he's in control of it.

Does he realize he could die?

A deeper chill wraps around my heart at that thought. Shadowkind aren't meant to be mortal in our natural playground, as un-playful as it is. The shadows are supposed to sustain us.

How has our world become so completely upended?

I nudge an illusion of serene music and calming currents around the being in distress. "Come farther away. Let the regular shadows heal you."

I don't know if they actually can, but if they *can't*, nothing else will.

The being's thrashing eases. With a shaky sigh, he propels himself past me, toward the thicker stretch of darkness I left behind.

The chorus of horror is still pealing through the air at full blast. So many other beings are caught up in confusion and pain—or possibly literally caught in the twisting strands of shadow Rollick mentioned.

When I creep a little closer, my whole presence squirms at the erratic energies resonating through me. I ease back and skirt the warped area as quickly as I can.

"Head this way!" I call out, projecting my voice into minds as well as shouting it into the atmosphere. I send it alongside a sense of soothing, cool darkness beckoning them and a dollop of butterscotch ice cream, because who wouldn't come for dessert? "Everything you could want is over here!"

The beings that were only disoriented start following my call. Some weave here and there as if they've forgotten what a straight line looks like; others flit past me like they're starving for buttery delights.

I hope they'll accept the consolation prize of being out of the warped area when the treat I teased doesn't materialize.

A few beings heave toward me at a sluggish pace, still gasping or groaning. The sounds remind me all too well of the scientists' laboratory, of the poking and prodding.

An icy shiver travels through my being. My essence wobbles with it, and I fight the urge to race off in search of my own ice cream cone.

Bracing myself, I project another call, another promise of good things this way. I lay out as clear as possible a trail for my fellow shadowkind to follow away from the writhing murk that's invaded our home.

As I send out my powers, I keep gliding along the edge of the most unnerving area. Yikes, it is huge. I feel as if I've been floating onward for an hour without finding the end of it.

Someone needs to tell these messed-up rifts that size isn't everything. And pacing yourself is healthier than going overboard. There's no need to be so ambitious.

If only there was a real chance they'd listen.

Not all of my fellow beings have gotten the short end of the stick from their warped encounters. One being passes me singing nonsense words to a bright tune. She doesn't reply when I greet her, too lost in her strange music, but she sounds happy enough.

Another rolls past me in what feels like a series of continual backflips, all shadowy gymnast. I'm not sure his limbs are exactly where he'd want them to be, but the change has left him extra limber, at least.

As I project another call, ignoring the first prickles of strain at the back of my mind, a thin cry that sounds almost familiar reaches my ears.

"No. I wasn't supposed to be here. This shouldn't be— It isn't fair!"

Frowning, I swivel toward the sound. It's coming from deeper within the thinned, unsettled area I've avoided doing more than dipping the edges of my being into.

A noise of pure agony follows the words. With a lurch of my pulse, I push myself forward.

As soon as I get close to the being, I recognize her. I never spent all that much time around Gloss at the academy, but her icy, polished attitude laces even her ephemeral presence.

That presence is stretched thin now, dispersing with her fading essence. The smoky substance leaches into the haze around us in jittery tendrils. She squirms and struggles, but I can't tell what she's fighting against.

Did she end up tangled in the twisted streams of shadow that have trapped other beings here? Or did the warping effect of the rift rake through her body, unraveling it in ways essence should never be pulled?

The memory of how she battered my mate makes me want to bare the fangs I don't exactly have here, but Gloss's anguish is undeniable. I'd be as bad as her if I leave her to suffer.

"Can you move?" I ask her. "Try to propel yourself this way. In the thicker shadows, you might heal."

I extend more of the soothing impressions I've been offering, but I don't want to over-promise. What I can sense of Gloss feels more like a tattered rag than a living being.

She lets out a gurgle that doesn't appear to be a response

and makes a wriggling motion that only dispels more essence. My innards tighten in horror.

I reach out and try to tug her with me, but the moment my essence touches hers, a spasm of energy shoots into me that sends me jerking back. Unfortunately, I think I snag another scrap of her fraying presence in the process.

"No, no, no," Gloss keeps muttering between gasps, but her voice is ebbing alongside her disintegrating form. I swivel around her, trying to figure out a way I can push or pull her someplace at least a little safer—and her words fade away completely.

The spark of life that energized her essence snuffs out. All at once, I can't detect anything in the atmosphere right in front of me except more aimless shadows.

As much as I disliked my cruel classmate, a cry of my own slips out of me. I grasp instinctively toward the spot where she was, but there's nothing left I can catch hold of.

And a wave of unnerving dissonance roars in the distance, surging toward me.

Yelping, I fling myself back the way I came. The wriggling quivers of warped energy nip at my heels.

Even in my panic, I don't forget my purpose. As I dash away from the expanding warped zone, I exude my power like I once colored the whole sky in rainbow hues to bring Peri back to me.

"Come with me! Come with me! It's safer this way! Happier, much more delightful! Everything you've ever dreamed of having, you can find it over here!"

Okay, I might really be overselling the situation with that pitch. But what do we all dream of more than staying *alive*?

Nothing else we could want is possible if these beings shatter apart like Gloss just did.

So technically, it's true.

Along with the words, I project a swell of tinkling music

both calming and uplifting, to encourage their spirits to take action. I add juicy hamburgers, pumpkin pie, and caviar to the imaginary buffet I'm offering, so there's something for all tastes. I guide the way not with a path of light like I did for the humans in the city but a streak of thicker darkness that'll lead to a shadowy embrace.

More and more presences flit over. Even as I flee the warped rift's onslaught myself, my spirits rise. So many other beings are soaring beside me.

I'm bringing them with me, out of danger this time. Toward something better. This is what my powers should always be used for.

I just hope we can shut down the rifts for good before there are no safe shadows left to hide in.

24

Periwinkle

Sorrel peers at the mass of murk that cloaks the city in front of us, her head cocked to one side and her mouth slanted at an even sharper angle. "So we just... think happy thoughts, and the darkness goes away?"

The skepticism lacing her voice is echoed on the faces of the group of shadowkind I've gathered. A couple dozen of the beings who answered Rollick's call for help when the rift first puked shadows all over the city agreed to come with me to attempt a larger clean-up. But that doesn't mean they won't question my methods.

I smile as brightly as I can in an attempt to inspire confidence. "It's a little more complicated than that, but only for me. I do all the talking. All you need to do is keep an open, friendly sort of attitude and let my energy flow through you."

A short, lumpy-headed figure who I've gathered is a toad

shifter—and looks the part—scratches his head. "Is it going to hurt us?"

"I… don't think so. It's all good feelings."

Mirage pipes up with a whirl of his five tails. "Like a warm hug, ever so snug! Even if it doesn't fix the city, we'll all feel happier."

I appreciate his words of support, even if I'm not sure I should be making promises like that.

Fen steps up next to me with an uncharacteristically firm expression. "Peri's already done a lot of work to clean up these shadows. We have to do whatever we can to stop the problem from spreading. *I'm* going to pitch in everything I can."

Not a single drip falls from her fingers, showing just how sure she is of her convictions. The beings around us who know her from school look a little chagrinned, as if embarrassed that the naiad most of them saw as weak might be showing them up.

The imp glances around us with twitchy eyes. "What if the hunters or the other angry humans attack us again? I'm not into bondage."

I ignore Hail's snort and motion to the scattered buildings around us. "That's why I picked a spot as far as possible from the camp and any other places the humans have been hanging out. They shouldn't even realize we've shown up here before we're done."

I only have the strength to keep at it for an hour or two.

Our efforts had better not fail because *I'm* a weakling.

I stuff that thought down and clap my hands. "But that does mean we should get started right away! My mates will stay next to me, and the rest of you spread out nearby. You don't need to touch each other, but keep close."

When my men and I tackled the rogue shadowkind who was destroying the city weeks ago, we created a barrier of light around Viscera while standing several feet distant from one another. But I don't want to count on my energies being able to flow so easily between a whole bunch of beings I barely know.

The crowd of shadowkind gathers just a few steps from the border of the strange murkiness. A gust of wind rattles a signpost, and a shifter on the fringes jumps out of her skin— literally. She shrinks into a cat with fur raised all along her back and tail puffy, and has to shake herself a few times before she can return to human-like form.

"What if the humans bring chainsaws?" someone says abruptly.

My gaze twitches in the direction of the voice. "What?"

"Sometimes the mean ones chop people up with chainsaws. I saw it on TV."

I'd like to point out that most things humans show on TV aren't real, but considering that any support I've gotten from our mortal friends came from *my* TV appearances, I'm not sure that's the best idea to put out there.

"I haven't seen any chainsaws," I say instead. "Even when they kidnapped me. I think that's more of a small-town thing than a city thing."

Another voice pipes up. "Yeah, in cities they don't have as much room to swing things around. They like butcher knives there. We can dodge those."

"But what if they're made out of silver and iron?"

"They still have to catch us."

"One time *I* saw a show where—"

Raze clears his throat with a sound like a growl. "There are no humans anywhere nearby right now. I'd smell them if there were. We need to let Peri work her powers before any of them *do* turn up."

The reminder that the weaponry they're talking about could appear if we don't get on with things quiets the conversation, but trickles of anxiety still lace the atmosphere. I tune out the sour prickles that cross my tongue as well as I can and turn toward the city.

Despite my insistence that we don't give up on the humans or their home, it takes longer than usual for me to dig into my reserves of compassion. When I stare into the shifting shadows, I don't think of figures wielding chainsaws and butcher knives... I remember the dark gazes of the humans who tied me up and interrogated me. The grim expression Colonel Hueber has when he talks about keeping shadowkind away.

Those people don't stand for all humans, I remind myself. I should think about the news reporters who've seemed interested in my story, about the refugees who spoke up about how we'd helped them, about Gracie trekking all the way out here to show how much she still cares about me.

"Hey," I say to the murk as if I'm talking to a being rather than a mass of shadow vomit. "I know things have been pretty chaotic around here, but we can still find a place for you. All of us can live together with peace and joy. Doesn't that sound nice? Let's see how you can fit in..."

I summon the vibrant blue-green light that's shone from me before. It tickles up inside me, wavering with the splashes of anxiety that hit my senses from all around.

Yes, this situation is a little scary, but I do want to find a common ground. I want us to be able to coexist without anyone getting hurt.

Is that really so much to ask for?

The light streams out of me to the four men standing around me. I nudge it farther, toward Fen and Brine and Sorrel, toward all the other beings gathered around us, ready to embrace it and the cooperation I'm talking about.

Except most of them still aren't in an embracing mood

after all. The glow flickers as it spreads rather than beaming brighter.

My pulse hiccups. I try to push more energy out of me, but my own doubts wriggle through my focus like worms brought out by the rain. While a few streaks of the light veer toward the shadows, most of it snuffs out.

Sorrel glances down at her hands and then at the murk, her brow knitting. "That wasn't much, was it? Maybe we should get, like, one of those big spotlights that can swing all over the place."

I swallow thickly. "I don't think that'll do anything to this kind of darkness. I'm sorry. I lost my concentration. If we can all focus on the things that make us happy here in the mortal realm, that should—"

A small, slender body springs out of the shadows to crash into my legs. Falkor gazes up at me, wriggles his furry snake form, and lets out an arf that sounds unmistakably urgent.

I frown down at him. "What's the matter, buddy?"

He gives a whine that ends in a serpentine hiss and squirms away from me—past Sorrel, who lets out a little yelp and looks around as if for a chair to jump onto. Maybe she sees him as a very large mouse.

My impression of his urgency only increases. I glance around at my men. "I think something's wrong. We should find out what's going on."

It's no good trying to clean up one disaster if an even bigger one is about to crash on our heads.

Jonah nods. "Anyone who wants to join us, jump in the van!"

While he hustles to the driver's seat, my other mates and I dive into the back through the shadows. Fen leaps after me, along with maybe a dozen of the other beings—including Sorrel, despite her shudder when my snake-puppy gives another arf from outside. Thankfully we all fit fine when we stick to the shadows.

Falkor seems to have picked up on what we're doing. He barks toward the driver's seat from where he's standing on the road, and Jonah gives him a wave. When our sorcerer starts the engine, the snake-puppy takes off as fast as he can slither-bound, keeping his physical form so Jonah can track him.

My self-declared pet leads us on a straight-forward route around the edge of the city, back toward the camp. My sense of the emotions wafting from the humans there had faded away with the distance. As we get closer, little jabs of panic and rage pierce my tongue, vinegar-sour and ghost-pepper-searing.

I materialize on the passenger seat next to Jonah. He's used enough to shadowkind habits that he only gives a slight twitch of surprise, his hands staying steady on the wheel.

"Something's happening at the camp," I say, a shiver rippling through my nerves as the impressions expand. "People are really upset. I don't know—"

We turn a corner that brings us into view of the army cabins, and my voice dies. Because now I do know, and what I know isn't good.

Dozens of soldiers stand shoulder to shoulder at the edge of their territory, their guns booming loud enough that I can hear the shots even though we're still half a mile distant. A few tanks are rolling over behind them.

In the first second, I can't tell who they're firing at. It quickly becomes clear with the blinking of bodies in and out of view.

Supernatural energy flashes in lightning bolts and blazes of fire. An eerie shriek pierces the air.

It's another army, one of shadowkind—more beings than I can count popping into view to hurl their powers at the humans and then vanishing before the bullets can tear into them.

The bottom of my stomach drops out. "Why are we attacking them? Well, not *us*, but... Did Rollick decide to drive the army away?"

Jonah shakes his head, his knuckles paling where he's gripping the steering wheel. "He wouldn't have done something like that—at all, I don't think, and definitely not without talking to us."

My voice shrinks. "Maybe he was worried I'd disagree and mess up his plans."

Jonah's gaze flicks away from the road just long enough to hold mine for a beat. "No, Peri. He might have been frustrated that you and he weren't seeing eye to eye, but— this is going to screw things up for all the shadowkind here. Make you all targets. He wouldn't put your life in danger like that."

That's true. Rollick might distrust humans to a massive degree, but only because of how they treat shadowkind. He wouldn't screw any of us over to screw them over too.

Only one-sided screwing is acceptable.

Jonah slows the van but keeps driving closer. I squint at the beings who briefly emerge, but I don't recognize any of them.

"The way they're acting, being careful in their strategy rather than just barging at the soldiers—they've got to be higher shadowkind, right? Do you think they're warped beings from the rift?"

Jonah's forehead furrows. "Maybe some, but I don't see how that many could have come through all at once or without us realizing it earlier. Have you seen *any* warped higher shadowkind other than Viscera?"

I shake my head. He has a point. Viscera didn't exactly arrive quietly.

Subtlety is not a typical quality of the warped shadowkind.

Hail must have been following our conversation from the shadows. He materializes to lean between our seats, his expression somber. "Plenty of humans are making their own groups to harass and capture us. It's not totally surprising that a bunch of shadowkind who don't feel like answering to Rollick might have decided to lash out, is it? Especially now that this rift situation is messing things up in the shadow realm too."

I hadn't thought of that. "They might blame the humans here for what's happening, just like the humans are blaming us."

Hail nods. "It's not as if humans haven't given many of us plenty of reasons to dislike them before now."

His own animosity toward humans doesn't ring quite as sharply through his voice as it used to, but I know he still would rather stay as far away from most of them as he can get.

The rattle of gunfire penetrates the van's walls, louder by the second. Jonah grimaces and pulls over onto the shoulder of the road. "I don't think we should get any closer. Not in the van, anyway."

I hug myself. "We can't let them keep fighting, can we?"

"I don't know if there's anything we can do to stop them. Maybe Mirage…" Jonah glances over his shoulder as he hesitates. "But most of the soldiers will be immune to his illusions with their badges."

I slip after him when he steps out of the van, peering toward the battle. "If I could project enough calming emotions to get all of them to settle down…"

The possibility of me ending the fighting with my power feels too huge for me to wrap my head around—so many beings both mortal and shadow, so much rage crackling through the air.

And then the idea becomes moot, because the tanks have jerked to a halt, their guns pointing toward the raging shadowkind.

A new line of humans appears amid the soldiers. Across the distance, I can't make out more than a mumble of the syllables they holler out, but the unnerving jitter over my skin tells me it's not words but sorcery.

The magic must be calling on the opposing beings to show themselves. The shadowkind on the attack emerge into physical form—here, there, and everywhere. Their heads whip around in confusion while their limbs jerk out defensively.

They definitely aren't warped beings if the sorcery worked that well on them.

I only have time for that one thought to pass through my head before the tanks open fire.

Their artillery booms even louder than the chorus of rifles, with puffs of smoke around the muzzles of their guns. Explosions flare amid the shadowkind force. Bursts of essence flood the air where several beings disintegrate beyond the point of healing, just like that.

A few of the rounds hit the factory buildings at the edge of the city. One roof crumples with a thunderous crash.

I wince, anguish squeezing my heart. The humans don't seem to care who *they* screw over while winning.

And the mutual screwing over is happening on an even larger scale than they probably realize. Because as I watch the flames dance amid the plumes of smoky essence, I notice something else that clenches the tension in my chest tighter.

The edges of murk around the city shiver—and creep a little forward.

At first, I think I must have imagined the effect in my horrified state. Then the tanks fire again, and I see it clearly.

One swath of thickened shadow looms closer, shifting from a porch across a lawn to the edge of the road.

The flood has never done that before, not since the original deluge. Even when more shadows belched from the rift, they only stirred up and condensed the darkness over the city rather than pushing it farther out.

My heart leaps to my throat. "Oh, no. The mess is spreading."

25

Raze

Few things set my nerves on edge like Rollick's frown. I'm a being so deadly I can kill without even meaning to, and the demon is many times more powerful than I am. It's hard to say what could be as disturbing as seeing even him unsettled.

"You're sure the flood expanded?" he says, peering at Peri, who delivered the news, and then the rest of us who are backing her up. "It wasn't simply fluctuating the way it's sometimes inclined to do?"

I speak up before Peri has to. "I could see the difference too. It wasn't a big expansion, but the border moved at least ten feet out from where it had been—and stayed there even after the fighting stopped."

Those last words bring a knot into my stomach. The fighting stopped because the soldiers managed to blast apart enough shadowkind that any who weren't totally trapped by the sorcerers' commands fled rather than continuing their attack.

It seems clear the group of shadowkind hit the humans first. I can't exactly blame the humans for striking back. But the memory of their methods makes my skin prickle with apprehension.

What if they decide to turn their tanks at all of us, even when we're trying to help?

If anyone comes at my Glowbug...

My fangs itch at my gums, and I have to flex my fingers to keep my claws retracted.

Jonah leans against the wall of the trailer. "With everything else we've seen, it makes sense, doesn't it? The shadowy stuff lightens up when Peri projects welcoming impressions at it. So why wouldn't it get worse in some way when people are being as *un*welcoming as possible? It might be as much the fault of the shadowkind who launched the attack as of the soldiers who retaliated."

Rollick nods slowly. "But either way, it all comes down to the conflict. And I don't see how we're sorting that out any time soon."

He shoots Peri a glance as if he thinks she might change her mind about trying to mind-wipe all the humans who know about our existence, but she stares back at him firmly. "We haven't had much time to make peace. And this time it was *our* kind who started the fight."

Hail clears his throat. "Does anyone else find it kind of concerning that the army was ready to aim tanks at shadowkind that quickly? And that the soldiers fired those guns even though they took down a few of their own buildings in the process?"

I suppress a shudder. "Like nothing mattered more to them than destroying us."

Peri nudges my arm with hers. "Not *us*. Only the ones who were trying to kill them. Bad behavior all around."

But how do we stop more of that badness?

"Have the soldiers said anything to you since the battle?" I ask Rollick. "They aren't blaming us for it, are they?"

Rollick splays his hands. "I have no idea what's on their minds. They've been clammed up for the past few days in general."

I don't like that either. Tension ripples through my muscles.

Peri spoke to that one major before, and he seemed open to her suggestions. She shouldn't have to be the only one sticking her neck out to try to find a common ground with the humans, though.

Am *I* really that scared of them when I could snuff out any of their lives in an instant?

I square my shoulders. "I think we should go to the military part of the camp. Stay in the shadows, listen in on their conversations, and get a sense of what they're planning next. It's not safe for Peri to go out and work on lightening the shadows if the soldiers might march on her."

Peri's forehead furrows. "But if I don't keep trying, the flood might get even worse."

Looking into her softly pretty face, my heart squeezes. "It'll get a million times worse if we lose you."

I don't know how I'd stand that.

I said "we," but really I expected my suggestion would be a solo mission, since I'm essentially volunteering. To my surprise, Sorsha's partner Thorn—a big shadowkind who gives off an aura of dour power—steps forward from where a bunch of the other shadowkind have been following the discussion.

"I agree," he says in his deep, somber voice. "We must

determine what the humans' current intentions are before we make further plans of our own."

Several more shadowkind materialize from the shadows, looking at Thorn and then at me… as if waiting for additional guidance.

Rollick raises his eyebrows with a hint of a smile aimed my way. "Sounds like you have our next step figured out, basilisk. Pick your team."

Even though the trust he's showing is nothing but a compliment, my pulse stutters. Do all these other beings trust me to lead the way too—even Thorn, who I have the sense has been through more battles than I can imagine?

Peri grasps my hand with an emphatic squeeze, and I shake myself into action. I won't be leading anyone anywhere if I freeze up before I can give the first orders.

I do know most of the beings around us better than Thorn does—they're people I went to the academy with, people I've worked alongside in our various minor missions over the past few weeks.

The first three choices are obvious… Well, mostly. "Peri, Hail—and Mirage, do you think you can stick to the shadows, no tricks?"

Mirage chuckles with a flick of his furry ears. "I might be as tricksy as a fox, but for this assignment I can be as quiet as a mouse."

I turn to the rest of our bunch. Thorn is obviously coming, and I don't need to worry about his sense of discipline. If anything, he'll be muttering about mine.

We'll want plenty of ears in plenty of places to make sure we overhear the most important conversations. Who's been loyal and reliable?

It has to be full shadowkind—the shadowbloods, skilled as they are, can't merge into the shadows. Neither can Jonah.

I pick out Peri's friends, the unassuming shadowkind

who nonetheless have stepped up and aren't likely to get any ideas about going rogue. "Fen and Brine." The centaur shifter whose attitude gets my hackles up but who I can admit has pitched in well under pressure. "Sorrel." The two school administrators who've joined us. "Gnash and Shanty, if you don't have other things you need to take care of."

I'm not sure I could ever get used to the beings who once debated banishing me dipping their heads respectfully. Gnash adds his gruff agreement in words. "I can't think of anything more important than finding out what the humans are scheming."

"My colleagues can join us as well," Thorn puts in. "Or —perhaps just Omen and Snap, not Ruse." He fixes the incubus standing next to Sorsha with a pointed look. "He is somewhat distractable."

Ruse raises his hands, his mouth curving into a wry grin. "Hey, I can stay focused when the situation calls for it! But I'll probably be more useful for cajoling the humans *out* of whatever plans they're making if we see the need."

I blink at him. "Can you convince the whole army to stop antagonizing us?"

The incubus's grin falters. "Well, that might be a bit much, even for me. And I'll admit I can't do anything at all when they're wearing the damned badges."

Sorsha pats his arm. "I'm sure we'll find plenty of other ways to put you to work."

Rollick motions toward the patches of darkness along the edges of the room, where more shadowkind are watching. "Crag, Torrent, why don't you go along too? That seems like plenty. Too many accounts and we'll have trouble picking them apart."

I'm not sure I agree with that idea, but the urge to get going is winding through my limbs. "All right. Let's move out."

That sounds like the sort of thing the colonel would say, doesn't it? Am I becoming a sort-of colonel to the shadowkind here?

I wouldn't mind that as long as I can be the non-asshole type. Hueber isn't anyone I want as a role model.

My expanded team weaves through the shadows across the increasingly vacant refugee camp to the area the army has claimed. We pause at the edge of their territory, considering our final approach.

A squadron of men and women in uniform marches past at strict attention, perfectly in sync.

One of Sorsha's other partners, Snap, eases up beside me. His bright voice reminds me a little of Peri's. "Why do they walk so close together like that? Does it help them fight?"

Thorn's tone manages to turn even gruffer. "It shows their discipline. They need to be able to work together utterly cohesively when a situation turns dire."

I suspect my current team won't be a match for the humans when it comes to walking in a straight line, but we definitely have them beat for stealth.

"Let's spread out," I say. "Ah, Shanty, Sorrel, and Snap, you can head to the north side of the camp. Gnash, Fen, and Omen can head south. I'll stick with my original team in the center here—"

"And I'll take whichever of our companions is left and go straight to the colonel," Thorn breaks in sternly.

Maybe he'd rather have been the one giving the orders. I could probably use a little more practice.

But everyone flits off in the directions I suggested without complaint. Thorn, Crag, Torrent, and Brine veer toward Colonel Hueber's cabin. I spot his boxy head passing the dusty window and grimace to myself.

I'd have liked to hear what the leader of these soldiers is plotting directly from his mouth. But I guess when you put yourself in charge, sometimes that means you delegate more than you do.

I travel straight ahead with Peri close by and Hail and Mirage trailing behind us farther out. When we reach the clumps of soldiers clustered around their tents and vehicles, Hail gives me a poke with a vague sense of direction. "I'm going to do my spying over here."

I don't see any reason to argue. "All right. We should all listen to different people. Call out through the shadows if you hear anything that seems important."

"Aye aye, captain," Mirage says jauntily, and darts off.

Peri brushes her presence against mine with enough affection through our bond to ease my concerns about the fox shifter's discipline. "We're going to dig up all the inside info so we can get the catastrophe back on track." She pauses. "Or the solution to the catastrophe, I guess I should say. Whatever makes things better."

"Of course." I offer the closest thing to a fond caress I can in our current state and move toward one of the army trucks that a few soldiers are standing by.

For a bunch of people who supposedly think they're here to solve the strangest crisis the human realm has ever faced, the soldiers seem incredibly unconcerned. The first group I listen to spends most of the time grumbling about their recent meals and making jokes about the hot medic who got stationed with them.

When I decide they're useless and move on to another cluster, I get a tedious rundown of one man's favorite guns in order from "most badass to least" and his female companion's opinions on a dozen different sports teams. I can't even tell from her comments about "domination," "amateurs," and "personal bests" what sport she's talking about.

Maybe it's actually some kind of military code? If so, I'm lost.

A twinge of envy runs through my essence at the thought of Thorn getting to listen in on the colonel's plans. Surely Hueber is talking about more than random everyday topics.

My frustration provokes a renewed jab of resolve. I can find someone who'll talk about something useful. I *am* a powerful shadowkind too, aren't I?

I stop in the middle of the camp and look around, letting my predator instincts rise to the surface. Who here looks like a good target for a very specific sort of hunt?

My gaze snags on a few uniformed men who are jostling against each other with obvious enthusiasm as they load another truck. They have more energy to their movements than any of the other soldiers I've seen.

It could be they're just excited about taking a day off or something like that, but it might also be that they're gearing up for a new mission.

As I prowl through the shadows toward them, their voices become audible.

"How long do you think it'll take before we get the go ahead?"

"I dunno. With something this big, it's got to go all the way up the chain of command. Like, ten different people who all need to sign off. But why wouldn't they? They have to let us."

"Can you imagine? All of it up in smoke just like that. That'll show them."

Apprehension coils around my gut. I creep even closer.

One of the men glances toward the shrouded city. He shifts restlessly from one foot to the other. "Do you figure it'll be enough to blow up that whole portal thing the monsters talk about? No more of the darkness coming through?"

Another guffaws. "Did you see how even the tank artillery tore through them? They won't stand a chance against an actual bomb. Blow up the city, blow up all the freaks in it."

A chill sweeps through every particle of my presence. They're talking about—they're really going to destroy the entire city?

A pang hits me from the other side of the truck. I leap over to find Peri there, watching like I was.

Worry ripples through her voice. "They can't really think bombing the city will clean up the warped flood, can they? Even shooting at a few buildings made the murk spread."

I swallow thickly. "I don't think they know that."

Shit, how bad could things get if the soldiers go through with this thoughtless plan?

Peri is obviously afraid of the same thing. "They might spread the messed-up shadows all over the country! We can't let them do this."

She dashes off without another word, only a sense of urgency that echoes right to my core.

"Peri!" I shoot after her, afraid as much for the woman I love as the horrible scenario we've uncovered.

My Glowbug can move fast when she wants to. She zips straight into Major Yin's cabin without hesitation.

I hurtle after her, but she's already taken physical form by the time I squeeze through the darkness around the doorframe.

"You can't bomb the city!" she's saying to the bewildered-looking major. "It won't get rid of the shadows that are hurting everyone—it'll spew them even farther, all over the place. You have to tell the colonel—"

Before she can finish her desperate appeal, two soldiers barge into the cabin with their guns pointing at Peri. "What are you doing in here? Get away from the major, *now*!"

They look like they're about to shoot whether she moves

or not, but Peri hasn't lost her usual stubbornness. She spins toward them. "I'm only trying—"

A finger tightens on a trigger, and I dive in. In one forceful leap, I emerge into physical form, tackle Peri as gently as you can tackle anyone while trying to save their life, and yank her with me back into the shadows.

The bang of a gunshot reverberates in her wake. Peri presses close to me with a sound like a sob.

"What's going to happen if they won't listen?"

As I tug her with me out of the cabin, I think of all the ways she's spread her light so far, all the people she has brought around. "Maybe we shouldn't be talking to the soldiers. There are a lot more humans out there who'd want to have a say, aren't there?"

26

Periwinkle

The clustered news vans have dwindled in number as some have followed the refugees to their new homes, but there are still several scattered along the edges of the camp. I watch a reporter interview a couple of men in hunter gear, the back of my neck prickling.

"Why do they want to talk to those jerks? Shouldn't they be focusing on the rift?"

Jonah lets out a short sigh from where he's standing next to me, peering around an abandoned tent. "That's the news cycle for you. As far as they've noticed, nothing about the rift has changed in the past couple of days. Telling everyone 'Things are still the same here' doesn't make for great news. I mean, it's not new."

A shudder runs down my spine. "Things will change a lot if the army starts dropping bombs. Are they even going to warn the other people still here?"

Jonah's mouth tightens. "They probably won't give any details, just evacuate the area."

"Of everyone except us," Hail mutters behind us. "They're hoping we all get caught in the blasts."

I'd like to tell him he's being overly cynical, but from what I've seen of Hueber and most of his soldiers, I'd guess he's probably right.

I draw my chin up. "We'll just have to let the other humans know now. Once the whole country finds out what the army is planning and how bad it'll be, they'll have to stop their plans."

Despite Jonah's comment about the news cycle, I assume it won't be too tricky getting back on camera. The reporters have seemed happy to film us lots of times before.

I wait until the interview with the hunters is finished and the jerks have walked far enough away that they won't see us, and then I march up to one of the other news vans nearby. No point in talking to people who like chatting with our enemies.

Jonah walks beside me, and my other mates follow through the shadows, along with most of the other beings who spied on the soldiers with us. Gnash stomped off to tell Rollick when I announced my intentions, and I have a feeling the demon is going to go straight to the nuclear option.

Destroy them before they can destroy us—and, well, most of their own world too. I can see the argument for it, but I can't shake the suspicion that going on the offensive against the humans is only going to make them *more* eager to bomb us.

If even one aspect of the memory wipe goes slightly wrong, then we're still screwed, just more so.

So why not end the conflict before anyone's bombing anyone? I won us a whole lot of support before.

Unfortunately, it turns out that Jonah's comments about fresh material apply to me too.

The first reporter I walk up to gives me a onceover and shakes her head before I've gotten one word out. "We've already done an interview with you. Got plenty of footage. We're moving on to other stories—sorry."

I don't think I've ever heard an apology that sounded less apologetic.

"We've got huge news!" I say with a broad gesture of my hands. "An even bigger catastrophe is coming. You need to—"

The reporter cuts me off with an upheld hand. "Colonel Hueber spread the word that some of… your kind of beings might try to create a panic. Is there anything you can actually give me that we can show our audience?"

What, do they want me to cart the bombs over as proof?

I grope for the right words to convince her. "It isn't happening *yet*. But we heard them talking—"

"Nope, sorry, that doesn't cut it. My producer says we need to stick to what's vivid and concrete."

She turns away.

When we head over to the next news van, I decide to get straight to the point. I stride up to the reporter who's drinking from one of those ever-present cups of coffee. "The army is going to bomb the city!"

Maybe I'm a little too emphatic about it. The guy sputters and coughs, apparently on the verge of choking on his caffeinated beverage.

My eyes widen. "Um, sorry, are you okay?"

He waves off my concern and swipes his hand across his mouth, appearing to recover. "What was that about bombs?"

I point toward the military area of the camp. "Colonel Hueber is trying to get permission to drop bombs on the city. That'll only—"

Like the first reporter, this one doesn't let me finish my story, even though I've already given him a juicy part of it. "I can't broadcast anything about impending military action unless they release the information to the public. Our instructions on that are very clear."

"But—"

"I'm not getting arrested! I'd look awful in orange."

He scrambles away into the van as if he's afraid I'm going to voodoo him into doing my bidding.

My shoulders slump. Jonah clasps my arm reassuringly. "We only need to find one person."

Raze shifts out of the shadows, a frown darkening his face. "But if the soldiers have threatened all the reporters… Humans are very scared of other humans with guns."

Having seen what those guns can do even to shadowkind, I guess that's reasonable. We can't stand around and twiddle our thumbs, though.

Any minute now, Rollick is going to come rushing in with his own plans that might cut humans right out of the equation.

Mirage pops into being at my other side and cocks his head. "Do we need reporters? It's the cameras and satellites that send the message to the TVs, isn't it?"

My hopes lift and plummet in the space of a heartbeat. "But we don't know how to use them."

Jonah clears his throat, looking suddenly awkward. "Er, I might. I helped out a lot with the A/V equipment when I was in high school, and I was in the broadcast club for a couple of years. I actually… always wondered about getting word out about the shadowkind somehow or other."

His gaze slides to the flood of murkiness at the other end of the camp. "I didn't think it'd happen because the shadow realm was about to collapse all over our world, but that part's already done. Desperate times… I guess we'd have to break into one of the vans to get the equipment, though."

His uncertainty flows into me like a gulp of over-sour lemonade. Jonah isn't really the criminal type.

He's only offering for me.

Guilt clamps around my gut. "You don't have to. I don't want you to get in trouble."

A rough chuckle tumbles out of Jonah. "It seems like there's going to be a lot more trouble for all of us if we don't do everything we can. Come on. The first thing we need is a van no one's monitoring so we have plenty of time to do our work."

He tips his head to Mirage. "Can you have a look around for a news crew where the employees aren't wearing protective badges? Your illusions work better than any other distraction."

Mirage grins. "Easy as pie." He flips through the air and into the shadows with a whoosh of his tails.

The rest of us shadowkind duck into the darkness as well so we don't draw unwanted attention from the humans around us. It only takes a few minutes before Mirage comes dashing back to us, pulling himself into solid form just long enough to give Jonah directions.

The fox shifter must have paid attention to all the reasons the reporters might have to balk. He can't pull off anything concrete, but vivid and startling is his wheelhouse.

Within view of the cameraman who's lounging outside the van, he conjures the impression of a few glowing figures darting past the nearby tents. Their bodies pulse with light as if they're radioactive.

The man jerks to attention. He snatches up his camera and calls to the reporter he's working with—in a hushed version of a shout, because he doesn't want anyone else getting in on the story if they can break it first.

The reporter scrambles out the back of the van, dabbing lipstick on her mouth as she comes. She shoves the tube into her pocket and hustles with the cameraman in the direction the glowing figures appeared to be running.

Mirage flits away through the shadows to lead them on his wild goose chase. Or I guess a wild fox chase?

The second the news team is out of view, I leap through the tiny, dark gap around the van's doors.

They locked automatically when the reporter shut them, but there's an easy switch to flip over. I nudge them just wide enough for Jonah to scramble inside. Hail, Fen, and a few of the other shadowkind dart in after him.

"I'll keep watch," Raze tells us, flexing his sinewy shoulders.

Jonah nods and peers at the equipment on the built-in shelves. "I'll make this as quick as possible."

He sits on the rolling stool in front of the displays mounted across from the shelves. Sucking his lower lip under his teeth in a way that looks adorable, he taps a button here and another there, and then speeds his fingers across the keyboard.

"I've got contact with the news station. Telling them we have an urgent story, breaking news, that they'll want to show live so we can get it out right away. We need to be ready. Grab that other camera there."

Shanty ripples into view and snatches the device in question off one of the shelves. Jonah jumps up to plug it into the control board, I guess so it'll transmit its recording to the waiting studio.

I'm going to need to talk. I'm going to need to talk *now* and *fast*. Because who knows how long the station will keep broadcasting once they see what we're sending them.

I drag in a breath, and Jonah lifts his hand. "We're on in

one minute. I'll count you down. Peri, are you going to talk alone?"

Before I need to answer, Hail steps in. His stance is stiff, but he holds his head high. "No. I think we should give them plenty to look at so we keep their attention."

With a glimmer over his body, he shifts into his fae form. The icy pallor and blue-tinged veins flow over his skin while his antlers sprout from amid his thickening hair.

Jonah blinks at him, never having seen this version of the winter fae before.

Fen jumps in too, scales sprouting over her arms and face, her hair rippling longer down her back like a waterfall. "I'll be in it too. You've got this, Peri."

I face the camera Shanty is holding, bolstered by the support I'm being offered on both sides.

Jonah starts counting. "Ten, nine, eight…"

He gives me the last three seconds with his fingers, in silence. Then a light flares on high on the control panel.

I launch myself into my appeal. "Hello, humans! I have urgent news for all of you. We've learned that the soldiers here at Jackson City are planning to drop bombs on it. They want to blow the whole place up! All those people's homes, all the living beings still stuck there. But even worse— aggression seems to rile up the shadows that've drowned the city. If the buildings are bombarded, the murky stuff could be tossed all over the place, all over the country, every other city and town! Please don't let that happen. I promise there are better ways to—"

Jonah lets out a grunt. "They cut us off."

Shanty lowers the camera. "You got most of the message out. Good job."

The administrator's praise barely touches the tension inside me. "What now?"

Jonah smiles crookedly. "We get the hell away from this van before they call the police. And then we wait and see what people made of your news."

27

Jonah

Th... he comments pop up under the news clip faster than I can read them.

We're going to bomb our own city with no idea how that'll solve the problem? Yeah, that sounds smart. /s

Did anyone tell the military bozos that bombs don't fix things, they destroy them?

Why the fuck are the monsters on our side more than our own soldiers? Come on, people!

Sure, there are a few comments mixed in that are supportive of the military plans—people saying no one should trust the "monsters" and that they're only looking out for themselves, others claiming it's all a big conspiracy and the shadows hazing the city are actually a top-secret experiment by humans that's gotten out of control. But that's to be expected.

Peri comes up behind me and leans her arms against my

shoulders, peering past me at the laptop screen. "You feel relieved. Is the response good?"

One corner of my mouth kicks up. "Nothing's resolved yet, but if the military tried to suppress that broadcast, they didn't manage to. The clips that've been uploaded on video-sharing sites have gotten millions of views. Most of the commenters are *very* against blowing cities up."

I catch a whiff of Peri's delight through our bond. "It worked, then! Colonel Hueber will have to rethink his plans if people are upset, won't he?"

"I hope so. It seems like he was figuring he could slip the bombing mission under the public's radar, and no one would mind the destruction if it got rid of the problem at the same time. With people already knowing about it and raising an outcry… Especially when you pointed out that it's likely to make the situation even worse instead of better… I think we're going to be okay."

Okay in the sense that no bombs should be dropping in our vicinity in the next few days. We still have a massive, warped rift belching shadows all over the city to deal with while avoiding all the hostile humans who've shown up to get in Peri's way.

That thought brings back the memory of the sorcerers we saw compelling the attacking shadowkind to take physical form… so the tanks could blow them apart. I swallow thickly, a sour flavor coating my mouth.

Peri tips her head next to mine. "Did you see some bad news? You got upset all of a sudden."

I'm never going to be able to keep any real secrets from her. Old habits die hard, though—a lie slips off my tongue automatically. "It's nothing."

Peri gives a soft little huff and pecks my cheek. "I *know* that's not true. What's bothering you? If you don't tell me, it'll only bother me too that something's wrong."

I exhale slowly and turn away from the little desk I've set up in my personal trailer. Peri swivels automatically to perch on my lap, her soft weight a comforting presence in my arms.

Why am I trying to hide anything from her? I know she doesn't judge me—she never has.

I've always been the person who's hardest on me.

"I was thinking about the sorcerers who were working with the army," I admit. "The way they set up the shadowkind so they'd die… I know the shadowkind started that fight, but I hate how most people who have the same power I do use it. They're *always* hurting shadowkind one way or another."

"That's because of who they are, not the power they have, right?" Peri nuzzles the edge of my jaw with a waft of affection. "Most of them were either brought up seeing shadowkind as inhuman monsters or went to the trouble of developing their powers because that's what they believed once they found out about us. You're lucky you got another perspective."

I grapple with the right words to explain how I'm feeling. "The talent still feels… tainted somehow. The whole point of it is to take away your will, to force you to do what I say. I'm always going to have that ability."

"You'd never use it in any way that would bother me, though. So it doesn't matter."

She says it as if it's the simplest thing in the world. I can't pick up on a trace of discomfort from her.

I shift Peri in my arms so I can look into her bright blue eyes. "It really doesn't get under your skin at all? Knowing that I have something so fundamental in common with so many people who want to manipulate and destroy beings like you?"

She doesn't hesitate even a split-second in her answer. "I don't see it that way even a little bit. The sorcery is like… like a gun or a tank. You can use it to hurt people or to protect them when they're threatened. Just because lots of other people decide to do the first thing doesn't mean it's not obvious to me that *you'd* always do the second."

She speaks so confidently the twist in my gut eases, but only partly. "I'm glad you feel that way. I don't know whether I'll ever be completely convinced."

Peri tsks her tongue at me. "Doesn't it make a difference that none of the shadowkind who've worked with you are unsettled by how you use sorcery anymore? When even Hail's okay with a human, you must be doing something right."

Her tone has turned teasing, but she does have a point.

A chuckle slips out of me, and I hug her tighter again. "I guess it's just something I'll have to keep working through in my own head. I'll try not to let it get to me in any way that'll worry you."

Peri hums. Her hand comes up to trace the line of my jaw, and heat sparks through my skin.

A thread of desire winds from her into me, stirring more of my own.

"Maybe you need to practice the better parts of sorcery more," she says in a voice that's still sweet but with a husky quality that sends a tingle of electricity straight to my groin. "It could be fun. People tie each other up with ropes and handcuffs to spice things up in the bedroom, don't they?"

My mouth has gone abruptly dry. "You want me to tie you up with sorcery?"

My heart is suddenly thumping twice as fast, but I can't say it isn't as much with a thrill at the thought as with nerves.

Peri presses a kiss to the side of my neck before answering. "I know you'd never put me in danger or treat me unkindly. How would you approach it if you *were* going to bind me with sorcery, for fun?"

The ideas flit through my mind giddingly fast. "I—I

guess I'd start… by giving you a command not to follow any other commands that you don't actually want to. That would give you a safety measure. I couldn't bend your will against your actual preferences."

Her voice drops to a whisper. "Then why don't you do that and take it from there?"

I swallow again in a moment of uncertainty, but the slight shift of her ass on my lap makes me starkly aware of how hard I am.

It *wouldn't* be risky to try this if I handle it the way I said, would it? Peri's asking me to give it a shot.

I can taste her eagerness the way she must be able to pick up on mine, with none of my apprehension mixed in. The magical bondage might make the experience extra enjoyable for her, just as she pointed out other kinds of bondage can for people.

The thought of her face flushing with pleasure convinces me.

The sorcerous syllables spill off my tongue, the meaning clear in my mind even if I couldn't explain why those sounds will have their intended effect. *"Only follow commands that you'd want to do even without sorcery."*

Peri's expression doesn't so much as tick. Of course, I haven't compelled her to do anything concrete right now, only set a boundary for future commands.

She squirms around on my legs so she can straddle me on the chair. The friction makes my dick ache.

The flush I imagined is already spreading across her cheeks, but she cups her hands against my jaw ever so tenderly. "What would you like me to do for you, my sorcerer?"

The answer comes to me like a bolt straight to my cock, tingling through my heart at the same time. And I understand why she's right to trust me. Why she's totally right in what she said about how the people we are use the talents we have.

Not one part of me wants me to ask her to do something for *my* benefit. All my thoughts immediately focus on what I can suggest that'll let me give *her* as much pleasure out of this encounter as possible.

My breath hitches around the heady thump of my pulse. My next command tumbles out in indecipherable syllables that nonetheless both our bodies understand. *"Tilt your head to one side."*

Peri follows the instruction automatically, peering at me only with curiosity. I take a second to confirm her cooperation before bringing my mouth to the crook of her neck now temptingly on display.

As I meld my lips to her soft skin with a flick of my tongue, Peri gasps. More desire flutters through our bond.

She runs her fingers up into my hair from the base of my skull, setting my scalp quivering with heady tingles. Her other hand grips the front of my shirt.

The slight tug gives me a suspicion of what she'd like to do with that shirt, but she doesn't proceed of her own accord. She's letting me call all the shots.

I tease my tongue from the corner of her jaw down to the hollow of her throat and murmur another command. *"Take off my shirt and touch whatever parts of me you'd like to."*

It's the loosest of orders—she could remove my clothes and then stop if she wasn't particularly inclined to cop a feel. But Peri makes an enthusiastic sound as she peels the shirt off my torso. The second she's tossed it aside, her hands are tracing over the lines of the muscles I've worked so hard to sculpt.

I've thrown myself into those workouts mainly to keep my strength somewhere close to what most shadowkind can wield. Feeling my mate caress my skin is an even better reward.

And the sight of the glow that beams from the small spot in the middle of my chest only lifts my spirits now. It's another reminder of just how much I earned this woman's trust.

I catch Peri's mouth in a kiss I didn't demand but that she gives herself over to happily. For a few minutes, I lose myself in the heat of her mouth and her exploring hands.

The throb of my erection brings me back to our supposed goal. I'm meant to be practicing—and even if the most recent crisis is averted, I don't know how much longer we'll have before we're called back to one duty or another.

I nip the lobe of her ear. *"Vanish your clothes."*

I've barely finished speaking before Peri blinks in and out of the shadows, returning in her full naked glory. Her own bond mark glimmers between her voluptuous breasts.

Mine. In this moment, *all* mine.

I can't restrain a groan before I bow down to lap one of her nipples into my mouth.

Peri whimpers, her hips rocking over me to torturous effect. When I dip one hand between her legs, her arousal slicks over my fingers.

I delve two fingers right inside her while strumming her clit with my thumb. A deeper moan reverberates up Peri's throat. She clutches my shoulders, swaying with my attentions.

Her voice comes out breathless but as tantalizingly heated as the emotions flowing between us. "You always make me feel amazing, Jonah. I want to do the same for you."

"You do," I promise, lifting my head so I can kiss her on the lips again. "So fucking good, Peri. It's never been like this with anyone else."

The pleased noise that emanates from her chest sounds

like a purr. Her breath is fracturing with the pumping of my hand, but I know I can make her feel even better than this.

"Push up on your knees," I murmur.

When she lifts her ass, I have just enough room to unzip my fly and wriggle my jeans partway down. It takes barely any effort at all for my cock to spring free, aching to stand at attention for her.

"Sink down until I stop you."

She lowers herself, but I catch her with a squeeze of her hip before she goes too far. Ever so carefully, I slide the head of my cock along her soaked slit.

Peri whimpers, burrowing her face against my shoulder. I exhale shakily. There's only one possible order I can give now.

"Tell me what you want."

"You," she mumbles immediately. "Inside me. All the way. So deep. Please."

God, does she really think she has to beg? There's nowhere in the world I'd rather be.

I guide her down onto me with a swift thrust that propels a groan out of our lungs. Peri's mouth crashes into mine again. We buck together, the pleasure of our merging radiating through my body and hers. The sensations swirl together into a whirlwind of bliss.

I can't tell where I end and she begins anymore. All I can do is chase my release and the ecstasy I can feel building in her all the way to the end.

Kissing her hard, I fondle her breast in time with my thrusts. Peri's gasp stutters across my lips. I barely hold on until she clamps around me with a cry and a flare of brilliant pink all through her hair.

At the clenching of her channel, my cock erupts. I spill myself into her with a few more pumps of my hips before easing us both down together.

Peri slumps into my arms with the most satisfied sigh I

can imagine. A flutter that's not desire but something sweeter passes through my chest.

There really wasn't anything the least bit horrifying about the sorcery I worked here this evening.

It's all in how you use it.

I'd like to revel in that understanding and the feel of the woman I love in my embrace for a while longer. Unfortunately, it's less than a minute before Mirage bursts out of the shadows by the door with an audible *pop*.

The fox shifter takes in our combined position with an upward twitch of his lips that fades just as quickly. "No more time for playing around. The bombs are coming."

28

Periwinkle

"How can they be bombing the city anyway?" I demand as I dash with Mirage through the shadows toward the military part of camp. "Haven't they seen how angry everyone is about the idea? Do they *want* all of human society pissed off at them?"

Mirage lets out a bemused sound. "Lots of big men making lots of big talk. I think the biggest of them is mad that everyone else is mad, and he thinks he's going to prove them wrong."

I guess that doesn't totally surprise me. I can way-too-easily picture Colonel Hueber ranting about how no one else is willing to be tough enough to "do what's necessary."

Well, I'm willing to be tough. In my own way, which looks nothing at all like his, but is obviously now more necessary than ever.

I propel myself out of the shadows at the edge of the military area, picking my clothes with particular emphasis on the sturdiness of the leather jacket. My sundress ripples with a flame pattern rather than flowers.

I'm a force to be reckoned with. They have to listen to me.

If only it was that easy.

As I set my hands on my hips, several of the soldiers hustling around the vehicles glance over and pause.

"You can't go through with this!" I declare in the most commanding tone I can summon. "You'll spread the shadows all over the place—over this camp, maybe all the way to your homes. I thought you wanted to get rid of the darkness, not blast it all over the place."

I catch a few snickers and plenty of narrowed eyes.

"Piss off!" one of the soldiers hollers at me, and goes back to tossing equipment into the back of a truck.

They're packing up, I realize. Evacuating the evacuation site—so they won't be in range of the aftershock.

Jonah jogs up behind me, slower for having needed to stick to the physical world.

"Peri," he starts, but at the same moment, three grim men with hunter whips slung on their belts march between the soldiers toward us.

One lets out a derisive grunt. "Time to deal with the vermin."

I'd point out that he looks much more like a rat than I do, but I don't think that will help my cause.

I aim my best glower at him, which I know is probably not particularly intimidating, but at least I've given it my all. "We're *trying* to save you."

"Right." He motions to his companions. "Don't bother with capture. This one's made enough trouble already."

"*I've* made trouble?"

I don't have much time to sputter at their slander, because they all unholster their whips and unleash the condensed beams of light. The guy who seems to be in charge also pulls a device from the other side of his belt that looks like a combination of a pistol and a fire extinguisher.

Does he think my dress is literally on fire?

I channel all the girl-boss attitude I've picked up from TV shows and movies. "We are *not* having this conversation."

And then I vanish into the shadows, because they can't follow me there anyway, neener-neener.

Okay, maybe that last bit wasn't very girl-boss-like. I'm a work in progress.

As I dash past the hunters, deeper into the military zone, Mirage flits after me. I pick up on my other mates' presences zooming over to join us: Raze resonating with urgent protectiveness, Hail all caustic frustration.

The winter fae is already muttering when he gets close enough for me to hear him. "Fucking humans. Always have to fuck everything up. They can't even resist fucking up what's already the most fucked-up thing that's ever happened here!"

I'll agree that there's a very high degree of fuckery going on at the moment, but I can't let my annoyance interfere with my goals. I veer in one direction and then another, peering around the tanks for a glimpse of one particularly tank-like human.

There.

Colonel Hueber stands near one of the cabins that's being hastily disassembled, glaring down his pointed nose at his underlings and barking out orders. Even with the protective badge shielding his emotions from me, the bullyish vibe he gives off makes my essence cringe.

I force myself to dart toward him anyway.

Because I don't want to put myself in easy range of those

blocky arms, I materialize perched on the hood of a nearby tank. Maybe that'll catch me a little more attention too.

I spread my arms so there's as much of me to draw attention as possible. "You have to call off the bombs! No one wants what's going to happen. It'll be an even bigger disaster."

The colonel spins toward me with a sneering curl of his lip. "Or maybe you're only protesting this much because you know how much of a disaster it'll be for *you* and the other monsters. We're going ahead. Everyone's going to see that it took *humans* to solve this problem, not freakish things like you."

His expression is so flinty I think I'd get farther arguing with a mountain. My heart sinks, but I hold on to my resolve.

If we can't talk him out of the operation, we'll just have to gum up the works.

Where are these bombs they're going to be dropping anyway? Even from my new, higher vantage point, I don't see any sign of massive explosives. Not that I'm totally sure what bombs big enough to level a city look like, but I don't spot anything here that wasn't in the camp yesterday.

Surely something powerful enough to blow up skyscrapers would be at least a little noticeable?

Hueber starts to stride toward me, and I decide I'm not getting anything useful out of him one way or another. I dive back into the shadows and zip away in pursuit of a likelier helper.

I just need to find one soldier who's not totally on board with this plan. One little quiver of doubt I can speak to.

My first thought is of Major Yin, but his cabin is already in pieces. I don't see his smooth, slim form anywhere nearby.

I don't stop weaving through the shadows until I stumble on a woman in soldier gear near the edge of camp.

Her emotions reach me in a waft of sauerkraut-sour uncertainty. Not my most favorite meal, but exactly what hits the spot right now.

And she's not wearing a badge. That's a good sign.

So I won't give her a heart attack, I step back into the physical world on the far side of a truck and ease around it. "Excuse me? I could use your help."

The soldier blinks at me. Recognition dawns in her eyes, and her stance stiffens, but she doesn't call out in alarm. Her voice stays quiet. "What?"

I hug myself, giving up my attempt at toughness to show the real nerves underneath. "I heard there are bombs coming. Are they already here in the camp? What if they explode before we can get out?"

The woman's gaze twitches. "They won't be on the ground here. They're coming from the base up north—"

Her mouth snaps shut around those words, but she's said enough.

I bob my head. "Thank you for letting me know."

I slip into the shadows once more, just as a much more forceful presence looms on me.

"So," Rollick says in a terse voice that still manages to be a little wry. "You're already chasing bombs. I should have figured."

My defiance surges back to the surface. "We have to stop them."

"I agree. And you've conveniently determined *where* we need to stop them. I've heard enough myself to know which base she means. It's a two-hour drive from here, so we'd better get going."

While Rollick calls for one of his assistants to bring the largest van around, I hustle around our trailers, popping back into physical form. I nearly crash right into Gracie, who's just coming around the corner.

She blinks at me, wide-eyed. "I heard—the army is going ahead with bombing the city?"

The acidic flavor of her fear mingles with my own queasiness. We've been keeping my old friend up to date on what's happening around the city—the last news I passed on was about our public appeal on TV.

So much for that.

The current development defies even my immense ability for finding a positive spin. I swallow hard. "Yeah. We're going out to the base where they're prepping the bombs to see if we can stop them."

Gracie's posture firms with a lift of her chin. "I want to come with you."

A different sort of fear flashes through my nerves. "It won't be safe—the soldiers will have guns—they're not going to be happy to see us."

"That doesn't matter. I came out here to help, and I haven't managed to do that yet. Maybe they'll listen more if you've got a few humans there agreeing with you."

That's why Jonah will come too, even though he's just as vulnerable to bullets as Gracie is. I'd never say no to him… so it wouldn't be fair for me to try to leave her out either, would it?

The van roars into view with several shadowkind emerging around it. Rollick appears and waves his arm toward the vehicle. "Let's go! We don't have time to waste."

I glance at Gracie. "All right. Come on."

Other than me and Gracie, "we" turns out to be my mates, Sorsha and her men, the shadowbloods, and a couple of dozen shadowkind associates. We all cram into the back of the van, those of us who can stay in the shadows doing so or we'd be pressed in tighter than sardines.

I find myself next to Vim's bristly presence. When we were fellow students at the academy, she seemed to take offense to anything I said, no matter how well-meaning, so I ignore her and peer out the back window instead.

Cars are starting to pull Rollick's trailers farther away from the city. My heart flipflops, and I pull myself out of the shadows to speak. "We're leaving the camp too—I mean, permanently?"

Rollick takes a dismissive tone. "Better safe than sorry." Then he turns to the assistant who's driving the van. "Pedal to the floor. Fast as the engine can handle. If we get cops on our tail, Ruse can charm them friendly again."

In tandem with the incubus's chuckle, the engine roars and the van hurtles forward.

Sorsha leans back on one of the van's benches and stretches out her legs. "Shouldn't we come up with a plan of attack? I don't think marching up to the base and asking them nicely not to bomb anyone is going to work."

No? That's a real shame. People don't put enough value in politeness these days.

Despite my disappointment in that fact, I know she's right. I'm not sure what *would* work on these military-focused humans, though. I don't even know what a "base" is exactly, in this context. Will we have to go running through dim hallways with beeping doors like in a hundred different action movies?

Gracie's mouth twists. "We have to *try* to talk to them. But… yeah, I don't know if that'll be enough."

"They'll be using planes," Jonah says. "Dropping the bombs from above. If we can mess with the controls so the planes won't even take off…"

Rollick shakes his head from where he's sitting on the front passenger seat, turned sideways to face us in the back. "They'll just call more planes in. We can't keep sabotaging them forever."

Riva sighs and swipes her hand over her pale face. "It'd buy us time, at least."

Dominic nods. "More time for public pressure to change the army's mind?"

I exchange an optimistic glance with Gracie. "That could help!"

"If it works." Rollick pauses, his silence grim. "The army might get on with things before we have the chance to find out. I don't normally advocate for coming in with a bang, but… it could be better if Sorsha and I simply burn the whole place down."

As Gracie winces, my whole body balks at the suggestion. "No! If we blow *them* up, they'll only want to blow us up more."

Vim emerges into physical form next to me, aiming a typical scowl my way. "You're still such a wimp."

Jonah frowns at her. "Peri's put herself in danger dozens of times in the past few months to help the rest of us. And she's not wrong."

He turns to Rollick. "Human opinions on the shadowkind are pretty mixed at the moment. Peri leaking the bomb plan actually seems to have swayed more of them to our side. If it comes out that we were responsible for burning down a whole military base—we're not going to have time to evacuate the soldiers…"

Sorsha sighs. She snaps her fingers, making a spark dance above them. "I don't like it either. But if it's that or blow this rift and its muck all over the place so millions of people could die… They can't blame us if they don't know it *was* us."

Riva raises her eyebrows. "You don't think they'd figure it out? They know we're against the plan. Entire military bases don't tend to burn down randomly. I think they'll put the pieces together no matter how subtle we are. Not that infernos are remotely subtle."

"We might set off the bombs too," I point out. "It'd look like we want to bomb *them*. That'll only make people like Colonel Hueber more determined to get back at us. Revenge makes humans do even crazier things than usual." At least, if their TV shows are anything to go by.

Gracie lets out a strained chuckle. "I can confirm that from personal experience."

Vim folds her arms over her chest, her attention fixed on me. "What do you think we should do then, if you're so smart?"

I open my mouth and close it again. I don't have a definite alternate plan. I just know this one feels wrong, all the way down to my bones.

Taking a deep breath, I focus on what I'm sure of. "For their plan to work, they need the planes, and they need the soldiers who'll fly those planes to think bombing is a good idea. The people in this base haven't been dealing with shadowkind directly—they shouldn't be wearing the badges. I can calm their fears and make them care about the horrible consequences. Mirage can distract them with illusions. You all have powers that could block them and challenge them rather than hurting them, don't you?"

"Risky," Rollick says with a tsk of his tongue.

"Do you really think it's more risky than getting into a bomb war with the humans? What if they bring out bigger ones next time? What if they convince the other countries with these weird rifts to bomb those too, and the shadows spread all over the whole world, and—"

My throat chokes up with the enormity of what I'm picturing. Just a big mess of toxic shadows, ones no kind of being can happily survive in. A big bath of misery without any warm towels to step out into.

Rollick's expression turns even more somber. I think he's picturing misery bathtubs too.

"We might not have a choice," he says finally. "We'll give the more peaceful approach our best shot, but if those planes take off with the bombs, all bets are off."

I nod, understanding his reasoning but unable to dislodge the lump from my throat.

~

A HEAVY FENCE surrounds the military base, but that only means Sorsha and the shadowbloods will hang back in the van for now. The rest of us can rush through the shadows into the compound unobstructed. Crag and Thorn carry Jonah and Gracie over the wall, with Mirage hiding them in an illusion until they're ready to make their human appeals.

I spot a row of jets beyond the low beige building with a flurry of activity going on around them. Panic flashes through my essence.

Without a second to lose, I sprint toward them.

My anxiety twists through me, straining with the need to spill out the darkness of my fears. I clamp those uncomfortable feelings down as well as I can and reach for my sense of light.

I have the support of my mates around me, their faith in me. I have the trust of all the humans who believed in my warning and have tried to stop this worse catastrophe from happening. Even these soldiers—they only want to protect their people and end the disaster. They just don't know how.

I leap out by the jets with a wash of warm light, bright enough to be noticed but not to burn. Heads all around the yard jerk toward me.

Alongside the glow, I project all the soothing, hopeful feelings I can toward the uniformed humans. "Let's not make a mistake. We can find a better way to protect Jackson City. Blowing it up definitely won't work. It'd be so sad to destroy all those pretty buildings, wouldn't it? You don't actually like the idea of ruining something beautiful. You want to make the world *more* beautiful."

I suspect the soldiers have never thought of their goals quite that way before, but my supernatural influence sinks in. The tension fades from some of the faces. A few do look abruptly sad.

Jonah and Gracie step into view on either side of me. Jonah lifts his voice. "We're humans like you, and we don't want to see all this destruction either."

Gracie's clenched hands wobble at her sides, but she speaks with total conviction. "We don't want to see other people like us hurt in the fallout."

Mirage joins us, sending an illusion of the city into the air—much brighter than it is right now, with no cloak of murk, and possibly better designed than the actual architecture. It's okay to fudge the details a little for a good cause, right?

"We're going to bring it back to how it should be, without blowing anything up!" he calls out.

"That's right." I propel another wave of reassurance over our audience, and Mirage makes the city buildings outright shine as if they're made of crystal, the Diamond Victory Tower living up to its name. "You can be heroes, restoring everyone's homes to how they're meant to be."

Faint smiles curve some of the soldiers' lips. My pulse thumps faster with a flicker of excitement.

But several of the uniformed figures haul themselves away from their companions. One clamps his hands over his ears; another starts humming as if trying to tune me out.

They dash toward the jets like they mean to take off right now.

29

Hail

At the sight of the soldiers sprinting toward the plane's cockpits, all I can think is, *Fuck, no.*

I'm not letting these assholes screw up Peri's peacemaking efforts—even if I don't particularly want peace with them myself. Every particle of her being vibrates with the certainty that our situation will go to hell if those jets manage to take off, regardless of what happens after.

And I trust her more than even myself.

I shoot a layer of ice across the paved ground. Time for a little slip-and-slide.

The unsuspecting soldiers skid on the suddenly slick ground. A couple fall to their hands and knees, others onto their asses. I can't restrain an upward tick of my mouth.

Serves the pricks right.

Peri is still calling out in her persistently sweet voice, and other magical effects warble past me, but I focus on my own powers. I turn the ice as slick as I can make it. The soldiers flail around as they try to stand up.

But I can't keep them down forever. One and then another manage to shove to their feet, stiffening their legs against the glass-smooth surface.

Fine. If what's on the ground isn't enough to stop them, I'll just have to throw some obstacles into the air too.

A gust of snow and frigid wind whips from me to whirl around the soldiers. The dense fall of snowflakes obscures their vision and turns them into a blur to even my eyes.

But they keep pushing through it. The assholes are fucking stubborn, I'll give them that much.

Why can't they be that determined about something that'll actually help us?

I'd blast them with even more snow, but outright freezing them would go against Peri's insistence that we don't hurt them—at least, not too badly. Where the hell is that brute of a basilisk shifter? Why isn't he toppling them?

I risk a glance around in time to see Raze roaring as he focuses his attention on a horde of soldiers barging toward us from the nearby buildings. His stance rigid, he aims his gaze at one and another, knocking them unconscious before they can finish raising their massive guns.

Okay, he's stopping our Cream Puff from being battered with bullets. I can't say his priorities are misguided.

Mirage leaps by with a swirl of his foxy tails through the air, and the image comes back to me of the glittering illusion he created minutes ago. Inspiration lights in my head.

"Fox boy," I holler. "Make my snow sparkle!"

The fox shifter doesn't appear to mind being bossed around. He spins toward me and peers at the blizzard I whip up even faster around the trudging soldiers.

The snowflakes flare with a sudden intense gleam. The

soldiers stumble and swing their arms as if trying to clear it, but it's obvious they're totally blinded now.

With wallops of wind—forceful but not bone-breaking—I shove them around on the ice they're still standing on until they're no longer facing the planes.

Shouts of consternation and yelps of fear bounce between them. They take a few straining steps in one direction, then in the other, squinting against the shimmering snow.

It's perfect, until some jerk I can't see starts hollering directions from another vantage point. "Kirkland, fifty degrees to your left then straight ahead. Alverez, you're going the right way now, just keep at it!"

The soldiers start making progress toward the jets again. Damn it.

I grit my teeth. I need a strategy that'll stop them in their tracks without literally freezing them in place.

With a wave of my arm, I send walls of solid ice shooting up around the soldiers. For good measure, I surround the jets too, walling them off from their prospective pilots.

That wuss of a naiad who Peri befriended, the one we always called "the Drip," sees what I'm doing—and it turns out she's not any more of a wuss than Peri is. Which maybe I should have expected at this point.

Setting her face with concentration, Fen extends her hands and tosses out not just drips but a whole torrent of water that rises against my walls. Catching on to her intent, I freeze the deluge as soon as it rushes into place, making my walls twice as thick.

The naiad flashes a grin at me, and a flicker of friendly warmth kindles in my chest despite all the wintery power I'm tossing around.

This is how I dreamed about my life being, isn't it? Supporting my fellow shadowkind, working together with them to create a place in this world we'd all be happy in.

Okay, so I didn't dream about pursuing that goal by hemming in soldiers on a military base, but it's progress all the same.

There are shadowkind who'll look to me for an example of what to do. Shadowkind who'll jump to help me the second I ask. That's all I really need to see my goals through, however exactly the safe haven I pictured comes into existence in the end.

I enjoy that sense of satisfaction for about five seconds before everything goes to hell again.

The soldier pilots have rifles too. A blare of gunfire rings out, and my icy walls start to crack.

Fuck.

Scowling, I push even more ice in to fill the cracks. Fen sloshes out more water for me to freeze, but her arms tremble as if she's on the verge of running dry. I'm not sure she's ever pushed her powers even this far before.

It's not enough. More cracks spider through the glistening walls with every passing moment and every new blast. Shards start to fragment off.

Any second now, my prison will shatter completely.

Anger twists inside me, and for an instant all I can see is those razor-sharp shards whipping around in the wind and spearing the assholes straight through. Tearing them apart like the men in the woods did to my fae mentor all those years ago. Splashing blood and gristle all across the icy yard.

They'd deserve it, wouldn't they? They want to blow up not just the rift but everything that's come out of it, including us.

I suck in a breath, and a ball of guilt sinks in my gut like a stone.

No.

I know that isn't the right way—not just because Peri

would be upset, but because I've seen how hanging on to resentment ruins everything.

I almost lost her, the best thing I've ever had in my life, because I couldn't see past the animosity that was eating away at me.

How much more awful will humans get if this situation devolves into a real war?

As the soldiers pummel the frozen walls, breaking off whole chunks now, I yank my gaze to the jets.

They're the real problem. If they can't get in the air, they can't drop any bombs.

And no one's going to get as upset about broken planes as they will about broken skulls.

My awareness of our environment prickles with an uneasy tremor. The materials that make up those aircraft started with natural sources, but they've been warped to human ends.

All the same… The fuel that fills the tank deep inside the steel-and-aluminum shell is a liquid like any other.

Every liquid has a freezing point.

My hands clench at my sides. I narrow all my attention onto the pockets of fuel I can sense in each of the jets.

I will wave after wave of cold into the planes. Sharpen the chill more and more, well past the point where water would be rock solid.

Not quite enough. Again. Again.

An ache forms behind my eyes and across the top of my head. Every inch of my frame has stiffened with the effort I'm exerting. But I'm not finished.

If I can just see this through…

Freeze. Freeze. *Freeze.*

My head feels as if it's cracking right open, but I taste the moment when the fuel goes solid. The tanks crack too, unprepared for that kind of pressure at such a low temperature. The massive metal bodies groan.

More shouts are bombarding me from all sides. My head is spinning.

I open my mouth, not even sure what I'd want to say, and all that comes out is a groan.

My legs give. I sag over, anticipating the smack against the ground in a distant sort of way.

It doesn't come. My body hits two solid arms instead.

Raze grips me, his voice turning growly as he speaks to someone—Peri? "I've got him! He's still alive."

Yes. The blare of pain in my head can confirm that, but it's overwhelming me.

As my consciousness fades into blackness, the last thing I hear is Mirage's wry tone roughened with a note of urgency. "Oh, look. Colonel Hubris has arrived."

30

Periwinkle

The squeal of the base's gate opening brings my head snapping around. Four boxy, desert-tan SUVs are pulling into the compound. Colonel Hueber's dull brown face hovers behind one windshield, his expression hard as steel.

I might not be able to taste his emotions, but I'm pretty sure he's not happy about recent developments.

He shoves open the passenger door before the vehicle has quite parked and pushes out into the yard at the edge of the chaos. Several soldiers spill out of his SUV and another; a bunch of people in civilian clothes emerge from the other two.

They aren't just regular civilians. I spot the gleam of metal-woven nets and the handles of hunter whips. A few of the faces I recognize from among the sorcerers who gathered in the city.

This is not good at all.

"Wait!" I cry out, throwing my hands to either side of me.

A blaze of light washes over the entire yard, bright enough to leave spots in my vision but not enough to actually hurt. At least, no one yelps or whimpers, which I'll take as a good sign.

The clamor of hollering soldiers and warbling powers dies down. Colonel Hueber strides a few steps forward but then stops with his soldiers flanking him.

I think... everyone *is* actually waiting to see what I'll say.

They probably won't wait for very long.

I stop closer to Hail's slack body with automatic protectiveness, though I'm not sure what I could do for him that Raze can't where he's poised over the winter fae.

My voice reverberates up my throat. "We don't want to fight. We're trying to prevent an even bigger disaster. Please, just *listen.* Can't you see how exploding the rift and all the toxic shadows that've come out of it could just blast the stuff all over the place?"

Hueber's lips draw back in a snarl. "I can see that it's no good listening to what you say about your own mess. You *things* would do whatever you can to protect yourselves. Is attacking our base supposed to prove your good intentions?"

"We didn't hurt anyone," I retort. "We're only stopping them from flying off with the bombs. They're a lot more likely to die carrying out your orders than staying here."

"So you'd like us to think." Hueber motions to the people around him. "Gentlemen?"

There are a few women in the crowd of sorcerers and hunters too, but I guess Hueber isn't worried about accuracy. They all jerk to attention anyway.

The hunters brandish their gleaming weapons. The

sorcerers open their mouths with a chorus of deep breaths that makes the hairs on the back of my neck stand on end.

A warning bursts out of me. "Don't let them use their magic!"

I didn't need to point out the obvious. Raze has already lunged forward from where he cushioned Hail's fall.

His eyes narrowing, he aims his deadly black glare at the crowd of sorcerers.

One topples over unconscious before any of them even manage to speak. With the first sorcerous syllable passing over their lips, another crumples to the ground.

My pulse jitters with the sense that it's not enough, but Raze isn't alone. A sudden spurt of water forms in the air and smacks into a few of the open mouths, leaving the sorcerers sputtering instead of ensorcering. Fen lets out a timid but bright crow of victory.

Nearby, Vim has hunched her shoulders with an impression of strain. Beneath a couple of the other sorcerers, the layer of asphalt erupts. They fall on their asses amid puffs of dry dirt.

And Jonah's voice is ringing out louder than we could hear any of the farther-off sorcerers. The power resonating through his supernatural words tingles through my bones, uncomfortable but steadying at the same time.

Don't listen to any other sorcery, he's commanding, like the defensive orders he gave our small team months ago when we were investigating the rift up north and stumbled on my former captor. *Ignore all other magical commands.*

I don't know how long that instruction will last against a full force of opposing sorcerers, but he's put all his strength into the attempt. The power of it crackles across my tongue like smoky chipotle.

As the sorcerers fall into disarray, the hunters march toward us. Whips lash through the air.

A few of them are holding those strange guns I noticed before—one fires at Raze before I have a chance to yelp a warning.

Raze dodges to the side, but he pulls Hail with him, and that slows him down. A projectile splats into his shoulder like a glittering paintball.

Whatever's in the stuff, it's obviously not friendly to shadowkind. Raze roars, a burst of essence puffing up from the spot the noxious paintball hit him.

It looks as if the substance is eating right into his flesh. Pain blares through our bond.

My throat constricts, but I have to do whatever I can to make sure that doesn't happen again.

"I'll try to help him!" Gracie calls to me, and sprints over to where Raze is crouched.

Girding myself, I swish my hands through the air. More light pours out of them. Our enemies stumble in momentary blindness.

With a battle cry, Sorrel charges into the hunters' midst in centaur form. Her well-muscled haunches heave one and another aside before their weapons can do more than graze her.

Flames leap up around the military force, penning them in. I spot Sorsha coming to stand on the top of the base's wall, her phoenix wings flickering like streaks of fire from her back.

She isn't incinerating our opponents, though, only caging them. She's trying to keep the peace, like I asked.

Colonel Hueber's face has reddened for reasons I don't think have anything to do with the fiery heat. As if he's annoyed that Sorsha now appears to outrank him, he hefts himself onto the hood of one of the SUVs so he can bellow at all of us from a little higher up than before.

"This is an act of war! You'll all stand down, or we'll bomb the bunch of you to smithereens too!"

I thought that was already the plan, not a new development. He's threatening us with what he was going to do anyway? I'm shaking in my boots.

Not that I'm wearing boots. Mary-janes go much better with my dress.

A tremor of supernatural energy passes through the air, and any hairs on my body that weren't already standing up get with the program fast. Is Rollick about to make an appearance—and make good on his offer to simply level this base and all the humans in it?

Before I can worry much about that, an unexpectedly familiar figure strides out of the base's nearest building.

The sunlight gleams off Major Yin's short black hair. He lifts his chin and folds his arms over his chest, staring at his boss from across the distance.

I had no idea the major was even here. Was *he* leading the bombing mission, even though he seemed like he might be open to hearing our side?

Or maybe he just wanted to stay close to the operation so he'd have more of a say.

"We need to stand down," he shouts to the colonel, sounding not at all pleased with his superior officer. "I've witnessed the entire confrontation. The shadowkind are telling the truth. They've avoided doing any major harm. No lives lost, even though it's clear these beings could easily have slaughtered us. We need to hear them out in good faith."

"Good faith?" Hueber lets out a strangled-sounding guffaw. "They've frozen the base *and* set it on fire."

"Only to stop us from going through with the bombing," Yin says. "They're pulling their punches. If it matters that much to them to avoid hurting us even when we're trying to destroy part of their world, I think we should assume they're telling the truth about the bombs too. They're trying to prevent us from hurting *ourselves*."

The colonel waves a meaty hand through the air in a dismissive gesture. "You've been brainwashed, Major. Get the fuck out of my sight and consider yourself relieved of duty."

Yin's jaw flexes with tension, but he stands his ground. "No, sir. I believe you're the one who's violated your duty to the American people. We swore to defend our nation with—"

"Yes," Hueber interrupts in a caustic tone. "We swore to defend them, and you're siding with the monsters who want to tear us apart. Now scram before I skip straight from court-marshalling you to telling my men to open fire."

A pang of protest shoots through me—but Major Yin must have been prepared for the colonel's reaction. Resignation tightens his expression and prickles through his emotions.

"I tried to give you a chance to do the right thing. *Another* chance, after you've thrown away the opportunities the shadowkind already gave you."

"What the fuck are you—"

"I'm relieving *you* of duty," Yin says, and gestures toward Raze, whose shoulder is still trickling essence but who's managed to scrape the worst of the paintball stuff off with Gracie's help.

Understanding gleams in my mate's eyes. He fixes his gaze on the colonel.

Hueber is still blustering. "Now look here—"

He never gets to finish his last threat. His eyes roll upward, and the rest of him sags down.

A couple of the nearby soldiers scramble to catch the colonel before he can slide right off the hood of the vehicle. The hunters glance between him and Major Yin, shifting on their feet uneasily behind the lines of dancing flames that still hem them in.

One of them points at Hueber. "We took our orders from him."

Yin draws his slim frame up straighter. He doesn't cut as imposing a figure as his—former?—boss, but he exudes plenty of authority all the same. "The colonel isn't giving any more orders today. I'm the highest ranking officer currently conscious on this base. Stand down and leave these beings alone." His gaze flicks to Sorsha. "And maybe our shadowkind helpers could simmer down too?"

Sorsha shrugs. Her flaming wings and the barriers of fire waver away at the same moment.

I brace myself, but Hueber's force of soldiers, hunters, and sorcerers stay where they are. I get the impression a lot of them would like to turn tail and run, but no one wants to break formation first.

Hail turns his head and mumbles, finally coming to. I bend down next to him and touch his cheek.

His eyelids flutter open. "Planes still on the ground?"

"Yep. You did it." A poignant smile tugs at my lips. I look over at the jets. "And they're leaking something out of their bellies, so I don't think they'll be flying anywhere anytime soon."

The winter fae struggles to push himself upright. "There'll be more. Too many fucking planes. Too many bombs. Stupid humans."

We'll just hope none of the humans standing around us heard that last part of his muttering.

Gracie sputters a laugh and swipes at her face. "He isn't wrong."

He isn't. Yin just bought us a reprieve, but how long will it last? For all we know, some other colonel is arranging a different bombing run at a different base right now.

We can't go running across the countryside, sabotaging every fighter jet in existence. And even if we could, it wouldn't solve the real problem of that warped rift still spewing its toxicity over the city and into the shadow realm on the other side.

Nothing will be fixed until we fix *that* catastrophe.

But how? It could take me years on my own or with just my mates. When I tried to bring more shadowkind into the mix to ramp up the effect of my power, we just distracted each other.

Because no one felt safe. Because we were worrying about the humans interrupting with their weapons at any moment.

"Hey!" Sorsha calls over from her perch on the wall and motions to the far side. "There's a news van over here that followed the colonel and them from the city. Anyone want to give them a good story?"

I don't think the phoenix meant her words this way, but her question sparks a strange quiver that races through my veins.

A good story.

That's what we need. Something that'll comfort people, make the humans feel secure so *we* can feel secure around them rather than worrying that they'll lash out.

Colonel Hueber's remark from just a few hours ago floats up from my memory: *Everyone's going to see that it took* humans *to solve this problem.*

I don't like how he sneered at us shadowkind. I don't like his strategy for "solving" the problem. But that doesn't mean there wasn't a kernel of truth in what he said.

Even though I realized the rift wanted to form some kind of cohesion with the mortal realm, I was still only counting on shadowkind to help me. How did I miss this before?

When we fight, the rift acts up more. If we could really

work together like we did with Gracie right here, but on a much larger scale…

I hustle forward, ignoring the panicked thudding of my heart and the familiar ache that's formed in my feet and ankles. "I'll talk to them. I have an important message."

No one moves to stop me. I guess I've established myself as the main shadowkind spokesperson inadvertently.

Oh, well. The humans watching their TVs can't be too scared of little old me, can they?

As I dart past the gate, the reporter poised beyond it stiffens. He and his camerawoman are staked out a careful distance from the wall but with their devices at the ready.

Despite his initial burst of nerves, he holds his microphone toward me. "What's going on in there? Did the mon—I mean, the 'shadowkind' destroy the base?"

"Not at all," I say with a cheery smile. "We stopped the planes from taking off with the bombs, but everyone and every building inside is perfectly okay." I won't mention the leaky jets. "And now we're going to get rid of this messy rift our way—a way that won't hurt anyone—once and for all. But we're going to need your help."

The camerawoman steps closer, maybe zooming in on my face.

The reporter's eyebrows leap up. "What do you mean?"

I aim my smile at the camera, picturing all those people who are watching this broadcast, worrying about what will become of their world. Who maybe, like me, like Gracie, are wishing they could contribute.

I've spent years trying to bring happiness to everyone, wanting to see them safe rather than hurting them. But isn't there an even deeper joy in facing the danger side by side and finding a way to tackle it?

"My power can calm and thin the darkness that's fallen over the city," I say. "But I can only do so much on my own.

The more people I've got working with me, the larger an effect I can have. So please, anyone who wants to see this disaster end and know they helped save the world, please come join us outside Jackson City as soon as you can. All are welcome."

By the time I'm finished speaking, the reporter's eyebrows have nearly reached his hairline. He says a quick wrap-up to the camera and then lowers his microphone. "You really need as many people as possible?"

I beam at him. "Absolutely. Will you come too?"

Before he can answer, Major Yin's voice reaches me from where he's approached the gate. "Whatever you're going to do, you'd better be quick about it. The top brass will already be on their way—and most of them believe in the bombs."

31

Periwinkle

The first part of my plan is to zip back to the rift as fast as the van's engine will carry us. My plan did not account for traffic jams.

The city with its draping of murk has just come into view in the distance when the van slows to a crawl. I slip through the shadows to a nook on the driver's seat where I can see out the front windshield.

The stretch of pavement ahead of us is packed with cars. More are pulling onto the highway from a crossroad farther along.

I stare for a few moments before my mind kicks back into gear. I materialize next to Rollick's seat. "What's going on? It'll take forever to get to the city now."

The demon shoots me a baleful look. "I believe this is your doing. You asked for people to come—they're coming. There are only so many routes into the city."

"They won't be able to help if I'm not there!"

"Maybe you should have thought of that before you put out your call from a hundred miles away."

I can't stop myself from grimacing at him, but my pulse thumps with more anxiety than annoyance. Major Yin said we didn't have much time. What will the "top brass" do once they get here?

If it involves bigger bombs, then we're in deep trouble.

Sorsha's hellhound-shifting partner—Omen—emerges into the physical world behind me. "I saw something half a mile back that might help. How many beings do we need to get to the city for your plan to work?"

I swallow hard. "As many as we can manage. But especially me and my mates. And Gracie."

The more humans we have involved from the start, the easier it should be to encourage others to join in.

Omen glances over at Jonah, who's sitting on one of the benches with a similarly tense expression, and lets out a gruff sigh. "Let's give it a shot. I'll be back in ten or so minutes. Hold tight."

It's not like we have much choice unless the van suddenly sprouts wings so it can fly over the traffic.

Actually that would be a really handy feature. Why haven't humans implemented it yet?

Omen vanishes, but I remain in physical form, gripping the seat back and peering at the cars ahead of us. "At least a lot of people want to help?"

Rollick gives a short guffaw. "Let's hope that is what they're coming for and they're not here to slam us for asking."

We creep forward a few inches at a time. At this rate, we'll be back at the city next year. But it has only been about ten minutes when a whirring engine sounds beyond the windows.

Omen pulls over to the shoulder of the highway steering

what looks like a miniature jeep. Its overlarge wheels bounce over the dips and bumps on the unpaved ground.

"We're borrowing an ATV," he calls over to us. "There's room for the two humans to perch behind me. Everyone else needs to stay in shadow form. Find whatever dark hollows you can. I figure we can fit more than a dozen if you squeeze tight."

My heart lifts. I glance around at the van's shadowy interior. This means we need to leave the shadowbloods behind for now, but most of our other allies can come along. "Let's go!"

I dip into the shadows and sidle up against Hail, who's totally awake now but whose presence still feels a little groggy. He leans into my touch with a waft of affection before we propel ourselves side by side across the gap between the vehicles and into the patch of darkness overtop one of the ATV's wheels.

A flurry of fellow shadowkind dart after us and settle into their own spots, cramming close. Jonah and Gracie scramble out of the van on their feet and dash over to Omen.

As our sorcerer and my former captor's daughter squish onto the seat, the hellhound shifter guns the engine. "Hold on tight!"

The little vehicle roars forward. It bounces across the uneven terrain, going not quite as fast as the van would on the road but moving a heck of a lot more swiftly than anyone's driving the highway right now.

Thankfully, our position in the shadows cushions us from most of the movement. I hate to think how Jonah's and Gracie's insides must be getting shaken and stirred.

Squished close to me in the darkness, Fen lets out a nervous giggle. "We're really going to do this."

To my surprise, it's Vim who answers, her voice still rough but less snarky than usual. "Yeah, I think we are." Her attention shifts to me with a sweet-and-sour mix of admiration and shame. "You were pretty incredible back there, Peri. If you think you know how to fix the rift… I want to see what you can do."

Despite my fears, a spark of joy lights in me. "What we all can do," I say. "It won't work without every one of us."

The ATV tears past the line of jammed cars toward the remains of the refugee camp, just scraps of a settlement after most of the evacuees have been relocated. I wonder how many of the people arriving here now came from the city to begin with.

It's their home. They have the most to gain by saving it. But from what I've seen, humans have a large capacity for looking out for each other, even if they're not always great at acting on it.

Rows of cars are already parked all along the sides of the highway in the camp and the smaller roads that branch off around the edges of the city. Omen brings us to a stop by the cluster of trailers Rollick had his people drive farther afield.

One of Rollick's assistants is standing outside one of them, wringing her hands. "What's happening? Where did all these people come from?"

As we sped back to the city, my certainty about what we're going to do—what *I'm* going to do—has grown. Resolve rises up in my chest as rich and potent as a perfectly glazed ham.

I materialize beside her. "I'm going to balance out the murk. Get the rift back into harmony with both realms so it stops messing things up. But I can only do that if all these people work with me."

I glance back at my companions who've disembarked behind me. "Let's round them up. Gracie, Jonah, I need you two especially. They might feel better seeing you with me, all normal-human-like."

Gracie snorts, but she hurries alongside me and Jonah as we head toward the gathering crowd of humans. "If you can call me 'normal.'"

The assistant follows us, not looking much less distressed than before. "The darkness over the city—it started fluctuating a couple of hours ago. Wavering back and forth like… like the wind was rippling through it. Except I think it came more out than in. It might have expanded over more territory."

Even as she finishes speaking, another of those currents flows through the murky area. Just like she said, the deluge of shadows wobbles and sways, out and in, out and in… but definitely a little more in the 'out' direction.

My lungs constrict. If that development started a couple of hours ago—that was when we were confronting the soldiers about the bombs. Did our fight rile the rift up again even though we were far away?

The murk might end up sloshing all over the countryside even if no bombs fall. Unless we can clean up the mess right now.

The nearest bunch of humans turns toward us. There must be several hundred gathered amid the few remaining tents, with more spilling out of newly parked cars every second.

A brief wave of dizziness rushes through me at the thought of all these people listening to me. I draw my spine straight against my nerves.

There were probably *millions* watching me on the TV. This is just talking to them without a screen. And they all *want* to listen to me.

I turn to my mates, who've slipped out of the shadows around me. "Mirage, can you project my voice far enough so that everyone can hear it?"

The fox shifter salutes me. "On the ball, helping you stand tall. I can handle it, Rainbow."

To make my short stature more visible, I clamber onto a crate someone left behind. Most of the crowd turns to look. Some people point and nudge each other, maybe recognizing me from TV.

I've become a celebrity. At what point do I start coming up with signature perfumes and clothing lines?

Definitely not today while we have a much bigger problem to worry about.

I lift my hands for attention and project my voice, trusting Mirage's illusions to spread it across the terrain before me.

"Thank you all so much for coming to help. I know the key to fixing this rift and the others like it. All it and the creatures it's warped have wanted is to merge with your world, to find a place where they belong, to be a part of the mortal realm. They've just been going about it in… a very destructive way, because no one knew how to offer a proper welcome. We're going to do that now, set the rift at ease and show it that it doesn't need to twist or drown anyone."

A voice hollers from the middle of the crowd. "What does that even mean? What are we supposed to do?"

I motion them toward the nearby factories. "We're going to surround the city by the edge of the murky area. I need you to focus on the most happy, friendly feelings you can. Think about your friends, your family, the people you love." Remembering my own confession of love to my men a few weeks ago, a pang resonates through my throat. "Both the pleasant parts and the painful parts that turned out okay in the end. Any feeling that brought you closer to the people in your life."

Murmurs pass through the crowd. Probably my explanation sounds too woo-woo for a lot of them. Maybe it'd have gone over better if I'd shown up with flowers woven into my hair and an embroidered shawl so I looked like some kind of mystic.

Gracie kicks over another crate and jumps up beside me. "Peri knows what she's talking about. She's an expert on emotions. Let's give it a try—what can it hurt? It's not like thinking about the people you care about is some huge ask, is it?"

Some of the muttering people now look abashed. They turn and start walking toward the city.

More of my shadowkind companions have emerged around me.

"What do you need us to do, Peri?" Fen asks. "Just join in?"

I wave toward the humans. "Mingle with them. Remind them of what they need to be doing and keep them on track. Encourage any other shadowkind you see to join in too." I glance around at all of the beings with me. "There's no need to be nervous. *These* humans trust us. They want to help. We're all safe."

They nod, but a little uncertainty flavors their determination.

I can't be there raising all of their spirits while I'm focusing on the rift.

My attention slides to my mates. The tension in my chest tightens, but I know what we have to do. A lighter twinge inside tells me it'll turn out right.

"Jonah, Mirage, Raze, Hail, I need you to spread out around the city so we're surrounding the whole thing. Like we did with Viscera, but on a larger scale. You'll know how to keep everyone's spirits up for me better than anyone else." I catch Mirage's bright eyes. "And if you can keep projecting my voice all around as much as you can, that would be perfect."

Raze frowns. "If we get that far away…"

I touch his arm. "It's not *that* far. And I can tell… it'll be okay now. Because there are no doubts left between us. Nothing shaking up our love. Our bonds won't hurt me, because you'll be there *for* me."

Jonah's expression is still solemn, but he tips his head in acknowledgment. "We should get moving. We'll need to fill in the people who've arrived at the other ends of the city."

A sly grin curves Mirage's lips. "They heard Peri's instructions too. I made sure of it."

Well, that might have confused people who couldn't even see who was speaking more than it guided them, but at least it's a start.

The group of us surges toward the city. As we get closer, my long-time companions veer away from me.

I watch them drift around and through the crowd of humans with a tug of loss. But enough gratitude and pride is welling up inside me to overcome my worries.

I brought all these beings together, shadowkind and mortal. I'm showing that we *can* tackle our problems together. That there's a place for all of us in the world, a way to coexist.

Now I just have to convince the rift of that before it decides to up its takeover-by-murk to another level.

I join the swarm of humans near the factories, which are now completely draped in shadows. Seeing how far the deluge has grown in just the past couple of days, a lump clogs my throat, but I gird myself against the discomfort.

It all stops here. We're going to show it a better way.

A furry body brushes my ankles. I look down to see Falkor curling around my legs, peering up at me with those big puppy-ish eyes that won me over to begin with.

He's ready to follow whatever orders I give. Even the lesser creatures among us are giving their all.

I lift my head and hold out my hands toward my new human companions. "We're going to start now. Remember, just keep thinking about all the ways you fit together with other people. The ways you can make something better with each other. The ways you make each other happy. Think about how we're all coming together right here to fix the craziest mess you've ever seen!"

A few laughs break out amid the crowd. With renewed confidence, I focus on the churning shadows in front of me and open my mind.

My mates aren't in place yet, still traveling around the edge of the city as quickly as they can, but that's all right. It's good to warm up, or I might sprain something.

My collaborators—most of them, anyway—have followed my instructions. Buttery affection and molasses-tangy delight flow from all around me, filling me with a different sort of flood.

I couldn't contain all that emotion even if I wanted to. I simply channel it into the glow of my own warmest feelings, the welcome I wish I could extend to every shadowkind who longs to spend time in the mortal realm, to all the energies twisting and contorting with the impulse to fit in.

The struggle between humans and shadowkind has been going on for so long without most of us even being aware of it. From the organizations that tormented shadowkind like Mirage to the individuals who caged me and tore apart Hail's mentor, from the powerful beings who tried to bend the whole world to their whims to Raze simply lashing out in anger—we've tangled and clashed and wrenched at each other.

All because being a part of this place mattered so much to us.

Is it any surprise that all that conflict ended up affecting the very atmosphere of our realms and, particularly, the portals that connect them? There's something magical about the way our different worlds exist alongside one another to begin with.

And magic can be bent and tainted, like sorcery can be used for evil no matter how much people like Jonah use it for good.

My blue-green glow washes over all the buildings in front of me and beams through the shadows. I send a silent but emphatic message with it.

It's so good to see you. Thank you for trying to work something out with us. We can all live here together. All these people want to see mortals and shadowkind existing side by side. Do you feel the love they have that they're sharing with you?

It's all right. You were confused and hurt, and you tried to grab what you believed should be yours. You don't have to claim or cling to anything. We can simply be, *existing next to one another, in harmony.*

My light spreads so much farther than I've ever managed before. I sense with a tingle through my nerves when Mirage, then Raze, then Hail, and finally Jonah find their places: five points around the ring. The current of shimmering warmth coursing out of me streams even faster and farther when it can reach out to them.

We're enveloping the city, the murk, and the rift above us in one massive embrace.

The edges of the portal twitch, and the impression of shrinking echoes into me. Some of the murk is thinning, brightening, but other whirls are rolling back up into the shadow realm where they came from.

It's really working!

I drag in a giddy breath—and a bang splits the quiet from somewhere behind me.

My nerves jump, and my glow falters. Splashes of acrid anxiety hit me from all sides.

A few more thumps and a faint impression of shouting reach my ears, but they're far enough away that I firm my stance.

We can't let ourselves be distracted. We're so close to our goal.

If we can fix this, every other problem will be so much easier to solve after. If we don't…

I'm not letting myself consider that possibility.

But my determination isn't enough to hold the thousands now gathered around the city in line. Sour threads are opening all through the currents of loving emotion that were reaching me.

No. We were doing this together. We can keep doing it.

I need to welcome all of *them* too.

I speak as loud as I can, hoping Mirage will be able to fling my voice wide even from his far-off position. "You're all such good people! Such caring, compassionate people. It's amazing that you came here and took this risk because you want the world to be a better, safer, happier place. You should feel so proud of yourselves."

The contrasting quivers start to fade.

I go on with a surge of renewed confidence. "We're changing the future into something brighter. It wouldn't be possible without all of you. You're amazing. You took a chance on me. You took a chance on this city. I've never met anyone braver."

A larger wave of satisfaction and contentment sweeps over and through me. I've never tasted a flavor so incredible.

This—this is what I've dreamed of. What I've wanted to offer, the total opposite of the pain I inadvertently caused before.

A gasp spills from my lips, and my glow erupts out of me again.

I manage to maintain enough control to stop it from

becoming outright burning. It isn't that hard anymore, not when my own heart is so full of joy.

The blaze of teal light spills through the entire city, caressing every sidewalk, every doorway and wall. The murk gives way in its wake, softening to accept it, twining with it as the darkness fades. The dissonant energy settles into serene stillness.

The exhilaration casts me higher and higher alongside the expanding glow, until I can taste the rift on the roof of my mouth. Sharp ripples of rejection smooth out. Tangs of resentment dwindle.

You can stay. You can be here with us. Meet us where we can all be happy. I'll show you the way.

The last splinters of animosity vanish one by one. Everything is warmth and light, comfort and happiness. On and on…

Until the sense of peace fills me enough that I let my arms drop to my sides. I blink and peer at the city before me.

A faint haze still hangs over the buildings, but it drifts and dances with the telephone poles rather than suffocating the atmosphere. Most of the unnatural shadows have either absorbed into the regular ones or returned through the rift.

I squint up at the sky and can only make out a faint dark spot against the brilliant blue. A relieved laugh tumbles out of me.

"We did it," I say. "We really did it!"

Falkor gives a joyful woof and wriggles his serpentine body. All around me, the humans and the shadowkind among them start chattering with excitement and awe. Their emotions radiate even more delight than I felt before.

And maybe this is what we've really healed today. Not just the rift but the reluctance to trust one another, to embrace the other kind of being with total openness.

At the thud of footsteps, I turn around. Rollick is

ambling over with Sorsha and the shadowbloods at his heels. Zian wipes his hands together with a satisfied expression.

"A bunch of hunters thought they'd try to join in the party," Riva informs me as they draw to a stop. "We took care of them before they could get in the way. Gently, of course."

She glances up at the brightened city. "Hopefully once they see this, they won't be in such a hurry to come at you again."

My smile slants. "I'm sure it'll be a work in progress. Not everyone is going to open up right away."

Rollick shakes his head at me. "Enough did. Remind me never to underestimate you again, Peri. You accomplished something not even I could have figured out how to do, with all my centuries."

Sorsha elbows him. "Yeah, yeah, old-timer. Ancient wisdom isn't all that matters." She waves to the crowd. "Who's ready to celebrate?"

At the whoops that carry through the gathering, my grin returns. "It's time for a re-opening party, and everyone's invited!"

32

One year later

Periwinkle

When I push past the coffee-shop door, a bugle sounds over my head. I glance up in surprise, but there's no sign of any actual instrument mounted on the frame.

"Sorry, sorry!" the barista calls over. "It's been doing that for the last couple of weeks. At least it gives you a dramatic entrance?"

It did. I laugh and go over to the table I've spotted Sorsha sitting at.

The phoenix shifter gets up with a swish of her scarlet hair, grinning wryly and holding a steaming cup in one hand.

"The city's still a little wacky, huh? On my way in, I passed a streetlamp doing a strobe effect and a tree that looked like it was growing fully formed loaves of bread."

"Yup. I'm not sure it'll ever get totally back to normal." The rift's strange flood has left its mark on the city—we did welcome it to join us here, after all. "At least it's hardly ever anything dangerous. The people who still live here and the new residents who moved in seem to see it as a plus. You never know what new special thing you'll encounter."

Sorsha chuckles. "It's like the Everymobile times a million. If I can manage to live in that bizarro RV, I can see making a home in a place like this. Why don't you show me what you've been up to?"

I buy a cup of hot chocolate to carry with me and lead Sorsha out into the street to more bugling.

Every month or so since we finished our clean-up efforts at all the warped rifts, one of the more established shadowkind has been stopping by to check on me in my role as the official ambassador to the shadow realm for Jackson City.

I've been on TV enough now, as well as speaking at conferences and rallies, that half of the pedestrians we pass wave to me or call out greetings. I really have become a sort of celebrity, although I haven't established any retail brands yet.

I've had lots of other responsibilities to keep me busy.

I picked this coffee shop because it's close to the things I want to show Sorsha—well, and also because the hot chocolate is the best blend of creamy and bitter darkness I've ever tasted. I sip it with a pleased hum and motion to the big wooden building with its vibrant paint up ahead.

"Mirage's theater has gotten very popular. He's doing two shows most days now, afternoon and evening. People are coming from all the way across the ocean just to see his illusionary performances."

Sorsha peers at the posters on the walls outside that promise vivid imagery and mind-tickling amusement. "Wow. I'll have to catch a show while I'm here. Maybe I can convince the guys to come along too—Snap will definitely want to check it out."

I beam at her. "I'll come with you. It's always fun to watch Mirage in his element."

I've never seen the fox shifter happier than he is now, getting to delight and startle crowds of people every day— and being applauded for his efforts.

A skinny weasel-like creature slips out of the shadows ahead of us, darts across the street, and pounces on a floating candy wrapper. Sorsha watches it go. "The creatures that came out of the weird rift haven't been causing any new problems, I take it?"

I shake my head. "It seems like whatever healing effect my glow had on them has been permanent too. They haven't been getting aggressive—at least, not any more than the occasional regular being does—and no one's disintegrating. Wins all around!"

And since things on the shadow-realm side of the rifts settled back into business as usual once I shrank them down, no new overly aggressive creatures have been forming and tumbling out. I just wish we could have saved the beings— both warped and regular—who got caught up in that chaos before we found the solution.

"How have people been reacting to the few beings that do lash out?" Sorsha asks.

More wins there. "We've held some informational seminars and put out public service announcements letting people know how to safely get away if they run into trouble. And our shadowkind police force that Raze is leading is always patrolling and ready to respond if there's a call for help. It seems like they usually catch the troublesome creatures before they do any major damage."

Vim and Sorrel were particularly proud of an elephantine beast they managed to apprehend together on the edge of the city a few days ago.

Sorsha arches an eyebrow. "I could see humans getting pretty pissed off about even minor damage."

I shrug. "I guess the kind of people who decide to live here are okay with taking the chance. Like explorers in the old days. It's a thrill for them."

A delicious kind of excitement laces the air everywhere I go, making sure I'm never the slightest bit hungry.

"I suppose that makes sense." Sorsha cocks her head at the sight of the park we're just coming up on. "This is new, isn't it?"

"Yes!" I motion to the elaborate water fountains that weave across the grassy lawn next to the playground. "My friend Fen helped set it up. She found an underground spring here that keeps the fountains going without any expense to the city."

We turn the corner at the park and continue along a few more blocks before a construction site comes into view up ahead. Beyond the plywood barrier, an elegant limestone face is partway through construction.

I sweep my arm toward it. "And here's the new halfway house that's going up!"

Sorsha perks up. "That's the one Quinn's helping design?"

I smile at her enthusiasm. "Yes! Hail's really liked getting to work with a real architect and making something that won't melt without magic."

Quinn, Rollick's partner from whom his academy got its name, did most of her work from afar in sketches and diagrams. But the couple of times she visited the city to see the site and talk with the people here, she was nothing but delightful. I'm guessing we can thank her for any softness the demon ever shows.

"When it's done," I go on, "it'll be a temporary residence for students who've graduated from the academies or are doing long-term practicums, where they can get some extra support while they're getting used to really living among humans. We've already got a bunch of beings volunteering to act as mentors."

"And speaking of academies…" Sorsha tips her head toward the sprawling brick complex the next block over.

With the existence of shadowkind now public knowledge, more and more beings have emerged from hiding —a lot of them seeking help from those of us who've established ourselves. Rollick founded a sister school right here in the city where voluntary students who present little danger to humans and each other can learn, while his more isolated original facility will focus on the involuntary students and those with dangerous talents.

Nobody was more surprised than me when he announced the new building was going to be called the Periwinkle Academy. I'd have pointed out that the name wasn't really fitting, since technically I was both an involuntary student and uncomfortably dangerous when I was first dragged in, but I've decided it's the spirit of the thing that matters.

And the spirit of this thing is very sweet.

As we approach the school, Sorsha's gaze sweeps over the streets. "Have you had any more trouble from the hunter groups lately?"

There've been a few incursions from shadowkind hunters insisting all of us "monsters" need to be taken down, the most recent one a couple of months ago. My smile tightens a bit at the memory.

"Thankfully, there are a lot fewer of them than there are people who are okay with us here in the city. I think the send-off they got last time made them afraid to make another attempt."

It was more human residents than shadowkind who ran them out of town. Since then, all I've seen is clips on the news of them ranting about the "monster invasion," but the more time passes without any further supernatural catastrophes, the more ridiculous they look.

I know I'm spreading all the joy I can. If some humans don't want to welcome it, that's on them.

We ease past the academy's doors into the broad front hall. Jonah glances over from where he's chatting with a couple of students in the front office. He finishes up with them, giving one a friendly clap on the shoulder, and comes out for our planned meeting.

"Hey," he says to both of us, and winces a little when Sorsha ruffles his hair with the oddly maternal air I only see when she's next to him.

She only does it briefly so as not to jeopardize his air of authority and then nudges him in the arm. "How's the new headmaster gig going?"

"Co-headmaster," Jonah corrects automatically.

Gnash moved to the city from the old academy to help run things here. I can't say the growly tiger shifter is my favorite being ever, but his fierce temper and Jonah's strict practicality seem to balance each other out well. Lilah, Jonah's temporary sorcerer colleague, has taken over his old wrangling duties for the original academy.

Sorsha rolls her eyes playfully. "Almost the same thing. You're not working too hard, I hope."

He grins back at her. "It can't be too hard when it's work I enjoy this much. Some of the new students… It's pretty incredible what they can do. Once they get a firm handle on their powers, I think the human world will be excited to have them join in."

Gracie pokes her head out of a room down the hall and hustles over. "Peri! Giving a bit of a tour?"

"Something like that. I hope we're not interrupting?"

She waves her hand dismissively. "Nah, I was just finishing some paperwork."

After the new academy opened, Gracie left her old job to come work here. I'm not sure what her exact title is, but she does a mix of guidance for the shadowkind students from a human perspective and outreach to the human community to encourage more acceptance.

It hasn't been smooth sailing across the board, after all. While the humans who live in the city see the supernatural elements as a bonus, there are still plenty around the world who are scared of the shadowkind. At least once a week, I stumble across a fear-mongering news story that makes me cringe.

But a year ago, I saw several of those a day. Things are definitely getting calmer as people have adjusted—and seen just how much shadowkind powers can make their lives easier when floods of darkness aren't suffocating their cities.

Some parts of the human world are more dangerous for us than others… but any time hunters or sorcerers have tried to make trouble here in Jackson City, they've been arrested before they got very far.

It helps that Colonel Hueber and Major Yin both got discharged from the army after the bombing mission was a flop—Hueber ending up in prison after he disputed the affront rather violently, and Yin taking a position consulting with federal law enforcement. The former major has helped nudge policies in a friendlier direction for shadowkind. Partly, I think, because he wants to recruit some beings to help with all that enforcing of laws.

"It's been too long since we really hung out," I say to Gracie. "We should do another girls' dinner sometime soon." Fen, Brine, Vim, and Sorrel usually join us for those.

Gracie gives me a thumbs up. "Pick the time, and I'm there."

I leave Sorsha to talk with Jonah for longer and head to another meeting I have scheduled to discuss a new project matching up human and shadowkind artists for collaborations. My days are a lot busier than they used to be—girl-bossing it for the win!

By the time the artistic planning is finished, I'm buoyed by satisfaction with the sense of a job if not well done yet then well on the way. With a spring in my step, I head back to the trim two-story house my mates and I call our own.

Mirage is already there, dancing around the kitchen tossing this and that into pots and pans. He's discovered a love of cooking and often comes up with intriguing combinations of flavors. Somehow they almost always work.

Tonight's dinner smells amazing. I take a deep breath of the scent—and giggle when Mirage pauses his slicing and stirring to spin me around in his embrace.

"Good day?" he asks, nuzzling my cheek before going in for a kiss.

I kiss him back with a caress of his foxy ears. "Very good."

Falkor comes bounding downstairs and squirms around my ankles in greeting. I grab his treats out of the cupboard—which emits a breeze most times of day as one of the city's lingering aftereffects, but I find it refreshing—and toss him a few.

Raze arrives next, humming with a cheerfulness that's new but increasingly normal over the past few months. He scoops me up and squeezes me close.

Hail arrives on the basilisk shifter's heels with a

disapproving tsk of his tongue that we all know is teasing. "Hoarding her all for yourself like usual, you lug."

I kiss Raze soundly and hop down to wrap the winter fae in an equally fond embrace. His mood softens as he strokes his fingers over my hair.

Jonah makes it just as Mirage is dishing out dinner. He inhales the wafting scent and smiles at all of us. "I can't wait to see what you've whipped up this time."

I tug him over to the table. "Did you have a good talk with Sorsha?"

He hooks his arm around mine and leans in to kiss the top of my head. "Yeah, she and the guys are going to stop by next week to do some workshops with the students. My third and fourth levels are already excited."

We settle in around the table like any family on TV—well, maybe composed slightly differently than the average family, but just as cozy. As I beam around at my men, an urge I can't totally explain brings my hand to my glass. "We should do a toast."

"To a year of collaboration?" Jonah asks.

"To that too." I lift my glass in the air. "But mostly to finding our way home, to making a place where *we* all belong, together."

"I'll drink to that!" Hail says.

We all clink glasses, gulp our drinks, and dig into our dinner. And all the while, the contentment radiating off all of my mates is the most satisfying meal I could ever have asked for.

ABOUT THE AUTHOR

Eva Chase lives in Canada with her family. She loves stories both swoony and supernatural, and strong women and the men who appreciate them.

Along with the Pack of Outcasts trilogy, she is the author of the Royal Spares series, the Rites of Possession series, the Shadowblood Souls series, the Heart of a Monster series, the Gang of Ghouls series, the Bound to the Fae series, the Flirting with Monsters series, the Cursed Studies trilogy, the Royals of Villain Academy series, the Moriarty's Men series, the Looking Glass Curse trilogy, the Their Dark Valkyrie series, the Witch's Consorts series, the Dragon Shifter's Mates series, the Demons of Fame series, and the Legends Reborn trilogy.

Connect with Eva online:
www.evachase.com
eva@evachase.com